# GHOSTS OF THE CHIT-CHAT

# Ghosts of the Chit-Chat

*edited by*

Robert Lloyd Parry

Swan River Press
Dublin, Ireland
MMXXI

*Ghosts of the Chit-Chat*
edited by Robert Lloyd Parry

Published by
Swan River Press
Dublin, Ireland
in April MMXXI

www.swanriverpress.ie
brian@swanriverpress.ie

*For Eryl and Nancy Lloyd Parry*

Twice a Fortnight photograph and James MacBryde's
illustration are courtesy of King's College Library, Cambridge;
Invitation to a Chit-Chat meeting courtesy of
the Syndics of Cambridge University Library.

Cover design by Meggan Kehrli
from artwork by John Coulthart

Set in Garamond by Ken Mackenzie

Published with assistance from Dublin UNESCO
City of Literature and Dublin City Libraries

Paperback Edition
ISBN 978-1-78380-744-4

Swan River Press published a limited hardback
edition of *Ghosts of the Chit-Chat* in December 2020.

# Contents

Preface . . . . . . . . vii

An Invitation to the Chit-Chat . . . . xi
  *Robert Lloyd Parry*

### *Ghosts of the Chit-Chat*

M. R. James (1862-1936) . . . . . 3
  "The Scrap-book of Canon Alberic" . . 11
  "Lost Hearts" . . . . . . . 25

E. F. Benson (1867-1940) . . . . . 37
  "The Other Bed" . . . . . . 42

R. C. Bosanquet (1871-1935) . . . . 55
  "The Dean's Story" . . . . . . 61
  "Red Gold" . . . . . . . 65

R. H. Benson (1871-1914) . . . . . 69
  "Father Bianchi's Tale" . . . . . 75

J. K. Stephen (1859-1892) . . . . . 83
  "Man Stories" . . . . . . . 89

A. C. Benson (1862-1925) . . . . . 99
  "Basil Netherby" . . . . . . 107

H. W. Tatham (1861-1909) . . . . 139
   "The Phonograph Bewitched" . . . . 143

Maurice Baring (1874-1945) . . . . 151
   "The Shadow of a Midnight" . . . . 155
   "The Ikon" . . . . . . . 160

Will Stone (1872-1901) . . . . . 167
   "A Fable" . . . . . . . . 173

Desmond MacCarthy (1877-1952) . . . 177
   "Pargiton and Harby" . . . . . 181

Gerald Warre Cornish (1875-1916) . . . 199
   "An Extract from 'Beneath the Surface' " . . 203

Appendix: *The Green Bay Tree* (1894) . . . 211
   "An Extract from *The Green Bay Tree*" . . 215
     *W. H. Wilkins and Herbert Vivian*

❧

Sources . . . . . . . . 227
Acknowledgements . . . . . . 229
About the Editor . . . . . . 231

# Preface

*"This Society shall be called the 'Chit-Chat Club', and consist of Members of the University, and have for its object the promotion of rational conversation."*

This rule, the first in the founding charter of the Chit-Chat, was not always strictly observed during the thirty-seven years of the club's existence. It's true that membership was only ever drawn from undergraduates and staff of Cambridge University, but the name was subject to variation, and it was for an evening of supernatural storytelling rather than rational conversation that the Chit-Chat has earned its modest place in the history of English literature.

On the evening of Saturday, 28 October 1893, members past and present ought to have been enjoying a dinner in celebration of the club's recently held 600th meeting. The secretary, A. B. Ramsay, had failed to make the necessary arrangements, however. So instead, ten current members and one guest gathered in the rooms of the Junior Dean of King's College and listened—with increasing absorption one suspects—as their host read "Two Ghost Stories".

*Ghosts of the Chit-Chat* is not the first book to celebrate this momentous event in the history of supernatural literature, the earliest dated record we have of M. R. James reading his ghost stories out loud. But it is the first to look more widely at the contributions that other club members made to the genre. The authors whose works appear in these pages are not a diverse group: they were the privately educated sons of bankers, lawyers, schoolmasters, and clergymen, who would themselves go on to careers in academia, journalism, the army and the church. But they were also men of imagination, curiosity, and wit, and the variety lies in the different approaches to supernatural fiction: here you'll find tales of ghostly retribution and black magic; spatterings of gore and glimpses "beyond the veil". You'll read stories written to edify schoolboys, and poems composed to tickle undergraduates. You'll encounter allegory, satire, and mysticism.

And while all the writers invoke ghosts in their work, many are also shades themselves; men whose remembrances have faded, whose voices are but faintly heard today. M. R. James and E. F. Benson remain in the mainstream, it's true. But while names like Maurice Baring, Desmond MacCarthy, and J. K. Stephen may still ring faint bells with the book-loving public, their works are long out of print. Whereas the writings of Robert Carr Bosanquet and Will Stone are found only in the pages of unread memorial volumes.

Each of the works selected here is preceded by an account of the author's life and his relationship to M. R. James and— except in one case—formal membership of the Chit-Chat Club is a prerequisite for inclusion in this volume. Celebrated Cambridge supernaturalists like Arthur Gray, E. G. Swain, R. H. Malden, and others find no place here for the simple reason that they never made the commitment to attend a meeting every Saturday evening at 10 p.m. during term, take a pinch of snuff, and listen to one of their friend's read a paper. Or perhaps they were never asked.

The designations of the Chit-Chat as a "club" and a "society" were interchangeable from the beginning—both appear in the first set of rules. The minute books, and the letters and memoirs of past members, variously render the name as "Chit-Chat", "Chit Chat", or "Chitchat". Except when quoting other sources, I shall follow rule one from the first set of rules, quoted above, and use Chit-Chat Club.

R.L.P.

# An Invitation to the Chit-Chat

## Winged Words

The Chit-Chat Club was inaugurated on Saturday, 27 October 1860, when Alsager Hay Hill, a Law undergraduate at Trinity Hall, Cambridge, entertained two friends in his rooms. The subject of the rational conversation that took place that night is not recorded, but the rules that were drawn up shortly afterwards established a clear and consistent format: on Saturday evenings during term, elected members were invited to present to their fellows "any original paper on any interesting topic by which conversation is likely to be promoted".

And so it worked out: over the next four decades, 211 men joined the club, their doings recorded in five minute books which were donated to Cambridge University Library in 1918 by M. R. James (henceforward MRJ). A letter accompanying this bequest gives us an idea of the comfortable atmosphere in which meetings took place: "[They] were held at 9.45–10 P.M. on Saturdays at the rooms of the reader of the paper who provided coffee, a cup & whales (anchovy toast). Minutes were read & a snuffbox (presented by F. W. Maitland) passed round (this snuffbox is still in my possession) of which all members were supposed to partake . . . A paper & discussion followed & out-college members departed at or around midnight."

New Chit-Chat members had to be elected by a majority of current members, one of whom acted as club secretary.

Though theoretically open to all Cambridge undergraduates, by the 1880s the club had come to be dominated by members of King's and Trinity colleges, who had schooled at Eton, Harrow, or Marlborough. On graduation membership became honorary and meetings regularly included a mixture of junior and senior members of the University. There was a nominal president, and there were printed sets of rules which were revised at various times during the club's existence.

E. F. Benson described the Chit-Chat as he first joined it, as "earnest and exclusive", but from an early stage there seems to have been an atmosphere of playfulness as well as scholarship. One of the founding fathers, Robert Francillon, had as a child owned a pet owl—Jacob—and this wise, nocturnal bird became the club's emblem. Jacob appears on the front cover of the first minute book, perched on a branch above a scroll bearing the Homeric motto "ΕΠΕΑ ΠΤΕΡΟΕΝΤΑ"—"winged words"—and he features on subsequent invitations to meetings.

The club's name suggests a light-heartedness too, though its original significance is unclear. The word "chit-chat" connotes informality, a friendly exchange of news and trivia rather than serious bilateral debate, and the name might have been a deliberate reaction against the self-importance of the Cambridge Conversazione Society, known also as the Apostles, an undergraduate group that had been around since 1820. The Apostles also met on Saturday nights and, according to A. C. Benson, "undertook highheartedly the reform of the world by the light of pure reason". The relationship between the two groups was complex: MRJ records that the Chit-Chat was seen as a recruiting ground for the more intellectual Apostles, and over the years there were defections to the older society.

Early on in its history there was a move to change the name of the Chit-Chat. "Owlet" was one proposal, which

On Saturday _____ the Meeting
will be in M<sup>r.</sup> _____ rooms
_____ College.

*An invitation to a Chit-Chat meeting (c. 1880).*

would have united name and emblem, and for a few months in 1862, the club became officially known as "The Round Table" before reverting to Chit-Chat again later the same year.

## *The Love-Feast of the Clan*

Related to the Chit-Chat was the Twice a Fortnight Club— the TAF—which had been founded by the spectacularly popular J. K. Stephen, when he was an undergraduate at King's in the late 1870s. Members met on Sunday nights during term to dine informally together.

MRJ described the TAF as "less exalted" than the Chit-Chat, and its scant surviving records suggest how much more informal it was; there were no rules or elections or hierarchy, no papers to be delivered. The TAF minute book simply lists members' names, and those who were present at a number of dinners, and a dance on 11 June 1889, perhaps the only TAF gathering at which women were present. The celebrated literary beauties Stella Duckworth and Kitty Lushington attended this, and MRJ invited his sister Grace: "I shall not dance myself," he warned her, "but . . . I will chaperone you and you can make what arrangements you please." Grace was thrilled: "I should very much like to see all your beautiful young ladies dressed for the evening . . . "

Like the Chit-Chat, the TAF drew its membership predominantly from King's and Trinity, and the two clubs had many members in common. Of the twelve men in a TAF group photograph, taken on 16 June 1891, six were also members of the Chit-Chat, and work by five of them is included in this book.

Robert Carr Bosanquet, seated at the far right, recalled the club's traditions when he was an undergraduate: "The host . . . was expected to provide certain traditional cold dishes and a reasonable quantity of hock, and it was an agreeable

*Twice a Fortnight Club (June 1891).* Seated—left to right: *Ted Sanderson, E. F. Benson\*, M. R. James\*, E. H. Douty, Marcus Dimsdale\*, Robert Carr Bosanquet\*;* Standing—left to right: *Gerald Duckworth, John Sanderson, R. H. Benson\*, J. K. Stephen, Walter Crum, Walter Headlam\* (\* Chit-Chat member).*

custom that the guests on their arrival should view the table with melancholy faces and murmur audibly that there seemed to be nothing to eat. Some of the party were excellent actors, and much of the chaff that went on through supper was conducted in the zassumed voices of certain well-known characters. Afterwards we adjourned to one of the larger sets of rooms in Fellows' Buildings, as often as not M. R. James's, where there was music, and more serious talk, frequently of French cathedrals, illuminated manuscripts, the lives of obscure saints and other medieval lore."

By the mid-1880s MRJ was the *de facto* leader of the TAF. Each time he won a University prize (which was often), he would host a dinner for the club, and later in life a fellow member, St. Clair Donaldson, made an intriguing suggestion: "I am not sure," he wrote, "that his bad habit of writing ghost stories was not fostered by the encouragement we gave him in those formative days." It's impossible to verify this, but Donaldson's memory of MRJ at TAF meetings was certainly vivid, and included an occasion on which he "lay writhing on the floor with Monty James's long fingers grasping at his vitals".

E. F. Benson described the TAF's Sunday night gatherings as "the Love-feast of the clan", and the phrase conveys well the cliquiness of the group—what could be perceived by outsiders as a smug exclusivity. The King's at which MRJ arrived as an undergraduate in the 1880s was a house divided: in 1861 the college statutes had been reformed and students from Eton, who had historically made up the majority of college members, found themselves sharing space with scholars from other, less traditional backgrounds. In his memoir, *Eton & King's* (1926), MRJ hinted at the tensions that existed: "I could tell unedifying stories of collisions such as youth rather welcomes and enjoys," he confessed. "Our elders saw, and regretted, and did all they could to heal breaches: but of course some irreconcilables on both sides stood out . . . "

Some of these irreconcilables were to be found in the ranks of the TAF and the Chit-Chat. And their evening activities were not always amiable.

## *The Stupid Party*

Robert Ross certainly fitted the profile of an outsider while King's was in this transitional state. Canadian, Roman Catholic, long-haired, physically slight: when he arrived at the college in October 1888, from a crammer school in London, he had already begun an affair with Oscar Wilde.

Ross resembled many of his contemporaries in the TAF and the Chit-Chat, however, in his literary ambitions, and as soon as he arrived in Cambridge, he began contributing to undergraduate magazines. On 1 March 1889, he wrote an article in *The Granta* attacking what he called "the stupid party" at King's, and describing the severance of its strong links with Eton as "the salvation of the college". He was particularly scathing about a plan to appoint E. H. Douty (who can be seen in the TAF photo immediately to MRJ's left) as one of the college's two Deans.

Ross set out to cause offence, and he succeeded. A week after the appearance of the article, on the evening of 8 March, six undergraduate vigilantes—among them Chit-Chat members E. F. Benson and Arthur Bather—seized its author and plunged him into the fountain in the middle of the front lawn at King's. Afterwards they went to dine with Arthur Tilley, a senior member of the college who was said to have encouraged the attack—Tilley was another prominent Chit-Chat member, who the month before had read a paper to the club entitled "The Art of Smiling". It was a deliberately public humiliation; and a physically harmful one—it has been suggested that Ross contracted pneumonia as a result.

The mood at King's was now more volatile than ever, but on the evening following the attack on Ross, MRJ gathered the junior members of college together and—in what *The Granta* described as "an oration à la Mark Antony"—made a successful plea for peace. The repercussions of the dunking continued for several weeks; Arthur Tilley was eventually required to make a public apology to the victim in the college hall, after which, it was said, he never dined there again; and for some time Ross considered bringing criminal charges against his assailants—he left Cambridge a few months later without taking a degree. But MRJ's management of the crisis won widespread admiration, and within a few weeks his leadership qualities were formally acknowledged when he was appointed Junior Dean of King's. There is some evidence that in the wake of this MRJ sought to distance himself from the TAF, but he was still there at a dinner in early 1891, and is prominent in the photo which was taken in June that year.

### Tenth Rate Prigs

Robert Ross's article in *The Granta* had been an affront to the Etonian set at King's, and the aftermath showed its members in a bad light; but it was a local difficulty, confined to the University. A more public assault on the cliques of Cambridge, and the Chit-Chat in particular, came a few years later.

At the 610th meeting, on 13 October 1894, a year after his night of ghost stories, MRJ once again entertained fellow members in his rooms by reading some fiction out loud. This time, however, the source was not his own imagination, but a recently published novel.

*The Green Bay Tree* is subtitled *A Tale of To-day*, and that day has long passed. The novel and its authors, W. H. Wilkins and Herbert Vivian, are long forgotten, and so are many of the objects of its satire. It was published in 1893, the same year as E. F. Benson's debut novel *Dodo* and, while it didn't achieve the high celebrity of Benson's book, it was well received and widely reviewed. "Clever" and "amusing" are the adjectives most critics reached for, and it went through several editions.

The title comes from Psalm 37: "I have seen the wicked in great power, and spreading himself like a green bay tree"—MRJ might have appreciated the biblical reference—and the story charts the Machiavellian rise of one Walpole Coryton, a self-styled "morologist", "a student of fools . . . " We follow his progress from school at Harrow, through Cambridge, to a career in Westminster, and along the way we encounter the dupes and fools that he uses and discards as he heeds his father's deathbed advice to "remember that your best friend is yourself". Many of the supporting characters are based on contemporary public figures, their identities thinly veiled behind cartoonish names. So Sir Keir Hardy, for instance, becomes Sir Beer Hardup. Other characters, less identifiable today, include Sir Cincinnatus Spreadeagle, Mr. Toadey-Snaile, and the Bishop of Bedlam. Like Benson's *Dodo*, *The Green Bay Tree* left the public guessing at the real-life models for its characters.

At Cambridge, the politically ambitious Coryton finds himself elected to a society called the Chit-Chat, and in the novel, as the club's real-life minute book notes, "the proceedings of the Society were slanderously reported". MRJ might have begun the 610th meeting by intoning the opening of Chapter Six: "The undergraduate with literary aspirations is about as precocious and insufferable a prig as may be found in the whole republic of letters . . . [and] the most pretentious coterie for such young men at Cambridge is a highly exclusive society known as the Chit-Chat."

That the authors had some knowledge of the real Chit-Chat, and hadn't simply borrowed a name that was at hand, is made clear as the passage continues: "[The society] meets once a week in the rooms of all the members in turn, when the host reads a dogmatic paper on a subject of frivolous solemnity and the other members discuss it. Punch is brewed, dried fruits are consumed, and the club snuff-box is handed round."

The authors of *The Green Bay Tree* were both younger contemporaries of MRJ at Cambridge, and Vivian's undergraduate career, in particular, closely matches that of Walpole Coryton: he had gone up to Trinity College from Harrow, and involved himself in undergraduate politics at the Cambridge Union Society. It's highly likely that Vivian and MRJ crossed paths: both were close friends of Leo Maxse, who in 1894 as editor of the *National Review* first published "The Scrap-book of Canon Alberic". Maxse was the President of the Union Society in 1885 when he invited MRJ to be the librarian, and Vivian himself was an active member.

Several of MRJ's contemporaries in the Chit-Chat are recognisable in *The Green Bay Tree*'s descriptions of the "tenth rate prigs" who constitute the club. The "man named Crust" must surely be Harry Cust who had joined the club in 1882. "A colourless young man named W. P. Jones, known to the intellectual circles of Cambridge as 'W.P.' and whose 'frightful cleverness' consisted merely in a knack of passing examinations in Latin and Greek" is probably Henry Babington Smith—known to his friends as H.B.—who indeed won several University prizes for Classics and was an exact contemporary of Vivian at Trinity. There seems to be an edge of genuine dislike on the authors' part in their description of Jones: "He had a thin, husky voice, which he used in the most supercilious way, as if it were amazing condescension to consent to speak at all. He was insignificant-looking, with a pug nose and mutton-chop whiskers, but it was the custom of the Chit-Chat to take men at their own valuation, and his was an unusually high one even for these select circles."

*Illustration for "Canon Alberic's Scrap-book"*
*by James MacBryde (1904).*

More affectionate is the description of "an effeminate young man named Freeman . . . [whose] father was a partner in a well-known firm of wholesale haberdashers". This is Ernest Debenham (of Debenham's department store fame), who joined the Chit-Chat in 1886 when MRJ was Secretary. *The Green Bay Tree* tells us that "he was good-looking . . . with a Roman nose and slight, well-curled moustache, and so long as he did not open his mouth, he made an impression on a stranger . . . He was eaten up with fads; from socialism and esoteric Buddhism to long hair and vegetable foods."

In his memoirs Herbert Vivian described Debenham "a dear friend" and tells us more about his spiritual practices: "One night he took some hashish (a compound of Indian hemp) to discover whether it would enable him to project his astral body across the court; but he swallowed so much of it that a doctor had to be sent for and three friends spent the night in walking him up and down the cloisters, to prevent his sinking into a sleep that would know no awakening." Unfortunately, Ernest Debenham never delivered a paper to the Chit-Chat.

The meeting described in *The Green Bay Tree*—reprinted in the appendix of this book—features the reading of a paper entitled "The Riddle of Life" which consists of "emasculated Rabelaisian language, with a few aphorisms modelled on Voltaire peeping out every now and then like truffles in *pâté de foie gras*". Afterwards Coryton's friend, Gaverigan, who has attended as a guest, wonders what the club's members get out of their meetings:

> "Mutual admiration here," [Coryton] replied . . . with a shrug of his shoulders, "And universal contempt hereafter."
>
> "But they are all coming men, aren't they?" said Gaverigan laughing.

"Coming men who never come. Or if they come at all, it will be as third-rate ushers in fourth-rate schools, quill-driving clerks, or literate 'ghosts' for illiterate hacks and quacks, doomed to spend their lives flitting on the top of a 'bus between the suburbs and the British Museum."

## Frivolous Solemnity

How fair was this satirical attack on the Chit-Chat? MRJ's first talk to the club, delivered on 19 May 1883, survives in draft form in Cambridge University Library, and can perhaps help us form a judgement.

"Useless Knowledge" is a rambling, sorry-not-sorry defence by MRJ of his niche academic interests, and the phrase used in *The Green Bay Tree* to characterise the typical Chit-Chat paper—"frivolous solemnity"—fits it well. The "serious" question the paper seeks to ask—Is the acquisition of knowledge, however obscure, a worthy educational end in itself?—is buried beneath long-winded digressions and ostentatiously obscure references and quotations. The whole thing lends substance to Wilkins' and Vivian's assertion that the talks at the Chit-Chat were intended to provoke the response: "How *frightfully* clever!"

If, then, we grant it some accuracy, how would *The Green Bay Tree*'s picture of the club have gone down with its real-world members? The minute book is typically laconic, but it would be hard to imagine MRJ's reading greeted by anything but laughter—derisive, but also perhaps grudgingly appreciative. Because while it is consistently disrespectful and occasionally really scathing, Wilkins' and Vivian's account of the Chit-Chat meeting is, in places, genuinely funny too. As the reviewer in *Punch* said of the novel as a whole, it is "smartly done". Would MRJ—the self-deprecatory author of *Eton and King's*, who was himself so ready to laugh at the foibles and follies of University life—have taken serious umbrage at so broad a comic swipe at his contemporaries? Or would not the man who took such delight in declaiming his favourite passages from Dickens, have relished the opportunity of impersonating men that he knew well and counted as friends? As well as a keen and infectious interest in antiquarian bypaths, MRJ had a resilient sense of humour, and it was these traits that largely set the tone for the Chit-Chat during the years of his membership.

According to the letter which accompanied the minute books that MRJ donated to the University Library, in 1897 the Chit-Chat Club "without ever being formally wound up, may be said to have expired of inanition, due I fear to the failure of the secretary to summon meetings & to the apathy of its members".

It had had a good run. By the end, 466 papers had been delivered, on an impressive variety of topics: from the literary—"On the genius of Edgar Allan Poe" (Thomas Wheeler, 1862) to the scientific—"Herbert Spencer's theory of the origin of nervous systems" (John Langley, 1877). From the general—"Fiction" (Benjamin Lock, 1870) to the specific—"Jean de la Force and his scheme for a French University—from a pamphlet in Peterhouse Library" (John Maxwell-Stirling, 1887). From the charmingly simple—"Bug hunting" (Francis Jenkinson, 1874) to the gravely intellectual—"The misuse of the words Knowledge & Belief in metaphysical controversy" (Sydney Vines, 1877). Religion was a perennially popular topic, and long before MRJ read his ghost stories, paranormal subjects had been covered—"Spirit Rapping" (Francis Adams, 1863), "Psychic Force" (Thomas Page, 1871), and, intriguingly, "A Recent Ghost Story" (Henry Wilson, 1880).

Only three of the works collected in this book were read at Chit-Chat meetings (MRJ's two stories and Robert Carr

Bosanquet's poem "The Dean's Story"); most were written long after their authors had left Cambridge. But it is notable how the undergraduate experience, the friendships and enthusiasms nurtured at university, underlie so many of them. And how the spirit of the MRJ's Chit-Chat—that impulse to display and share knowledge, but above all to entertain—informs them all.

So, let's join them now, old fellow. Fix yourself a beaker of claret-cup (Bordeaux, Amontillado, a twist of lemon peel and a squirt of soda water). Find a comfortable chair. And picture yourself in a Cambridge college room, sometime in the last three decades of the nineteenth century.

The chill of the Fenland wind has been driven out by a crackling log fire. The candles are casting curious shadows upon the wall. There's the smell of pipe smoke and tweed, anchovy toast and old books. Former schoolfellows and bright new acquaintances laugh and chatter and argue, while a friendly don sneezes and swears that he'll "never get the hang of snuff".

And now, as the distant bells of Great St. Mary's church strike ten, a respectful silence descends on the room. Your host clears his throat, shuffles a sheaf of papers on his knee, smiles to himself, and begins to read.

Business is underway at the Chit-Chat Club . . .

Robert Lloyd Parry
Southport, Merseyside
October 2020

*Ghosts of the Chit-Chat*

# M. R. James
## (1862-1936)

*"I am going to an institution called the Chitchat ... Benson, Cust, HB and others are members but it is not a large society at all, only about 11 people and the subjects terrible deep sometimes."*

– MRJ in a letter to his father (March 1883)

M. R. James joined the Chit-Chat in January 1883 at the beginning of his second term in Cambridge, and he was there for its final meeting in May 1897. Years later he reflected in a letter that his sole "programme" in life had been "to find out all I could about various matters and to make friends", and in the pursuit of these goals, the Chit-Chat played an important part. In turn MRJ provided the club's backbone during its final years. He was the longest-serving secretary, from 1885 to 1888, and he was recorded as president in 1892. He was also the club's most prolific contributor of papers, addressing his fellow members on twenty-one different occasions.

MRJ doesn't ever seem to have descended to the "terrible depth" of the papers that he had anticipated when he first joined the Chit-Chat. The titles and surviving notes for his talks suggest a desire to entertain as much as inform; to excite the kind of curiosity that he so valued in others; and to share the fruits of his own offbeat research. So in 1884, for instance, he spoke about "Art Magic"; the following year "The Grotesque". Obscure literary topics regularly cropped up: "The Beginnings of Christian Fiction" in 1885; "Breton Ballads" in 1894; in 1889 "Caesarius of Heisterbach", a thirteenth-century German monk who wrote the influential and amusing *Dialogue on Visions and Miracles*; and in 1892, "Walter Map" whose twelfth-century book *Courtiers' Trifles*, brimming with jokes, curious stories, and anecdotes, was edited and translated by MRJ in 1923. On 4 February 1893 he spoke about "Sheridan Le Fanu", the Irish novelist and writer of supernatural tales, whom he acknowledged as his own inspiration in the genre and whose works he later edited and anthologised. But it is for his offering at the 601st meeting of the club on 28 October 1893, that the name of the Chit-Chat is remembered today. On this occasion, the minute book tells us, "Mr. James read 'Two Ghost Stories'."

MRJ was thirty-one years old by then, and already well advanced on a successful career at Cambridge University, both as an administrator and an academic. He was one of the two Deans of King's College, in which office he was expected, according to the college's statutes, "to provide for the solemn and decorous performance of divine worship in the College Chapel . . . [and] to maintain, as far as in them lies, discipline and good order amongst such members of the College as are *in statu pupillari*".

More congenial, perhaps, and relevant to his tastes, had been his appointment a few months earlier to the Directorship of the Fitzwilliam Museum, Cambridge's collection of art and antiquities, which was (and remains) housed in a magnificent classical building just down the road from King's College. MRJ was still an undergraduate when, in 1884, he began cataloguing the museum's large collection of medieval manuscripts. This work was eventually published in 1895, along with detailed descriptions of four other important manuscript collections, the first of twenty-six such catalogues that MRJ compiled in his lifetime—a body of work for which he is still admired by medievalists today.

The minute for the 601st meeting doesn't give us the titles of the stories that he read that night (we learn that from S. G. Lubbock's 1939 *A Memoir of Montague Rhodes James*). The first of the two to be published appeared in March 1895, in the *National Review*, the editor of which, Leo Maxse, had been an undergraduate contemporary of MRJ at King's (though not a member of the Chit-Chat). When Maxse first wrote to accept the story for publication, he referred to it as "A Curious Book", but by the time it was published, it had become "The Scrap-book of Canon Alberic".

It's the text of this first magazine appearance that is reprinted here and, apart from the subtly different title to that by which it is known today, readers familiar with the story will notice only one major difference: the name of the protagonist. Why, between its publication in the *National Review* and its reappearance in *Ghost Stories of an Antiquary* (1904), the name "Anderson" was changed to "Dennistoun", is unclear. Anderson is also the name of the protagonist in "Number 13", so perhaps MRJ didn't want to be burdened by a recurring character—although Dennistoun does make a fleeting reappearance in "The Mezzotint".

Whatever one calls him, though, the central character of "The Scrap-book of Canon Alberic" is clearly an authorial self-portrait. His interests and habits—the travelling in France, the close inspection of medieval churches, the obsessive note-taking, the pipe smoking—precisely match those of his creator. MRJ himself had visited St. Bertrand de Comminges, the scene of the story, with friends in the spring of 1892, and been struck by the ancient, strangely appointed cathedral, and the down-at-heel little town in which it stood.

This idea of the protagonist as a portrait of the author is brought home in James MacBryde's illustrations to the story, where he is clearly modelled physically on MRJ: bespectacled and stooping as he takes notes in the magnificent carved choir stalls at St. Bertrand; or sitting before an open manuscript, smoking his pipe by the light of an oil lamp, oblivious to the demon-haunted gloom around him. But for the bug-eyed being at his elbow, the latter picture could be MRJ himself, working late on his catalogue in the Founder's Library of the Fitzwilliam.

In different ways, medieval manuscripts lie behind both the stories that MRJ read to the Chit-Chat that night. And while they received their first readings in his room in King's in October 1893, important elements of both "The Scrap-book of Canon Alberic" and "Lost Hearts" can be traced back to an event three years earlier.

In 1890 MRJ had been tipped off, by a friendly archdeacon, about the existence of a number of ancient books in the possession of the church at Brent Eleigh, a tiny village in Suffolk. On investigation, he discovered, "in a small, dank building in the churchyard", nine long-neglected manuscripts which, while not quite matching the contents of Canon Alberic's scrap-book for glamour and value, were each significant finds. MRJ must have felt something of the incredulous thrill that he attributes to his alter ego on opening the scrap-book ("such a collection Anderson had hardly dreamed of in his wildest moments"), and like the Cambridge man in the story, he lost no time in acquiring the volumes for his University.

This discovery brought MRJ into contact with Augustus Jessopp, the vicar of Scarning in Norfolk and a well-known East Anglian antiquary. Jessopp had been a contemporary of MRJ's father at Cambridge and was there too early to have been a member of the Chit-Chat, but one senses that he'd have fitted in well at the club had he had the opportunity to join. As the headmaster of King Edward VI Grammar School in Norwich, Jessopp had, it was said, "been beloved for his kindliness, and magnificent moments of indiscretion and frivolity"; and his obituary in *The Times* described him as "a remarkable example of the lettered cleric with interests extending widely outside his own profession . . . "

He also had a well-developed interest in the supernatural, and in January 1880 *The Athenaeum* published his account of a strange personal experience. The title of this piece—"An Antiquary's Ghost Story"—clearly inspired that of MRJ's 1904 collection, *Ghost Stories of an Antiquary*, and the story itself is echoed in the climactic scene of "The Scrap-book of Canon Alberic".

Sitting up alone, late at night on 10 October 1879, in the library of Mannington Hall, Norfolk, examining "some very rare books", Jessopp is surprised by the sudden appearance of "a large white hand within a foot of my elbow", and is convinced that the body to which this hand is attached "was not a reality". He himself responds with the utmost calm to this visitation, but while his "simple, unvarnished narrative of facts", lacks the drama, artfulness, and sense of terror that mark out his younger friend's fictions, it's clear that MRJ had heard of Jessopp's experience by the time he came to describe the terrifying nocturnal apparition in the Chapeau Rouge.

But if the circumstances of the discovery at Brent Eleigh informed "The Scrap-book of Canon Alberic", the contents of one of the books that MRJ found there, directly inspired the other story he read that night, "Lost Hearts".

Of the nine manuscripts that were recovered from that churchyard outhouse, the one with perhaps the widest general interest contained the text of a long-lost account of the life and miracles of Saint William of Norwich by Thomas of Monmouth, written around 1173. It was MRJ's collaboration with Augustus Jessopp on the publication of this, that first bought the two men into contact; and MRJ spoke about the discovery at the 559th meeting of the Chit-Chat on 21 November 1891.

The legend of William, a twelve-year-old boy who was said to have been murdered by Jews in Norwich at Easter 1144, perfectly aligned with the passion for obscure saints' lives and East Anglian history that MRJ had cherished since his childhood; and in his introduction to *The Life and Miracles of St. William of Norwich* (1896), he looks closely and critically at the story that Thomas of Monmouth has to tell.

As the earliest medieval expression of what MRJ calls "the myth of Jewish ritual murders," (what is known as "the blood libel"), Thomas's book had a far reaching and terrible effect. His account of William's martyrdom was followed by a slew of similar stories throughout Europe, fabrications which have been used to justify outbreaks of violent anti-Semitic persecution ever since. MRJ estimated that over one hundred variations on the legend had been circulated by the time he was writing, and he had researched enough of these to be able to discuss them with some authority in his introduction. The idea of ritual child murder was therefore firmly lodged in his mind when he came to write "Lost Hearts" sometime in 1893, and aspects of William's story found their way into his ghostly entertainment.

While allowing for the possibility that a child called William was violently killed in Norwich in 1144, MRJ swiftly dismisses the idea that the Jews of the city murdered him for religious purposes. "The accusations of child-murder, of cannibalism and of other horrid practices," he points out, "are among the first that any set of uneducated people is likely to bring against a tribe or sect whose practices they do not understand." And he refers to accusations "against Christians by Pagan Greeks and Romans, against heretical sects by orthodox Christians, against the Templars by their contemporaries, against Christian missionaries (in 1870 and in 1895) by the Chinese". He might have added that false accusations of "horrid practices" were also directed at pagan worshippers by Christians in the late Roman Empire.

MRJ locates the earliest literary account of Jews killing a Christian child in the *Historia Ecclesiastica*, a fifth-century church history by one Socrates of Constantinople. He presumably, therefore, also knew of the charge—mentioned in the same work—of human sacrifice against worshippers of Mithras, the popular Roman solar deity, in whose mysteries Mr. Abney in "Lost Hearts" is said to be an expert, and whose statue—engaged in an act of sacrificing a bull—is found in the vestibule of Aswarby Hall.

While MRJ is emphatic in his rejection of the idea that William was ritually murdered by Jews, he does allow himself to speculate about what might really have happened in Norwich in 1144, and wonders what "a reversion to half-forgotten practices of a darker age, might effect in the case of an ignorant Jew seven centuries back". Might an "insane, superstitious" individual Jew have taken it upon himself to murder William, he asks? In this case his imagination does not take him any further. But what the scholar backed away from, the writer of fantastic tales pursued; the idea of a lone, murderous, religious zealot stuck with MRJ and found its way into "Lost Hearts". For what is Mr. Abney's vague, cannibalistic nineteenth century Neoplatonism if not a grotesque return to "half forgotten practises of a darker age"? Or, to use the killer's own words, to "processes, which to us moderns have something of a barbaric complexion"?

Apart from the violent slaughter of children, the most obvious detail that the stories of William of Norwich and "Lost Hearts" share is a date: March 24th. This is when Mr. Abney plans to murder Stephen Elliot, and it is the date that

MRJ (erroneously) gives as the Feast Day of St. William in his introduction to *The Life and Miracles* . . .

In Thomas of Monmouth's story, and several of the legends that it inspired, the murderers commit their outrages at the time of the Passover—in some cases the blood of the murdered child is used as an ingredient in the Passover bread; the victim's life-stuff is literally consumed, like the hearts of Mr. Abney's victims. William's blood is not so used in Thomas's account, but he does die, in a grotesque parody of the crucifixion of Christ, on the great Jewish feast day. The date of Passover traditionally falls on the first full moon after the vernal equinox, and this is precisely the night that Mr. Abney chooses for Stephen Elliott's murder: as the boy stands at his bedroom window waiting to join Mr. Abney in his study, on 24 March 1812, he looks out over "a still night and a full moon". There is a clear parallel, then, in MRJ's mind between Mr. Abney's fictional victims and those of the—equally fictional but much less entertaining—Jewish "murderers".

"Lost Hearts" was first published in the *Pall Mall Magazine* in December 1895, and it is that version that is reprinted here, for the first time. It differs only slightly from the text that appeared in *Ghost Stories of an Antiquary* in 1904, but when MRJ came to collect his earliest tales for publication he admitted that he didn't "much care about" "Lost Hearts," and he included it only when his publisher requested a longer book. It's not obvious why he was so dismissive. The story remains an effective and entertaining spine chiller; gory perhaps, but not out of keeping with the rest of MRJ's oeuvre. Thirty-four years later he would happily evoke the violent death of a child in order to entertain the Eton Boy Scout Troop on their summer holiday—"Wailing Well" was first read in 1927. Did he feel a qualm about "Lost Hearts" because behind it—although filtered through his imagination—lay so grave a historical reality?

# The Scrap-book of Canon Alberic

M. R. James

S. Bertrand de Comminges is a decayed town on the spurs of the Pyrenees, not very far from Toulouse, and still nearer to Bagnéres-de-Luchon. It was the site of a bishopric until the Revolution, and has a cathedral which is visited by a certain number of tourists. In the spring of 188— an Englishman arrived at this old world place—city, I might call it, but there are not a thousand inhabitants. He was a Cambridge man, who had come specially from Toulouse to see St. Bertrand's Church, and had left two friends, who were less keen archaeologists than himself, in their hotel at Toulouse, under promise to join him on the following morning. Half an hour at the church would satisfy *them*, and all three could then pursue their journey in the direction of Auch. But our Englishman had come early on the day in question, and proposed to himself to fill a note-book and to use several dozens of plates in the process of describing and photographing every corner of the wonderful church that dominates the little hill of Comminges. In order to carry out this design satisfactorily, it was clearly necessary to monopolize the verger of the church for the day. The verger or sacristan (I prefer the latter appellation, inaccurate as it may be) was accordingly sent for by the somewhat brusque lady who keeps the inn of the *Chapeau Rouge*; and when he came, the Englishman found him an unexpectedly interesting object of study. It was not in the personal appearance of the little, dry, wizened old man that the interest lay, for he was precisely like dozens of other church guardians in France, but in a curious furtive, or rather hunted and oppressed, air which he had. He was perpetually half-glancing behind him; the muscles of his back and shoulders seemed to be hunched in a continual nervous contraction, as if he were expecting every moment to find himself in the clutch of an enemy. The Englishman hardly knew whether to put him down as a man haunted by a fixed delusion, or as one oppressed by a guilty conscience, or as an unbearably henpecked husband. The probabilities when reckoned up certainly pointed to the last idea, but still, the impression conveyed was that of a more formidable persecutor even than a termagant wife.

However, the Englishman (let us call him Anderson) was soon too deep in his note-book and too busy with his camera to give more than an occasional glance to the sacristan. Whenever he did look at him he found him at no great distance, either huddling himself back against the wall, or crouching in one of the gorgeous stalls. Anderson became rather fidgetty after a time. Mingled suspicions that he was keeping the old man from his *déjeûner*, that he was regarded as likely to make away with St. Bertrand's ivory crozier, or with the dusty stuffed crocodile that hangs over the font, began to torment him.

"Won't you go home?" he said at last; "I'm quite well able to finish my notes alone; you can lock me in if you like. I shall want at least two hours more here, and it must be cold for you, isn't it?"

"Good heavens!" said the little man, whom the suggestion seemed to throw into a state of unaccountable terror, "such a thing cannot be thought of for a moment. Leave monsieur alone in the church? No, no; two hours, three hours, all will be the same to me. I have breakfasted, I am not at all cold, with many thanks to monsieur."

"Very well, my little man," quoth Anderson to himself, "you have been warned and you must take the consequences."

Before the expiration of the two hours, the stalls, the enormous dilapidated organ, the choir-screen of Bishop John de Mauléon, the remnants of glass and tapestry, and the objects in the treasure chamber, had been well and truly examined; the sacristan still keeping at Anderson's heels, and every now and then whipping round as if he had been stung, when one or other of the strange noises that trouble a large empty building fell on his ear. Curious noises they were sometimes. "Once," Anderson said to me, "I could have sworn I heard a thin metallic voice laughing high up in the tower. I shot an inquiring glance at my sacristan. He was white to the lips. 'It is he, that is—it is no one; the door is locked,' was all he said, and we looked at each other for a full minute."

Another little incident puzzled Anderson a good deal. He was examining a large dark picture that hangs behind the altar, one of a series illustrating the miracles of St. Bertrand. The composition of the picture is well-nigh indecipherable, but there is a Latin legend below, which runs thus: *"Qualiter S. Bertrandus liberavit hominem quem diabolus diu volebat strangulare!"* (How St. Bertrand delivered a man whom the Devil long sought to strangle.) Anderson was turning to the sacristan with a smile and a jocular remark of some sort on his lips, but he was confounded to see the old man on his knees, gazing at the picture with the eye of a suppliant in agony, his hands tightly clasped, and a rain of tears on his cheeks. Anderson naturally pretended to have noticed nothing, but the question would not away from him, "Why should a daub of this kind affect anyone so strongly?" He seemed to himself to be getting some sort of clue to the reason of the strange look that had been puzzling him all the day; the man must be a monomaniac; but what was his monomania?

It was nearly five o'clock; the short day was drawing in, and the church began to fill with shadows, while the curious noises—the muffled foot-falls and distant talking voices that had been perceptible all day—seemed, no doubt because of the fading light and the consequently quickened sense of hearing, to become more frequent and insistent. The sacristan began for the first time to show signs of hurry and impatience. He heaved a sigh of relief when camera and note-book were finally packed up and stowed away, and hurriedly beckoned Anderson to the western door of the church, under the tower. It was time to ring the *Angelus*: a few pulls at the reluctant rope, and the great bell *Bertrande*, high in the tower, began to speak, and swung her voice up among the pines, and down to the valleys, loud with mountain-streams, calling the dwellers on those lonely hills to remember and repeat the Salutation of the Angel to her whom He called Blessed among women. With that a profound quiet seemed to fall for the first time that day upon the little town, and Anderson and the sacristan went out of the church.

On the doorstep they fell into conversation.

"Monsieur seemed to interest himself in the old choir-books in the sacristy."

"Undoubtedly; I was going to ask you if there were a library in the town."

"No, monsieur; perhaps there used to be one belonging to the Chapter, but it is now such a small place——" Here came a strange pause of irresolution, as it seemed. Then, with a sort of plunge, he went on; "But if monsieur is *amateur des vieux livres*, I have at home something that might interest him. It is not a hundred yards."

At once all Anderson's cherished dreams of finding priceless manuscripts in untrodden corners of France flashed up, to die down again the next moment. It was probably a stupid missal of Plantin's printing, about 1580; where was the likelihood that a place so near Toulouse would not have been ransacked long ago by collectors? However, it would be foolish not to go; he would reproach himself for ever after if he refused. So they set off. On the way the curious irresolution and sudden determination of the sacristan recurred to Anderson, and he wondered in a shame-faced way whether he was being decoyed into some purlieu to be made away with as a supposed rich Englishman. He contrived, therefore, to begin talking with his guide, and to drag in, in a rather clumsy fashion, the fact that he expected two friends to join him early the next morning. To his surprise, the announcement seemed to relieve the sacristan at once of some of the anxiety that oppressed him.

"That is well," he said, quite brightly, "that is very well. Monsieur will travel in company with his friends; they will be always near him. It is a good thing to travel thus in company—sometimes." The last word appeared to be added as an afterthought, and to bring with it a relapse into gloom for the poor little man.

They were soon at the house, which was one rather larger than its neighbours, stone-built, with a shield carved over the door, the shield of Alberic de Mauléon, a collateral descendant, Anderson tells me, of Bishop John de Mauléon. This Alberic was a Canon of Comminges from 1680-1701. The upper windows of the mansion were boarded up, and the whole place bore, as does the rest of Comminges, the aspect of decaying age.

Arrived on his doorstep, the sacristan paused a moment.

"Perhaps," he said, "perhaps after all monsieur has not the time?"

"Not at all—lots of time—nothing to do till to-morrow. Let us see what it is you have got."

The door was opened at this point, and a face looked out, a face far younger than the sacristan's, but bearing something

15

of the same distressing look, only here it seemed to be the mark, not so much of fear for personal safety as of acute anxiety on behalf of another. Plainly, the owner of the face was the sacristan's daughter; and, but for the expression I have described, she was a handsome girl enough. She brightened up considerably on seeing her father accompanied by an able-bodied stranger. A few remarks passed between father and daughter, of which Anderson only caught these words, said by the sacristan, "He was laughing in the church," words which were answered only by a look of terror from the girl.

But in another minute they were in the sitting-room of the house, a small, high chamber with a stone floor, full of moving shadows cast by a wood-fire that flickered on a great hearth. Something of the character of an oratory was imparted to it by a tall crucifix which reached almost to the ceiling on one side; the figure was painted of the natural colours, the cross was black. Under this stood a chest of some age and solidity, and when a lamp had been brought, and chairs set, the sacristan went to this chest, and produced therefrom, with growing excitement and nervousness, as Anderson thought, a large book, wrapped in a white cloth, on which cloth a cross was rudely embroidered in red thread. Even before the wrapping had been removed, Anderson began to be interested by the size and shape of the volume. "Two large for a missal," he thought, "and not the shape of an antiphoner; perhaps it may be something good after all." The next moment the book was open, and Anderson felt that he had at last lit upon something better than good. Before him lay a large folio, bound, perhaps, late in the seventeenth century, with the arms of Canon Alberic de Mauléon stamped in gold on the sides. There may have been a hundred and fifty leaves of paper in the book, and on almost every one of them was fastened a leaf from an illuminated manuscript. Such a collection Anderson had hardly dreamed of in his wildest moments. Here were ten leaves from a copy of Genesis, illustrated with pictures, which could not be later than 700 A.D. Further on was a complete set of pictures from the Psalter of English execution, of the very best kind that the thirteenth century could produce; and, perhaps, best of all, there were twenty leaves of uncial writing in Latin, which, as a few words seen here and there told him at once, must belong to some very early unknown patristic treatise. Could it possibly be a fragment of the copy of Papias *On the Words of Our Lord*, which was known to have existed as late as the twelfth century at Nismes?[†] In any case, his mind was made up; that book must return to Cambridge with him, even if he had to draw the whole of his balance from the bank and stay at S. Bertrand till the money came. He glanced up at the sacristan to see if his face yielded any hint that the book was for sale. The sacristan was pale, and his lips were working.

"If monsieur will turn on to the end," he said.

So monsieur turned on, meeting new treasures at every rise of a leaf; and at the end of the book he came upon two sheets of paper, of much more recent date than anything he had yet seen, which puzzled him considerably. They must be contemporary, he decided, with the unprincipled Canon Alberic, who had doubtless plundered the Chapter library of S. Bertrand to form this priceless scrap-book. On the first of the paper sheets was a plan, carefully drawn and instantly recognizable by a person who knew the ground, of the south aisle and cloisters of S. Bertrand's. There were curious signs looking like planetary symbols, and a few Hebrew words in the corners; and in the north-west angle of the cloister was a cross drawn in gold paint. Below the plan were some lines of writing in Latin which ran thus: "*Responsa* 12 *mi Dec.* 1694.

---

[†] We now know that these leaves did contain a considerable fragment of that work, if not of that actual copy of it.

*Interrogatum est: Si inveniam? Responsum est. Invenies. Si fiam dives? Fies. Si vivam invidendus? Vives. Si moriar in lecto meo! Ita.* "(Answers of the 12th of December, 1694. It was asked: Shall I find it? Answer: Thou shalt. Shall I become rich? Thou wilt. Shall I live an object of envy? Thou wilt. Shall I die in my bed? Thou wilt.)

"A good specimen of the treasure-hunter's record: quite reminds one of Mr. Minor-Canon Quatremain in *Old St. Paul's*," was Anderson's comment, and he turned the leaf.

What he then saw impressed him, as he has often told me, more than he could have conceived any drawing or picture capable of impressing him. And, though the drawing he saw is no longer in existence, there is a photograph of it (which I possess), which fully bears out Anderson's statement. The picture in question was a sepia drawing of the end of the seventeenth century, representing, one would say at first sight, a Biblical scene; for the architecture (the picture represented an interior) and the figures had that semi-classical flavour about them which the artists of two hundred years ago thought appropriate to illustrations of the Bible. On the right was a king on his throne, the throne elevated on twelve steps, a canopy overhead, soldiers on either side—evidently King Solomon. He was bending forward with outstretched sceptre, in attitude of command: his face expressed horror and disgust, yet there was in it also the mark of imperious command and confident power. The left half of the picture was the strangest, however. The interest plainly centred there. On the pavement before the throne were grouped four soldiers, surrounding a crouching figure which must be described in a moment. A fifth soldier lay dead on the pavement, his neck distorted and his eye-balls starting from his head. The four surrounding guards were looking at the King. In their faces the sentiment of horror was intensified: they seemed, in fact, only restrained from flight by their implicit trust in their master. All this terror was plainly excited by the being that crouched in their midst. I entirely despair of conveying by any words the impression which this figure makes upon anyone who looks at it. I recollect once showing the photograph of the drawing to a lecturer on Morphology, a person of, I was going to say, abnormally sane and unimaginative habits of mind. He absolutely refused to be alone for the rest of that evening, and he told me afterwards that for many nights he had not dared to put out his light before going to sleep. However, the main traits of the figure I can at least indicate. At first you saw only a mass of coarse matted black hair; presently it was seen that this covered a body of fearful thinness, almost a skeleton, but with the muscles standing out like wires. The hands were of a dusky pallor, covered, like the body, with long coarse hairs, and hideously taloned. The eyes, touched in with a burning yellow, had intensely black pupils, and were fixed upon the throned King with a look of beast-like hate. Imagine one of the awful bird-catching spiders of South America translated into human form and endowed with intelligence just less than human, and you will have some faint conception of the terror inspired by the appalling effigy. One remark is universally made by those to whom I have shown the picture, "It was drawn from the life."

As soon as the first shock of his irresistible fright had subsided, Anderson stole a look at his hosts. The sacristan's hands were pressed upon his eyes; his daughter, looking up at the cross on the wall, was telling her beads feverishly.

At last the question was asked. "Is this book for sale?"

There was the same hesitation, the same plunge of determination that he had noticed before, and then came the welcome answer, "If monsieur pleases."

"How much do you ask for it?"

"I will take 250 francs."

This was confounding. Even a collector's conscience is sometimes stirred, and Anderson's conscience was tenderer than a collector's. "My good man!" he said again and again, "your book is worth far more than 250 francs, I assure you, far more."

But the answer did not vary. "I will take 250 francs, not more."

There was really no possibility of refusing such a chance. The money was paid, the receipt signed, a glass of wine (Vin de Limoux, not to be recommended) drunk over the transaction, and then the sacristan seemed to become a new man. He stood upright, he ceased to throw those suspicious glances behind him, he actually laughed or tried to laugh. Anderson rose to go.

"I shall have the honour of accompanying monsieur to his hotel?" said the sacristan.

"Oh no, thanks! it isn't a hundred yards. I know the way perfectly, and there is a moon."

The offer was pressed three or four times, and refused as often.

"Then monsieur will summon me if—if he finds occasion; he will keep the middle of the road, the sides are so rough."

"Certainly, certainly," said Anderson, who was impatient to examine his prize by himself; and he stepped out into the passage with his book under his arm. Here he was met by the daughter; she, it appeared, was anxious to do a little business on her account; perhaps, like Gehazi, to "take somewhat" from the foreigner whom her father had spared.

"A silver crucifix and chain for the neck; monsieur would perhaps be good enough to accept it?"

Well really, Anderson hadn't much use for these things; what did mademoiselle want for it?

"Nothing, nothing in the world. Monsieur is more than welcome to it."

The tone in which this, and much more, was said was unmistakably genuine, so that Anderson was reduced to profuse thanks, and submitted to have the chain put round his neck. It really seemed as if he had rendered the father and daughter some service which they hardly knew how to repay. As he set off with his book they stood at the door looking after him, and they were still looking when he waved them a last good-night from the steps of the *Chapeau Rouge*.

Dinner was over, and Anderson was in his bedroom, shut up alone with his acquisition. The landlady had manifested a particular interest in him since he had told her that he had paid a visit to the sacristan and bought an old book from him. He thought, too, that he had heard a hurried dialogue between her and the said sacristan in the passage outside the *salle á manger*, some words to the effect that "Pierre and Bertrand would be sleeping in the house" had closed the conversation. At this time a growing feeling of discomfort had been creeping over him, nervous reaction perhaps, after the delight of his discovery. Whatever it was, it resulted in a conviction that there was someone behind him, and that he was far more comfortable with his back to the wall. All this, of course, weighed light in the balance as against the obvious value of the collection he had acquired. And now, as I said, he was alone in his bedroom, taking stock of Canon Alberic's treasures, in which every moment revealed something more charming. "Bless Canon Alberic," said Anderson, who had an inveterate habit of talking to himself, "I wonder where he is now? Dear me! I wish that landlady would learn to laugh in a more cheering manner. It makes one feel as if there was someone dead in the house. Half a pipe more, did you say? I think perhaps you are right. I wonder what that crucifix is that the young woman insisted on giving me? Last century, I suppose—Yes, probably. It is rather a nuisance of a thing to have round one's neck—just too heavy. Most likely her father has been wearing it for years. I think I might give it a clean up before I put it away."

He had taken the crucifix off, and laid it on the table, when his attention was caught by an object lying on the red cloth just by his left elbow. Two or three ideas of what it might be flitted through his brain with their own incalculable quickness. "A penwiper? No, no such thing in the house. A rat? No, too black. A large spider? I trust to goodness not—no. Good God! a hand like the hand in that picture!" In another infinitesimal flash he had taken it in. Pale, dusky skin covering nothing but bones and tendons of appalling strength; coarse black hairs, longer than ever grew on a human hand; nails rising from the ends of the fingers and curving sharply down and forward, grey, horny, and wrinkled. He flew out of his chair with deadly inconceivable terror clutching at his heart. The shape, whose left hand rested on the table, was rising to a standing posture behind his seat, its right hand crooked above his scalp. There was black and tattered drapery about it; the coarse hair covered it as in the drawing. The lower jaw was thin—what can I call it?—shallow, like a beast's; teeth showed behind the black lips; there was no nose; the eyes, of a fiery yellow against which the pupils showed black and intense, and the exulting hate and thirst to destroy life which shone there, were the most horrifying feature in the whole vision. There was intelligence of a kind in them, intelligence beyond that of a beast, below that of a man.

The feelings which this horror stirred in Anderson were the intensest physical fear and the most profound mental loathing. What did he do? What could he do? He has never been quite certain what words he said, but he knows that he spoke, that he grasped blindly at the silver crucifix, that he was conscious of a movement towards him on the part of the demon, and that he screamed with the voice of an animal in hideous pain. Pierre and Bertrand, the two sturdy little serving-men, who rushed in saw nothing, but felt themselves thrust aside by something that passed out between them, and found Anderson in a swoon. They sat up with him that night, and his two friends were at S. Bertrand by nine o'clock next morning. Anderson, though still shaken and nervous, was almost himself by that time, and his story found credence with them—though not until they had seen the drawing and talked with the sacristan. Almost at dawn the little man had come to the inn on some pretence and had listened with the deepest interest to the story retailed by the landlady. He showed no surprise. "It is he, it is he! I have seen him myself," was his only comment; and Anderson's friends elicited but one reply to all their questions: "*Deux fois je l'ai vu; mille fois je l'ai senti.*" He would tell them nothing of the provenance of the book, nor any details of his experiences. "I shall soon sleep, and my rest will be sweet; why should you trouble me?" he said.[†]

We shall never know what he or Canon Alberic de Mauléon suffered. At the back of that fateful drawing were some lines of writing, which throw some light on the situation.

"*Contradictio Salomonis cum demonio nocturno.*
*Albericus de Mauleone delineavit.*
*V. Deus in adiutorium. Ps. Qui habitat.*
*Sancte Bertrande, demoniorum, effugator, intercede pro me miserrimo.*
*Primum uidi nocte 12mi Dec. 1694: uidebo mox ultimum. Peccaui et passus sum, plura adhuc passurus. Dec. 29, 1701.*"[‡]

---

[†] He died that summer; his daughter married, and settled at S. Papoul. She never understood the circumstances of her father's "obsession".

[‡] The *Gallia Christiana* gives the date of the Canon's death as Dec. 31, 1701, "in bed, of a sudden seizure". Details of this kind are not common in the great work of the Sammarthani.

I have never quite understood what was Anderson's view of the events I have narrated. He quoted to me once a text from Ecclesiasticus: "Some spirits there be that are created for vengeance and in their fury lay on sore strokes." On another occasion he said: "Isaiah was a very sensible man; doesn't he say something about night monsters living in the ruins of Babylon? These things are rather beyond us at present."

Another confidence of his impressed me rather, and I sympathized with it. We had been, last year, to Comminges, to see Canon Alberic's tomb. It is a great marble erection with an effigy of the Canon in a large wig and *soutane*, and an elaborate eulogy of his learning below. I saw Anderson talking for some time with the Vicar of S. Bertrand's, and as we drove away he said to me: "I hope it isn't wrong: you know I am a Presbyterian—but—I have just ordered a trental of masses for Alberic de Mauléon's rest." Then he added, with a touch of the Northern British in his tone, "I had no notion they came so dear."

The book is in the Wentworth Collection at Cambridge. The drawing was photographed and then burnt by Anderson on the day when he left Comminges on the occasion of his first visit.

# Lost Hearts

## M. R. James

I t was, as far as I can ascertain, in September of the year 1811, that a postchaise drew up before the door of Aswarby Hall, in the heart of Lincolnshire. The little boy, who was the only passenger in it, and who jumped out as soon as the chaise had stopped, looked about him with the keenest curiosity during the short interval that elapsed between the ringing of the bell and the opening of the hall door. He saw a tall, square, red-brick house, built in the reign of Anne; a stone-pillared porch had been added in the purer classical style of 1790; the windows of the house were many, tall and narrow, with small panes and thick white woodwork. A pediment, pierced with a round window, crowned the front. There were wings to right and left, connected by curious glazed galleries, supported by colonnades, with the central block. These wings plainly contained the stables and offices of the house. Each was surmounted by an ornamental cupola with a gilded vane. An evening light shone on the building, making the window-panes glow like so many fires. Away from the Hall in front stretched a flat park studded with oaks and fringed with firs, which stood out against the sky. The clock in the church-tower, buried in trees on the edge of the park—only its golden weather-cock catching the light—was striking six, and the sound came gently beating down the wind. It was altogether a pleasant impression, though tinged with the sort of melancholy appropriate to an evening in early autumn, that was conveyed to the mind of the boy who was standing in the porch waiting for the door to open to him.

He had just come from Warwickshire, and was an orphan of some six months' standing: now, owing to the generous and unexpected offer of his elderly cousin, Mr. Abney, he had come to live at Aswarby. The offer was unexpected, because all who knew anything of Mr. Abney looked upon him as a somewhat austere recluse, into whose steady-going household the advent of a small boy would import a new and, it seemed, incongruous element. The truth is that very little was known of Mr. Abney's pursuits or temper. The Professor of Greek at Cambridge had been known to say that no one knew more of the religious beliefs of the later pagans than did the owner of Aswarby. Certainly the library at the Hall contained all the then available literature of the Mysteries, the Orphic poems, the worship of Mithras, and the Neo-Platonists. In the marble-paved hall stood a fine group of Mithras slaying a bull, which had been imported from the Levant at great expense by the owner. He had contributed a description of it to the *Gentleman's Magazine*; and he had written a remarkable series of articles in the *Critical Museum* on the superstitions of the Romans of the Lower Empire. He was looked upon, in fine, as a man wrapped up in his books, and it was a matter of great surprise among his neighbours that he should ever have heard of his orphan cousin, Stephen Elliott, much more that he should have volunteered to make him an inmate of Aswarby Hall.

Whatever may have been expected by his neighbours, it is certain that Mr. Abney, the tall, the thin, the austere, seemed inclined to give his young cousin a kindly reception. The moment the front-door was opened he darted out of his study, rubbing his hands with delight.

"How are you, my boy?—how are you? How old are you?" said he—"that is, you are not too much tired, I hope, by your journey to eat your supper?"

"No, thank you, sir," said Master Elliott; "I am pretty well."

"That's a good lad," said Mr. Abney. "And how old are you, my boy?" It seemed a little odd that he should have asked the question twice in the first two minutes of their acquaintance.

"I'm twelve years old next birthday, sir," said Stephen.

"And when is your birthday, my dear boy? Eleventh of September, eh? That's well—that's very well: nearly a year hence, isn't it? I like—ha, ha!—I like to get these things down in my book. Sure it's twelve?—certain?"

"Yes, quite sure, sir."

"Well, well; take him to Mrs. Bunch's room, Parkes, and let him have his tea—supper—whatever it is."

"Yes, sir," answered the staid Mr. Parkes; and conducted Stephen to the lower regions.

Mrs. Bunch was the most comfortable and human person whom Stephen had as yet met in Aswarby. She made him completely at home. and they were great friends after the first quarter of an hour—as indeed they continued. Mrs. Bunch had been born in the neighbourhood some fifty-five years before the date of Stephen's arrival, and her residence at the Hall was of twenty years' standing. Consequently, if anyone knew the ins and outs of the house and the district, Mrs. Bunch knew them; and she was by no means disinclined to communicate her information. Certainly there were plenty of things about the Hall and the Hall gardens which Stephen, who was of an adventurous and inquiring turn, was anxious to have explained to him. "Who built the temple at the end of the laurel walk? Who was the old man whose picture hung on the staircase—sitting at a table, with a skull under his hand?" These and many similar points were cleared up by the resources of Mrs. Bunch's powerful intellect. There were others, however, of which the explanations furnished were less satisfactory. One November evening Stephen was sitting by the fire in the housekeeper's room reflecting on his surroundings. "Is Mr. Abney a good man, and will he go to heaven?" he suddenly asked, with the peculiar confidence which children possess in the ability of their elders to settle these questions—the decision of which is believed to be reserved for other tribunals.

"Good?—bless the child!" said Mrs. Bunch. "Master's as kind a soul as ever I see! Didn't I never tell you of the little boy as he took in out of the street, as you may say, this seven years back? and the little girl, two years after I first come here?"

"No: do tell me all about them, Mrs. Bunch—now this minute!"

"Well," said Mrs. Bunch, "the little girl I don't seem to recollect so much about. I know Master brought her back with him from his walk one day, and give orders to Mrs. Ellis, as was housekeeper then, as she should be took every care with. And the pore child hadn't no one belonging to her—she telled me so her own self: and here she lived with us a matter of three weeks it might be: and then, whether she were somethink of a gipsy in her blood or what not, but one morning she out of her bed afore any of us had opened a eye, and neither track nor yet trace of her have I set eyes on since. Master was wonderful put about, and had all the ponds dragged: but it's my belief she was had away by them gipsies, for there was singing round the house for as much as an hour the night she went and Parkes, he declares as he heard them a-calling in the woods all that afternoon. Dear, dear! an odd child she was, so silent in her ways and all; but I was wonderful taken up with her, so domesticated she was—surprising."

"And what about the little boy?" said Stephen.

"Ah, that pore boy!" sighed Mrs. Bunch. "He were a foreigner—Jevanny he called hisself—and he come a-tweaking his urdy gurdy round and about the drive one winter day, and Master ad him in that minute, and ast all about where he came from, and how old he was, and how he made his way, and where was his relatives, and all as kind as heart could wish. But it went the same way with him. They're a hunruly lot, them foreign nations, I do suppose, and he was off one fine morning just the same as the girl. Why he went and what he done was our question for as much as a year after: for he never took his urdy gurdy, and there it lays on the shelf."

The remainder of the evening was spent by Stephen in miscellaneous cross-examination of Mrs. Bunch and in efforts to extract a tune from the hurdy-gurdy.

That night he had a curious dream. At the end of the passage at the top of the house, in which his bedroom was situated, there was an old disused bathroom. It was kept locked, but the upper half of the door was glazed, and, since the muslin curtains which used to hang there had long been gone, you could look in and see the lead-lined bath affixed to the wall on the right hand, with its head towards the window. On the night of which I am speaking, Stephen Elliott found himself, as he thought, looking through the glazed door. The moon was shining through the window, and he was gazing at a figure which lay in the bath. His description of what he saw reminds me of what I once beheld myself in the famous vaults of St. Michan's Church in Dublin, which possess the horrid property of preserving corpses from decay for centuries. A figure inexpressibly thin and pathetic, of a dusty leaden colour, enveloped in a shroud-like garment, the thin lips crooked into a faint and dreadful smile, the hands pressed tightly over the region of the heart. As he looked upon it, a distant, almost inaudible moan seemed to issue from its lips, and the arms began to stir. The terror of the sight forced Stephen backwards, and he awoke to the fact that he was indeed standing on the cold boarded floor of the passage in the full light of the moon. With a courage which I do not think can be common among boys of his age he went to the door of the bathroom to ascertain if the figure of his dream were really there. It was not, and he went back to bed. Mrs. Bunch was much impressed next morning by his story, and went so far as to replace the muslin curtain over the glazed door of the bathroom. Mr. Abney, moreover, to whom he confided his experiences at breakfast, was greatly interested, and made notes of the matter in what he called "his book".

The spring equinox was approaching, as Mr. Abney frequently reminded his young cousin, adding that this had been always considered by the ancients to be a critical time for the young: that Stephen would do well to take care of himself, and to shut his bedroom window at night; and that Censorinus had some valuable remarks on the subject. Two incidents that occurred about this time made an impression upon Stephen's mind.

The first was after an unusually uneasy and oppressed night that he had passed—though he could not recall any particular dream that he had had.

The following evening Mrs. Bunch was occupying herself in mending his nightgown. "Gracious me, Master Stephen!" she broke forth rather irritably, "how do you manage to tear your nightdress all to flinders this way? Look here, sir, what trouble you do give to poor servants that have to darn and mend after you!"

There was indeed a most destructive and apparently wanton series of slits or scorings in the garment, which would undoubtedly require a skilful needle to make good. They were confined to the left side of the chest—long, parallel slits, about six inches in length, some of them not quite piercing the texture of the linen. Stephen could only express his entire ignorance of their origin: he was sure they were not there the night before. "But," he said, "Mrs. Bunch, they're just the same as the scratches on the outside of my bedroom door; and I'm sure I never had anything to do with making *them*."

Mrs. Bunch gazed at him open-mouthed, then snatched up a candle, departed hastily from the room, and was heard making her way upstairs. In a few minutes she came down. "Well," she said, "Master Stephen, it's a funny thing to me how them marks and scratches can a come there—too high up for any cat or dog to ave made 'em, much less a rat: for all the world like a Chinaman's finger nails, as my uncle in the tea trade used to tell us of when we was girls together. I wouldn't say nothink to Master, not if I was you, Master Stephen, my dear; and just turn the key of the door when you go to your bed."

"I always do, Mrs. Bunch, as soon as I've said my prayers."

"Ah, that's a good child: always say your prayers, and then no one can't hurt you."

Herewith Mrs. Bunch addressed herself to mending the injured nightgown, with intervals of meditation, until bed-time. This was on a Friday night in March, 1812.

On the following evening the usual duet of Stephen and Mrs. Bunch was augmented by the sudden arrival of Mr. Parkes, the butler, who as a rule kept himself rather to himself in his own pantry. He did not see that Stephen was there: he was, moreover, flustered and less slow of speech than was his wont. "Master may get up his own wine, if he likes, of an evening," was his first remark. "Either I do it in the daytime or not at all, Mrs. Bunch. I don't know what it may be: very like it's the rats, or the wind got into the cellars; but I'm not so young as I was, and I can't go through with it as I have done."

"Well, Mr. Parkes, you know it is a surprising place for the rats, is the Hall."

"I'm not denying that, Mrs. Bunch; and, to be sure, many a time I've heard the tale from the men in the shipyards about the rat that could speak. I never laid no confidence in that before; but to-night, if I'd demeaned myself to lay my ear to the door of the further bin, I could pretty much have heard what they was saying."

"Oh, there, Mr. Parkes, I've no patience with your fancies! Rats talking in the wine-cellar indeed!"

"Well, Mrs. Bunch, I've no wish to argue with you: all I say is, if you choose to go to the far bin, and lay your ear to the door, you may prove my words this minute."

"What nonsense you do talk, Mr. Parkes—not fit for children to listen to! Why, you'll be frightening Master Stephen there out of his wits."

"What! Master Stephen?" said Parkes, awaking to the consciousness of his presence. "Master Stephen knows well enough when I'm a playing a joke with you, Mrs. Bunch."

In fact, Master Stephen knew much too well to suppose that Mr. Parkes had in the first instance intended a joke. He was interested, not altogether pleasantly, in the situation; but all his questions were unsuccessful in inducing the butler to give any more detailed account of his experiences in the wine-cellar.

We have now arrived at March 24, 1812. It was a day of curious experiences for Stephen: a windy, noisy day, which filled the house and the gardens with a restless impression. As Stephen stood by the fence of the grounds, and looked out into the park, he felt as if an endless procession of unseen people were sweeping past him on the wind, borne on resistlessly and aimlessly, vainly striving to stop themselves, to catch at something that might arrest their flight and bring them once again into contact with the living world of which they had formed a part. After luncheon that day Mr. Abney said: "Stephen, my boy, do you think you could manage to come to me to-night as late as eleven o'clock in my study? I shall be busy until that time, and I wish to show you something connected with your future life which it is most important that you should know. You are not to mention this matter to Mrs. Bunch nor to anyone else in the house; and you had better go to your room at the usual time."

Here was a new excitement added to life: Stephen eagerly grasped at the opportunity of sitting up till eleven o'clock. He looked in at the library door on his way upstairs that evening, and saw a brazier, which he had often noticed in the corner of the room, moved out before the fire; an old silver-gilt cup stood on the table, filled with red wine, and some written sheets of paper lay near it. Mr. Abney was sprinkling some incense on the brazier from a round silver box as Stephen passed, but did not seem to notice his step.

The wind had fallen, and there was a still night and a full moon. At about ten o'clock Stephen was standing at the open window of his bedroom looking out over the country. Still as the night was, the mysterious population of the distant moonlit woods was not yet lulled to rest. From time to time strange cries as of lost and despairing wanderers sounded from across the mere. They might be the notes of owls or water birds, yet they did not quite resemble either sound. Were not they coming nearer? Now they sounded from the nearer side of the water, and in a few moments they seemed to be floating about among the shrubberies. Then they ceased; but just as Stephen was thinking of shutting the window and resuming his reading of *Robinson Crusoe*, he caught sight of two figures standing on the gravelled terrace that ran along the garden side of the Hall—two figures of a boy and girl, as it seemed: they stood side by side, looking up at the windows. Something in the form of the girl recalled irresistibly his dream of the figure in the bath. The boy inspired him with more acute fear. Whilst the girl stood still, half smiling, with her hands clasped over her heart, the boy, a thin shape, with black hair and ragged clothing, raised his arms in the air

33

with an appearance of menace and of unappeasable hunger and longing. The moon shone upon his almost transparent hands, and Stephen saw that the nails were fearfully long and that the light shone through them. As he stood with his arms thus raised, he disclosed a terrifying spectacle. On the left side of his chest there opened a black and gaping rent; and there fell upon Stephen's brain, rather than upon his ear, the impression of one of those hungry and desolate cries that he had heard resounding over the woods of Aswarby all that evening. In another moment this dreadful pair had moved swiftly and noiselessly over the dry gravel, and he saw them no more. Inexpressibly frightened as he was, he determined to take his candle and go down to Mr. Abney's study; for the hour appointed for their meeting was near at hand. The study or library opened out of the front hall on one side; and Stephen, urged on by his terrors, did not take long in getting there. To effect an entrance was not so easy. It was not locked, he felt sure, for the key was on the outside of the door as usual. His repeated knocks produced no answer. Mr. Abney was engaged: he was speaking. What? why did he try to cry out? and why was the cry choked in his throat? Had he, too, seen the mysterious children who were tracking their prey around that house of horrors? But now everything was quiet, and the door yielded to Stephen's terrified and frantic pushing. He did not come to himself for many hours after he had looked in.

On the table in Mr. Abney's study certain papers were found which explained the situation to Stephen Elliott when he was of an age to understand them. The most important sentences were as follows:—

"It was a belief very strongly and generally held by the ancients—of whose wisdom in these matters I have had such experience as induces me to place confidence in their assertions—that by enacting certain processes, which to us moderns have something of a barbaric complexion, a very remarkable enlightenment of the spiritual faculties in man may be attained: that, for example, by absorbing the personalities of a certain number of his fellow-creatures, an individual may gain a complete ascendancy over those orders of spiritual beings which control the elemental forces of our universe. "It is recorded of Simon Magus that he was able to fly in the air, to become invisible, or to assume any form he pleased, by the agency of the soul of a boy whom, to use the libellous phrase employed by the author of the *Clementine Recognitions*, he had 'murdered'. I find it set down, moreover, with considerable detail in the writings of Hermes Trismegistus that similar happy results may be produced by the absorption of the hearts of not less than three human beings below the age of twenty-one years. To the testing of the truth of this receipt I have devoted the greater part of the last twenty years, selecting as the *corpora vilia* of my experiment such persons as could conveniently be removed without occasioning a sensible gap in society. The first step I effected by the removal of one Phoebe Stanley, a girl of gipsy extraction, on March 24th, 1792. The second, by the removal of a wandering Italian lad, named Giovanni Paoli, on the night of March 23rd, 1805. The final 'victim'—to employ a word repugnant in the highest degree to my feelings—must be my cousin, Stephen Elliott. His day must be this March 24th, 1812.

"The best means of effecting the required absorption is to remove the heart from the *living* subject, to reduce it to ashes, and to mingle them with about a pint of some red wine, preferably port. The remains of the first two subjects, at least, it will be well to conceal: a disused bathroom—or wine-cellar will be found convenient for such a purpose. Some annoyance may be experienced from the psychic portion of the subjects—which popular language dignifies with the name of ghosts. But the man of philosophic temperament—to whom alone the experiment is appropriate—will be little prone to attach importance to the feeble efforts of these beings to wreak their vengeance on him. I contemplate with the liveliest satisfaction the enlarged and emancipated existence which the experiment, if successful, will confer on me; not only placing me beyond the reach of human justice, but eliminating to a great extent the prospect of death itself."

Mr. Abney was found in his chair, his hair thrown back, his face stamped with an expression of rage, fright, and mortal pain. In his left side was a terrible lacerated wound, exposing the heart. There was no blood on his hands, and a long knife that lay on the table was perfectly clean. A savage wild cat might have inflicted the injuries. The window of the study was open, and it was the opinion of the coroner that Mr. Abney had met his death by the agency of some wild creature. But Stephen Elliott's study of the papers I have quoted led him to a very different conclusion.

# E. F. Benson
## (1867-1940)

O ne of the Chit-Chat members who heard M. R. James read his ghost stories that October night, was himself already a literary celebrity. Edward Frederic Benson had taken a double first in Classics at King's in 1891, and he spent much of the following four years pursuing a passion for Greek archaeology at the British School in Athens. But in May 1893 he'd also published a novel, *Dodo: A Detail of the Day*, and by the time the Chit-Chat met for the 601st time, this "tour de force and . . . social bomb" was already in its eighth edition. The fact that *Dodo* had been written by the youthful son of the then Archbishop of Canterbury added to its notoriety.

Benson was one of three ghost story writing siblings to belong to the Chit-Chat at various points in the club's history—works by his brothers, A.C. and R.H., can be found elsewhere in this volume. E.F. himself had been elected to the club in October 1888, at the start of his second year at Cambridge, and he delivered four papers during his membership: "A Course of Nature" (precise subject unknown), "The Englishman Abroad" (ditto), "Marie Bashkirtseff" (about a Russian painter and diarist), and "Marlowe" (the Elizabethan playwright). During this last, read on 1 March 1890, the society's snuff box had done the rounds earlier than the speaker would have liked.

"I remember (still with pain)," he recalled in his 1921 memoir *Our Family Affairs*, "reading a paper on Marlowe's *Faustus*, during which embarrassing explosions unnerved me.

I had reason to quote (at a very impressive stage of this essay) certain lines from that tragedy, which with stage directions came out as follows:

*Faustus*: Where are you damned? (sneezings)

*Mephistopheles*: In Hell. (sneezings and loud laughter)
For where I am is hell (sneezing and more laughter)
And where hell is (uproar) there must I ever be."

Benson was also a member of the Twice a Fortnight Club, the photo of which shows him in 1891 looking notably self-assured, immediately to MRJ's right. Five years his junior, Benson was frank about his fealty to the then Dean of King's: "Intellectually (or perhaps aesthetically) I, like many others, made an unconditional surrender to his tastes, and, with a strong prepossession already in that direction, I became convinced for the time—and the time was long—that Dickens was the St. Peter who held the keys of the heavenly kingdom of literature . . . He almost made me dethrone Bach from his legitimate seat, and by a revolutionary movement place Handel there instead . . . " (*Our Family Affairs*, 1921).

There was something, perhaps, of the older/younger brother dynamic to the two men's relationship. In 1890, at the bidding of Archbishop Benson, MRJ had led E.F. on a tour of the great cathedral cities of Normandy; he'd have recognised at once the kind of high-brow, ecclesiastical sightseeing trip described in "The Scrap-book of Canon Alberic" (1895).

But as well as cultural and aesthetic tastes, the two men shared a boyish sense of humour, and Benson was, after MRJ, the most prolific and creative contributor to a long-running joke about the eccentric Cambridge don, J. E. Nixon: "the oddest of mortals . . . " according to *Our Family Affairs*, with one hand, one eye, and a mind "like a cage-full of monkeys".

An elaborate mythology was constructed around Nixon and the imagined indignities that he suffered at the hands of Professor Brooke Foss Westcott, another Fellow of King's, and Canon of Westminster Cathedral. Benson recalled how, on his cathedral tour of Normandy, "the Nixon saga was enriched by a Pindaric ode in praise of Pnyxon, winner of the tricycle race against two Divinity professors . . . " and this fantasy survives in a letter that he wrote to MRJ, now in Cambridge University Library: "But on that day came there one from the back lawn of King's, who sped like black night on a tricycle, and he had only one glove. And the parasitic eye gleamed like the lightning of Zeus to the left of his forehead and his tawny beard shone like the unharvested sea when the sun strikes it . . . " So it goes on, for three pages.

The publication of *Dodo* seems to have put some strain on the friendship: MRJ wrote to A. C. Benson complaining that the book's extraordinary success had gone to his younger brother's head. But if that debut novel didn't impress him much, then the collections of "spook tales" that E.F. began publishing in 1912 did. They "rank high", MRJ wrote in "Some Remarks on Ghost Stories" (*The Bookman*, 1929), though he added that the author "sins occasionally by stepping over the line of legitimate horridness". Given that one of MRJ's own earliest tales involves a scholar who rips the hearts from the living bodies of children and eats them, it would be interesting to know more precisely where he thought that line lay. The moment of gory revelation in "The Other Bed", printed here, might be thought to hover around it.

"The Other Bed", first published in *The Popular Magazine* (April 1908), illustrates well the relationship between the two writers. An account of nocturnal horror in a twin-bedded hotel room, it reads like a self-conscious response to MRJ's "Oh, Whistle and I'll Come to You, My Lad" (1904). The spare bed with its restless linen is only the most obvious of several common features. Both protagonists are bookish travellers whose complacency is eroded by the strange phenomena that accrue. Both men take part in after-dinner discussions on the supernatural, and experience upsetting dream visions. And in both stories adverse December weather plays an active role in the narrative. Smaller details chime too: the reading of a book to induce sleep; a throwaway Biblical joke. Benson's tale feels like both a tribute to MRJ and a challenge; as if he has tasked himself with surpassing the tension and horror of those events in the Globe Inn at Burnstow.

If so, I think he falls short. Benson was a more prolific producer of ghost stories than MRJ, and he was the more versatile writer; there's a greater variety of horror and settings to be found in his collections *Visible and Invisible* (1923), *Spook Stories* (1928), and *More Spook Stories* (1934). And he published plenty of high quality non-supernatural fiction too: the comic novels about the bickering neighbours Mapp and Lucia, which first appeared in 1930, remain popular and amusing today. But while the sense of terror in "The Other Bed" mounts effectively enough, it flounders at the end. The well-paced set-up deserves more than the deflating coincidence that concludes it, and the kind of exposition that MRJ's stories so effectively eschew.

Where Benson excelled MRJ was as a writer of memoirs, and his greatest contribution to the Chit-Chat was as its funniest and most prolific chronicler. The anecdote that follows from *Our Family Affairs*, is also found, with variations, in another of Benson's memoirs, *As We Were* (1930), and in one of his novels, *David of King's* (1924). He wasn't even in Cambridge when the meeting that he describes took place; and MRJ, who was there, cast doubt upon accuracy of his account in his own memoir. But his older brother Arthur was an eye witness, and E. F. Benson's sketch bears repeating here for what it tells us about the atmosphere at the Chit-Chat in MRJ's day:

"A prominent philologist whose turn it was to regale us, found that he had not had leisure to write his paper on 'Manners' and proposed to address us on the subject instead. He strode about the room gesticulating and vehement, stumbling over the hearthrug, lighting cigarettes and throwing them away instead of his match, while he harangued us on this interesting ethical topic, with interspersed phrases of French and German, and odd English words like 'cocksuredom'. As this ludicrously proceeded, a rather tense silence settled down on 'The Chitchat'; its decorous members bit their lips, and prudently refrained from looking each other in the face, and there were little stifled noises like hiccups or birds in bushes going about the room, and the sofa where three sat trembled, as when a kettle is on the boil. Then he diverged, via, I think, the exquisite urbanity of the ancient Greeks, to Greek sculpture, and proceeded as a practical illustration to throw himself into the attitude of Discobolus. At that precise moment, Dr. Cunningham of Trinity, who was drinking claret-cup and trembling a great deal, completely lost control of himself. Claret-cup spurted from his nose and mouth; I should not have thought a man could have so violently choked and laughed simultaneously, without fatal damage to himself. That explosion, of course, instantaneously spread round the entire company, except the amazed lecturer, and Dr. Cunningham, finding he could not stop laughing at all, seized his cap and gown and left the room with a rapid and unsteady step. Even when he had gone wild yells and slappings of the leg came resonantly in through the open windows as he crossed the court . . . "

# The Other Bed

### E. F. Benson

I had gone out to Switzerland just before Christmas, expecting, from experience, a month of divinely renovating weather, of skating all day in brilliant sun, and basking in the hot frost of that windless atmosphere. Occasionally, as I knew, there might be a snowfall, which would last perhaps for forty-eight hours at the outside, and would be succeeded by another ten days of cloudless perfection, cold even to zero at night, but irradiated all day long by the unflecked splendour of the sun.

Instead the climatic conditions were horrible. Day after day a gale screamed through this upland valley that should have been so windless and serene, bringing with it a tornado of sleet that changed to snow by night. For ten days there was no abatement of it, and evening after evening, as I consulted my barometer, feeling sure that the black finger would show that we were coming to the end of these abominations, I found that it had sunk a little lower yet, till it stayed, like a homing pigeon, on the S of storm. I mention these things in depredation of the story that follows, in order that the intelligent reader may say at once, if he wishes, that all that occurred was merely a result of the malaise of nerves and digestion that perhaps arose from those storm-bound and disturbing conditions. And now to go back to the beginning again.

I had written to engage a room at the Hôtel Beau Site, and had been agreeably surprised on arrival to find that for the modest sum of twelve francs a day I was allotted a room on the first floor with two beds in it. Otherwise the hotel was quite full. Fearing to be billeted in a twenty-two franc room, by mistake, I instantly confirmed my arrangements at the bureau. There was no mistake: I had ordered a twelve-franc room and had been given one. The very civil clerk hoped that I was satisfied with it, for otherwise there was nothing vacant. I hastened to say that I was more than satisfied, fearing the fate of Esau.

I arrived about three in the afternoon of a cloudless and glorious day, the last of the series. I hurried down to the rink, having had the prudence to put skates in the forefront of my luggage, and spent a divine but struggling hour or two, coming up to the hotel about sunset. I had letters to write, and after ordering tea to be sent up to my gorgeous apartment, No. 23, on the first floor, I went straight up there.

The door was ajar and—I feel certain I should not even remember this now except in the light of what followed—just as I got close to it, I heard some faint movement inside the room and instinctively knew that my servant was there unpacking. Next moment I was in the room myself, and it was empty. The unpacking had been finished, and everything was neat, orderly, and comfortable. My barometer was on the table, and I observed with dismay that it had gone down nearly half an inch. I did not give another thought to the movement I thought I had heard from outside.

Certainly I had a delightful room for my twelve francs a day. There were, as I have said, two beds in it, on one of which were already laid out my dress-clothes, while night-things were disposed on the other. There were two windows, between which stood a large washing-stand, with plenty of room on it; a sofa with its back to the light stood conveniently near the pipes of central heating, there were a couple of good arm-chairs, a writing table, and, rarest of luxuries, another table, so that every time one had breakfast it was not necessary to pile up a drift of books and papers to make room for the tray. My window looked east, and sunset still flamed on the western faces of the virgin snows, while above, in spite of the dejected barometer, the sky was bare of clouds, and a thin slip of pale crescent moon was swung high among the stars that still burned dimly in these first moments of their kindling. Tea came up for me without delay, and, as I ate, I regarded my surroundings with extreme complacency.

Then, quite suddenly and without cause, I saw that the disposition of the beds would never do; I could not possibly sleep in the bed that my servant had chosen for me, and without pause I jumped up, transferred my dress clothes to the other bed, and put my night things where they had been. It was done breathlessly almost, and not till then did I ask myself why I had done it. I found I had not the slightest idea. I had merely felt that I could not sleep in the other bed. But having made the change I felt perfectly content.

My letters took me an hour or so to finish, and I had yawned and blinked considerably over the last one or two, in part from their inherent dullness, in part from quite natural sleepiness. For I had been in the train for twenty-four hours, and was fresh to these bracing airs which so conduce to appetite, activity, and sleep, and as there was still an hour before I need dress, I lay down on my sofa with a book for excuse, but the intention to slumber as reason. And consciousness ceased as if a tap had been turned off.

Then—I dreamed. I dreamed that my servant came very quietly into the room, to tell me no doubt that it was time to dress. I supposed there were a few minutes to spare yet, and that he saw I was dozing, for, instead of rousing me, he moved quietly about the room, setting things in order. The light appeared to me to be very dim, for I could not see him with any distinctness, indeed, I only knew it was he because it could not be any body else. Then he paused by my washing-stand, which had a shelf for brushes and razors above it, and I saw him take a razor from its case and begin stropping it; the light was strongly reflected on the blade of the razor. He tried the edge once or twice on his thumb-nail, and then to my horror I saw him trying it on his throat. Instantaneously one of those deafening dream-crashes awoke me, and I saw the door half open, and my servant in the very act of coming in. No doubt the opening of the door had constituted the crash.

I had joined a previously-arrived party of five, all of us old friends, and accustomed to see each other often; and at dinner, and afterwards in intervals of bridge, the conversation roamed agreeably over a variety of topics, rocking-turns and the prospects of weather (a thing of vast importance in Switzerland, and not a commonplace subject) and the performances at the opera, and under what circumstances as revealed in dummy's hand, is it justifiable for a player to refuse to return his partner's original lead in no trumps. Then over whisky and soda and the repeated "last cigarette", it veered back via the Zantzigs to thought transference and the transference of emotion. Here one of the party, Harry Lambert, put forward the much discussed explanation of haunted houses based on this principle. He put it very concisely.

"Everything that happens," he said, "whether it is a step we take, or a thought that crosses our mind, makes some change in its immediate material world. Now the most violent and concentrated emotion we can imagine is the emotion that leads a man to take so extreme a step as killing himself or somebody else. I can easily imagine such a deed so eating into the material scene, the room or the haunted heath, where it happens, that its mark lasts an enormous time. The air rings with the cry of the slain and still drips with his blood. It is not everybody who will perceive it, but sensitives will. By the way, I am sure that man who waits on us at dinner is a sensitive."

It was already late, and I rose.

"Let us hurry him to the scene of a crime," I said. "For myself I shall hurry to the scene of sleep."

Outside the threatening promise of the barometer was already finding fulfilment, and a cold ugly wind was complaining among the pines, and hooting round the peaks, and snow had begun to fall. The night was thickly overcast, and it seemed as if uneasy presences were going to and fro in the darkness. But there was no use in ill augury, and certainly if we were to be house-bound for a few days I was lucky in having so commodious a lodging. I had plenty to occupy myself with indoors, though I should vastly have preferred to be engaged outside, and in the immediate present how good it was to lie free in a proper bed after a cramped night in the train.

I was half-undressed when there came a tap at my door, and the waiter who had served us at dinner came in carrying a bottle of whisky. He was a tall young fellow, and though I had not noticed him at dinner, I saw at once now, as he stood in the glare of the electric light, what Harry had meant when he said he was sure he was a sensitive. There is no mistaking that look: it is exhibited in a peculiar "inlooking" of the eye. Those eyes, one knows, see further than the surface . . .

"The bottle of whisky for monsieur," he said putting it down on the table.

"But I ordered no whisky," said I. He looked puzzled.

"Number twenty-three?" he said. Then he glanced at the other bed.

"Ah, for the other gentleman, without doubt," he said.

"But there is no other gentleman," said I. "I am alone here."

He took up the bottle again.

"Pardon, monsieur," he said. "There must be a mistake. I am new here; I only came today. But I thought—"

"Yes?" said I.

"I thought that number twenty-three had ordered a bottle of whisky," he repeated. "Goodnight, monsieur, and pardon."

I got into bed, extinguished the light, and feeling very sleepy and heavy with the oppression, no doubt, of the snow that was coming, expected to fall asleep at once. Instead my mind would not quite go to roost, but kept sleepily stumbling about among the little events of the day, as some tired pedestrian in the dark stumbles over stones instead of lifting his feet. And as I got sleepier it seemed to me that my mind kept moving in a tiny little circle. At one moment it drowsily recollected how I had thought I had heard movement inside my room, at the next it remembered my dream of some figure going stealthily about and stropping a razor, at a third it wondered why this Swiss waiter with the eyes of a "sensitive" thought that number twenty-three had ordered a bottle of whisky. But at the time I made no guess as to any coherence between these little isolated facts; I only dwelt on them with drowsy persistence. Then a fourth fact came to join the sleepy circle, and I wondered why I had felt a repugnance against using the other bed.

But there was no explanation of this forthcoming, either, and the outlines of thought grew more blurred and hazy, until I lost consciousness altogether.

Next morning began the series of awful days, sleet and snow falling relentlessly with gusts of chilly wind, making any out-of-door amusement next to impossible. The snow was too soft for tobogganing, it balled on the skis, and as for the rink it was but a series of pools of slushy snow.

This in itself, of course, was quite enough to account for any ordinary depression and heaviness of spirit, but all the time I felt there was something more than that to which I owed the utter blackness that hung over those days. I was beset too by fear that at first was only vague, but which gradually became more definite, until it resolved itself into a fear of number twenty-three and in particular a terror of the other bed. I had no notion why or how I was afraid of it, the thing was perfectly causeless, but the shape and the outline of it grew slowly clearer, as detail after detail of ordinary life, each minute and trivial in itself, carved and moulded this fear, till it became definite. Yet the whole thing was so causeless and childish that I could speak to no one of it; I could but assure myself that it was all a figment of nerves disordered by this unseemly weather.

However, as to the details, there were plenty of them. Once I woke up from strangling nightmare, unable at first to move, but in a panic of terror, believing that I was sleeping in the other bed. More than once, too, awaking before I was called, and getting out of bed to look at the aspect of the morning, I saw with a sense of dreadful misgiving that the bed-clothes on the other bed were strangely disarranged, as if some one had slept there, and smoothed them down afterwards, but not so well as not to give notice of the occupation. So one night I laid a trap, so to speak, for the intruder of which the real object was to calm my own nervousness (for I still told myself that I was frightened of nothing), and tucked in the sheet very carefully, laying the pillow on the top of it. But in the morning it seemed as if my interference had not been to the taste of the occupant, for there was more impatient disorder than usual in the bed-clothes, and on the pillow was an indentation, round and rather deep, such as we may see any morning in our own beds. Yet by day these things did not frighten me, but it was when I went to bed at night that I quaked at the thought of further developments.

It happened also from time to time that I wanted something brought me, or wanted my servant. On three or four of these occasions my bell was answered by the "Sensitive", as we called him, but the Sensitive, I noticed, never came into the room. He would open the door a chink to receive my order and on returning would again open it a chink to say that my boots, or whatever it was, were at the door. Once I made him come in, but I saw him cross himself as, with a face of icy terror, he stepped into the room, and the sight somehow did not reassure me. Twice also he came up in the evening, when I had not rung at all, even as he came up the first night, and opened the door a chink to say that my bottle of whisky was outside. But the poor fellow was in a state of such bewilderment when I went out and told him that I had not ordered whisky, that I did not press for an explanation. He begged my pardon profusely; he thought a bottle of whisky had been ordered for number twenty-three. It was his mistake, entirely—I should not be charged for it; it must have been the other gentleman. Pardon again; he remembered there was no other gentleman, the other bed was unoccupied.

It was on the night when this happened for the second time that I definitely began to wish that I too was quite certain that the other bed was unoccupied. The ten days of snow and sleet were at an end, and to-night the moon once more, grown from a mere slip to a shining shield, swung serenely among the stars. But though at dinner everyone exhibited an extraordinary change of spirit, with the rising of the barometer and the discharge of this huge snow-fall, the intolerable gloom which had been mine so long but deepened and blackened. The fear was to me now like some statue, nearly finished, modelled by the carving hands of these details, and though it still stood below its moistened sheet, any moment, I felt, the sheet might be twitched away, and I be confronted with it. Twice that evening I had started to go to the bureau, to ask to have a bed made up for me, anywhere, in the billiard-room or the smoking-room, since the hotel was full, but the intolerable childishness of the proceeding revolted me. What was I afraid of? A dream of my own, a mere nightmare? Some fortuitous disarrangement of bed linen? The fact that a Swiss waiter made mistakes about bottles of whisky? It was an impossible cowardice.

But equally impossible that night were billiards or bridge, or any form of diversion. My only salvation seemed to lie in downright hard work, and soon after dinner I went to my room (in order to make my first real counter-move against fear) and sat down solidly to several hours of proof-correcting, a menial and monotonous employment, but one which is necessary, and engages the entire attention. But first I looked thoroughly round the room, to reassure myself, and found all modern and solid; a bright paper of daisies on the wall, a floor parquetted, the hot-water pipes chuckling to themselves in the corner, my bed-clothes turned down for the night, the other bed. The electric light was burning brightly, and there seemed to me to be a curious stain, as of a shadow, on the lower part of the pillow and the top of the sheet, definite and suggestive, and for a moment I stood there again throttled by a nameless terror. Then taking my courage in my hands I went closer and looked at it. Then I touched it; the sheet, where the stain or shadow was, seemed damp to the hand, so also was the pillow. And then I remembered; I had thrown some wet clothes on the bed before dinner. No doubt that was the reason. And fortified by this extremely simple dissipation of my fear, I sat down and began on my proofs. But my fear had been this, that the stain had not in that first moment looked like the mere greyness of water-moistened linen.

From below, at first came the sound of music, for they were dancing to-night, but I grew absorbed in my work, and only recorded the fact that after a time there was no more music. Steps went along the passages, and I heard the buzz of conversation on landings, and the closing of doors till by degrees the silence became noticeable. The loneliness of night had come.

It was after the silence had become lonely that I made the first pause in my work, and by the watch on my table saw that it was already past midnight. But I had little more to do; another half-hour would see the end of the business, but there were certain notes I had to make for future reference, and my stock of paper was already exhausted. However, I had bought some in the village that afternoon, and it was in the bureau downstairs, where I had left it, when I came in and had subsequently forgotten to bring it upstairs. It would be the work of a minute only to get it.

The electric light had brightened considerably during the last hour, owing no doubt to many burners being put out in the hotel, and as I left the room I saw again the stain on the pillow and sheet of the other bed. I had really forgotten all about it for the last hour, and its presence there came as an unwelcome surprise. Then I remembered the explanation of it, which had struck me before, and for purposes of self-reassurement I again touched it. It was still damp, but—Had I got chilly with my work? For it was warm to the hand. Warm, and surely rather sticky. It did not seem like the touch of the water-damp. And at the same moment I knew I was not alone in the room. There was something there, something silent as yet, and as yet invisible. But it was there.

Now for the consolation of persons who are inclined to be fearful, I may say at once that I am in no way brave, but that terror which, God knows, was real enough, was yet so interesting, that interest overruled it. I stood for a moment by the other bed, and, half-consciously only, wiped the hand that had felt the stain, for the touch of it, though all the time I told myself that it was but the touch of the melted snow on the coat I had put there, was unpleasant and unclean. More than that I did not feel, because in the presence of the unknown and the perhaps awful, the sense of curiosity, one of the strongest instincts we have, came to the fore. So, rather eager to get back to my room again, I ran downstairs to get the packet of paper. There was still a light in the bureau, and the Sensitive, on night-duty, I suppose, was sitting there dozing. My entrance did not disturb him, for I had on noiseless felt slippers, and seeing at once the package I was in search of, I took it, and left him still unawakened. That was somehow of a fortifying nature. The Sensitive anyhow could sleep in his hard chair; the occupant of the unoccupied bed was not calling to him to-night.

I closed my door quietly, as one does at night when the house is silent, and sat down at once to open my packet of paper and finish my work. It was wrapped up in an old news-sheet, and struggling with the last of the string that bound it, certain words caught my eye. Also the date at the top of the paper caught my eye, a date nearly a year old, or, to be quite accurate, a date fifty-one weeks old. It was an American paper and what it recorded was this:

"The body of Mr. Silas R. Hume, who committed suicide last week at the Hôtel Beau Site, Moulin sur Chalons, is to be buried at his house in Boston, Mass. The inquest held in Switzerland showed that he cut his throat with a razor, in an attack of delirium tremens induced by drink. In the cupboard of his room were found three dozen empty bottles of Scotch whisky . . . "

So far I had read when without warning the electric light went out, and I was left in, what seemed for the moment, absolute darkness. And again I knew I was not alone, and I knew now who it was who was with me in the room.

Then the absolute paralysis of fear seized me. As if a wind had blown over my head, I felt the hair of it stir and rise a little. My eyes also, I suppose, became accustomed to the sudden darkness, for they could now perceive the shape of the furniture in the room from the light of the starlit sky outside. They saw more too than the mere furniture. There was standing by the wash-stand between the two windows a figure, clothed only in night-garments, and its hands moved among the objects on the shelf above the basin. Then with two steps it made a sort of dive for the other bed, which was in shadow. And then the sweat poured on to my forehead.

Though the other bed stood in shadow I could still see dimly, but sufficiently, what was there. The shape of a head lay on the pillow, the shape of an arm lifted its hand to the electric bell that was close by on the wall, and I fancied I could hear it distantly ringing. Then a moment later came hurrying feet up the stairs and along the passage outside, and a quick rapping at my door.

"Monsieur's whisky, monsieur's whisky," said a voice just outside. "Pardon, monsieur, I brought it as quickly as I could."

The impotent paralysis of cold terror was still on me. Once I tried to speak and failed, and still the gentle tapping went on at the door, and the voice telling some one that his whisky was there. Then at a second attempt, I heard a voice which was mine saying hoarsely:

"For God's sake come in; I am alone with it."

There was the click of a turned door-handle, and as suddenly as it had gone out a few seconds before, the electric light came back again, and the room was in full illumination. I saw a face peer round the corner of the door, but it was at another face I looked, the face of a man sallow and shrunken, who lay in the other bed, staring at me with glazed eyes. He lay high in bed, and his throat was cut from ear to ear; and the lower part of the pillow was soaked in blood, and the sheet streamed with it.

53

Then suddenly that hideous vision vanished, and there was only a sleepy-eyed waiter looking into the room. But below the sleepiness terror was awake, and his voice shook when he spoke.

"Monsieur rang?" he asked.

No, monsieur had not rung. But monsieur made himself a couch in the billiard-room.

# Robert Carr Bosanquet
## (1871-1935)

*"At Cambridge . . . [Carr Bosanquet] wrote as wittily as he talked and spoke. He had rather a dry, kind sense of humour… which pervaded his talk, his speeches, his finished and scholarly verse. We thought he was certain to be a bright star in English literature . . . "*

– Maurice Baring,
*The Puppet Show of Memory* (1922)

Like E. F. Benson, Robert Carr Bosanquet was present to hear M. R. James read "The Scrap-book of Canon Alberic" and "Lost Hearts" for the first time in October 1893. Unlike Benson, the literary promise that he showed as a schoolboy and undergraduate was not fulfilled in later life.

Bosanquet arrived in Cambridge from Eton in October 1890 to read Classics at Trinity, and he joined the Chit-Chat straightaway. His reputation as a wit and raconteur was already high. As a schoolboy he'd once written home with the proud news that a friend had "tried to make me a medal for telling him stories at dinner, with the inscription 'For Good Ta*i*ls'. But it was rather a failure, so he made one with a simple 'S' on (for stories). I melted it for bullets." A. C. Benson, his tutor at Eton, encouraged his literary pursuits, and the young Bosanquet edited a highly acclaimed school magazine called *The Parachute*, contributed topical light verse to the *Eton Chronicle* and, in his final year, co-wrote a book.

*Seven Summers* was published at the authors' expense in July 1890 and dedicated partially to A. C. Benson, "who first sowed in our breast the fatal ambition to perpetuate our thoughts in black and white . . . " Aimed at Etonians past, present, and future, it's a lively account of public school life, with chapter titles like "On Getting Up" and "The Shiny Fag". And it shone brightly during the brief time it was available—years later Maurice Baring described it as "the best book about Eton life that has ever been written". But a few days after publication, having been once vetted and approved by those in authority, it was suddenly withdrawn from circulation on the grounds that "it gave a picture of the school that was 'unpleasing and untrue'."

"The disappointment and financial loss were severe," recalled Bosanquet's widow fifty years later, and she couldn't account for the sudden act of censorship. "The strongest epithet used is 'ring-tailed roarer'," she noted, "and the worst crime the concealment of a case of claret".

Undeterred, Bosanquet brought his literary and comic talents to the Chit-Chat. On 24 November 1894 he delivered a paper on "the elephant in the ancient world", which was reported appreciatively by Will Stone in a letter to his mother. On other occasions he spoke on "*Lorna Doone*", "Dry Bones", and "Early English Theatres". The only contribution of his which has survived, however, was given on 7 March 1891, when the minute book tells us that "original poems were read by Mr. James 'A College Council', Mr. Benson 'Tobogganing' . . . Mr. Bosanquet 'The Dean's Story', [and] Mr. Bather 'Organgrinder' (by Mr. J. K. Stephen)." All these poets and readers were also members of the Twice a Fortnight club, and Bosanquet can be seen seated on the far right of the group photograph.

Apart from MRJ's evening of ghost stories, this meeting of the Chit-Chat seems to have been the only one that was devoted solely to members' literary compositions. "A College Council" has not survived, but it doubtless treated of the committee meetings that MRJ so loathed, yet as Dean was obliged to attend. Complaints about these pepper his memoir *Eton and King's* (1926) and it would have been a treat to have heard his exasperation versified. E. F. Benson's "Tobogganing" is likewise lost, though his thoughts on the subject survive in prose in a chapter of his *Winter Sports in Switzerland* (1913). J. K. Stephen's "Organgrinder" was published a month later in the *Pall Mall Gazette* under the title "The Street Organs Bill, 1891". It's a response to government plans to impose a curfew on the playing of organs in public and has perhaps lost some of the comic urgency it once had: "If they pass their cruel measure, / If the House is true to them, / You must never give us pleasure, / Grinder, after 8 P.M."

More entertaining, and timeless, is Bosanquet's "The Dean's Story" reprinted here. I had hoped at first that the college official of the title might be MRJ himself, who was the Junior Dean of King's at the time the poem was written, and an avowed cat-lover. But Bosanquet was a Trinity man, and we're probably meant to imagine the action taking place there. The poem is a sprightly variation on an old theme: the vengefulness of cats upon their human abusers, what Bosanquet calls "the wrath of Pasht". Works like Edgar Allan Poe's "The Black Cat" (1843), Bram Stoker's "The Squaw" (1893), and H. P. Lovecraft's "The Cats of Ulthar" (1920) mine the same tradition.

"The Dean's Story" was published a few weeks after the meeting at which it was read, in *The Granta* (April 1891). Bosanquet was a valued early contributor to this undergraduate magazine, and in January 1893 he attended a dinner at the Reform Club to celebrate its 100th edition. The guest of honour was Sir Arthur Conan Doyle, a friend of *The Granta*'s then editor Bertrand Fletcher Robinson, and it was recalled that "festivities were kept up to a late hour, and the solemn palace of Liberalism in Pall Mall re-echoed with laughter produced by many good stories" (*The Granta and Its Contributors, 1889-1914* [1924]).

The seating plan for the dinner survives, and alongside those of notable ex-Cambridge writers like Barry Pain and Anstey Guthrie, it includes an intriguing, single name: James. There's no indication whether this is a surname or a Christian name, and the official history of the magazine, published in 1924, tells us only that "The identity of 'James' remains a mystery." Now, MRJ never wrote for *The Granta* himself, but he was praised in its pages, on 31 May 1889, and friends other than Bosanquet contributed in the 1890s: J. K. Stephen, and fellow Chit-Chat members E. F. Benson and Eustace Talbot, who was the editor from 1895/6 (both men were present to hear MRJ read his two ghost stories at the 601st meeting). *Might* MRJ have been a guest at this dinner? Can we fantasise about the possibility that he and Arthur Conan Doyle shared stories and jokes around the same table in early 1893? We probably shouldn't . . .

The second poem printed here, "Red Gold: A Cosmic Poem" by Bludyard Skribling, appeared in another university magazine, *The Cambridge ABC*, which ran for four issues during May Week, the end-of-academic-year celebrations, in 1894 and was edited by Richard Austen-Leigh, Maurice Baring, and Hubert Cornish—the last two of whom were also members of the Chit-Chat. With its broad dialect and rollicking rhythm, it's an impressively sustained pastiche of Rudyard Kipling whose *Barrack Room Ballads* had been published in 1892.

But for all his literary and comic flair, Bosanquet had a more serious calling. The week before MRJ's night of ghost stories, he read a paper to the Chit-Chat on "The Festival of Tenos". This gathering of Greek Orthodox pilgrims on the Cycladic island of Tenos, home to an ancient, miraculous icon of the Annunciation, takes place annually on 25 March, and in 1893 Bosanquet had witnessed it, during a break from his studies at the British School in Athens.

His time in Greece shaped his future career. Fearing that his reputation as a "professional funny-man" had damaged his chances of winning a Fellowship of Trinity, Bosanquet put aside his pen and devoted his working life to Classical archaeology—at which he excelled.

After his death his literary remains were gathered into a commemorative volume, *Letters and Light Verse*, which was published privately in 1938. That's where "The Dean's Story" and "Red Gold" can be found today, and where we can read a limerick about a fellow Chit-Chat member, John Stewart Shearme, who was also present at the 601st meeting.

> "There once was a fellow called Shearme
> Who said to his tutor, 'You Worm.'
>     The tutor replied,
>     'You had better decide
> To go down at the end of the term.' "

# The Dean's Story

R. C. Bosanquet

"That cat, sir, black and yellow
    And blind and deaf and lame,
Is on the books as Fellow,
    And ranks in all but name
As Master," said the Junior Dean,
And told this tale to me between
Our efforts on the bowling-green,
    As I repeat the same.

"There entered at this College
    Some dozen years ago,
A man that hated knowledge
    And held that books were low.
Your thorough-bred patrician weed
Can run uncommon quick to seed—
I judge by Chapels—to proceed,
    He lived on Staircase O.

"He never stinted tenners
    His tip was seldom less,
And when he ran at Fenner's
    He ran in evening dress:
Became what you would call a Blood,
One part whisky, three parts mud,

The kind that chews the devil's cud,
    And chews it to excess.

"His sinful soul was spotted
    As any groom's cravat,
And grew so far besotted
    With self-indulgence that
Impelled one night by freak of fate
Or liquors that intoxicate,
At any rate returning late
In passing through the College gate
    He kicked the Senior Cat.

"She rose in silent sorrow,
    Inscrutable, obese,
Resolved that on the morrow
    Indignities should cease.
Her couriers, the Chapel bats,
Proclaimed the tryst to fens and flats,
And midnight found three hundred cats
    Encamped on Parker's Piece.

"That night, about a quarter
    To one or something more,
Men say the college porter
    Sat up in bed and swore.
He cursed the bell that broke his sleep
In tones to make a Bursar weep,
In metaphors as broad and deep,
    Then loth unbarred the door.

"It was no common cabby
    That pealed the midnight bell;
It was a grizzled tabby,

A cat he knew right well;
And lo! behind her through the night
A long procession loomed in sight,
Cats black and yellow, dun and white,
 Blue-grey and tortoise-shell.

"Their pace was soft and solemn,
 Their claws were bared to wound,
In dim fantastic column
 A dreadful dirge they crooned.
He counted near three hundred pass
In single file across the grass,
He heard the crash of breaking glass,
 That heard, and hearing swooned.

"Against his shoulder creaking
 The gate swung to and fro,
And round the turrets shrieking
 Came gusts of wind and snow.
Yet men that are not wont to dream
Declare they heard a human scream
That unmistakeably did seem
 To come from staircase O.

"A Help about the dawning,
 Unlocked the outer door;
She found the window yawning
 And snow across the floor,—
An empty bed, no blood, no tracks:
No corpse in Cam or on the Backs:
For whom the wrath of Pasht attacks
 Is seen on earth no more.
The only clue that fact supplied
I personally verified—

63

*The cats in all the countryside*
    *Were sleeker than before.*

"No Proctor, Dean or Master
    Has more despotic right
Of dealing out disaster
    And satisfying spite.
The most unbending democrat
Does homage to the Senior Cat,
    And—*verbum sapienti sat*—
It's just as well to lift your hat
    In passing, so—Good-night."

# Red Gold:
## A Cosmic Poem

by Bludyard Skribling
[R. C. Bosanquet]

There be three strong men that curse the fates
    In the mists of a wet Quay-side;
For through the Mediterranean Gates
The news is come from Behring Straits
    That Cain O'Kane has died.

*And it's O to find the Isle he knew*
    *And where the gold is hid,*
*And the chart he stole from a Spanish Jew,*
*The chart that a priest in Lima drew*
*From the dying tale of one of the crew*
    *That was there with Captain Kidd.*

The first swore low—"His hammocked bones
    "In forty fathoms are:
"But himself's in the locker of David Jones,
"And I guess there ain't no telephones
    "From there to Eternal Tar."

And the Second spake—"For the red gold's sake
    "There's many a man in Leith
"Had up and swum to Kingdom Come
    "With a knife between his teeth."

And the Third laughed out—"By Bottled Stout
    "Ye be drunk or not far from it:
"If ye lie so large at dawn, by noon
"Ye'll steal the Shoon of the Man in the Moon
    "And ride on the tail of a Comet."

And the Scot swore back—"Ye doubt too soon;
"What's said at dawn may be done by noon;
"I havena robbit the Man in the Moon,
    "I havena bridled a comet:
"But I plumbed the pool where Pilate lies,
"And I rode to Mecca and took for a prize
"From under a hundred Hadjis' eyes
    "The eye-tooth of Mahomet."

He has sworn on the tooth to win the truth
    From the soul of Cain O'Kane.
He has sought the home of the North Sea Gled
That is a Presbyterian bred
And shrieking dives with the sinking dead,
    And there has counsel ta'en.

And the shrieking Gled, "Go North," she said,
    "and O 'tis a madman's search,
"And pluck from its roots the Northern Pole
    for a Rod or Pole or Perch.
"Then for two long years ye maun tickle the ears
    of the Hyperborean Ass,
"And then ye maun yoke him in Charles his Wain,
    and drive to the Hills of Glass.
"And O! but a valley lies thereby where
    the Milky Way runs deep,
"Too deep to wade, but not so braid
    that a Scotsman daurna leap:

"Then lean on the Pole and fling your soul
    to the Kirk o' the North to keep.
"And if ye win to the further side where
    all dead mariners are
"Ye may meet again with Cain O'Kane
    at the Sea of Eternal Tar.
"But beware of the Reeling Beaches
    and beware of Hunger Bay
"And the tall king-crabs like hansom cabs
    that stand in rank all day."

By Matyushin and Wilczek-land he is come
    to the Northern Pole,
Whose tap-roots bite on the Oolite and
    Palaeozoic coal:
He set his knee and his haunch to the tree,
    he plucked it up by the root,
And the lines of longitude upward sprung
    like the broken chords of a lute;
And over against the Hills of Glass he came
    to the spate of stars,
And the Pole it sank, but he swam to bank
    and warmed himself on Mars;
Till he came to the Reeling Beaches
    between the night and the day,
Where tall king-crabs like hansom-cabs
    and black bull-lobsters lay.
Then thrice he called the dead man's name
    across the Sea of Tar,
And a bubble brake on the shadowy lake
    and a voice came thin and far:
"Go say to him who sent you here

I have not what he seeks,
"For I gave a part of the pirate chart
    to clout my bosun's breeks;
"And part was took by a blamed Chinook,
    and part by a Polar bear,
"And my old sea-chest that held the rest is gone
    the sea knows where.
" 'Twas pirate gold, 'twas ill-got gold,
    and better let it lie
"Forgotten and forgiven like sailors
    when they die;
"For it's bedded in the white, white sand,
    and in the white sand we,
"A-chewing of eternal quids below
    a land-locked sea."

There be two grey men that curse the Fates
And stand long hours at Bedlam gates
    To see the third again;
And the third he gibbers, and weeps and sings
Of bricks of gold and emerald rings,
And the jewelled crowns of Inca Kings,
    And calls on Cain O'Kane.

*And it's O to find the Isle he knew*
    *And where the gold is hid,*
*And the chart he stole from a Spanish Jew,*
*The chart that a priest in Lima drew*
*From the dying tale of one of the crew*
    *That was there with Captain Kidd.*

# R. H. Benson
*(1871-1914)*

When Robert Hugh Benson was five years old, one of his godfathers visited the family home with a gift for his young ward. His older brother, Arthur, recalled the occasion in *Hugh, Memoirs of a Brother* (1915):

> "After luncheon . . . Hugh, in a little black velvet suit, his flaxen hair brushed till it glowed with radiance . . . entered the room, and said with his little stammer: 'Tha-a-ank you, Godpapa, for this beautiful Bible! Will you read me some of it?' . . .
> 'And what shall I read about?'
> 'The de-e-evil!' said Hugh without the least hesitation."

R. H. Benson was a strange child, and he grew up to be a strange man: a devout, if restless, Christian, his interest in and relish for matters demonological lasted long into adulthood.

After an academically undistinguished career at Eton, and a failed attempt to join the Indian Civil Service, Benson arrived at Trinity College, Cambridge, in October 1890 to study Classics. A few months later he joined the Chit-Chat and the Twice a Fortnight club where, like his older brother E. F. Benson, he came under the influence of M. R. James. "In those years," recalled Robert Carr Bosanquet, "Mr. James was full of the reconstruction of the library and church of the Monastery of St. Edmund at Bury . . . and I have no doubt that the talks in which he sketched the life of that great house . . . furnished some of the colour which Hugh was to use so skilfully when he came to write of the medieval church".

Benson and MRJ were both attracted to the less frequented byways of Christian belief and legend. He was present in MRJ's rooms in November 1891 to hear the host read a paper about St. William of Norwich—the boy-martyr who was said to have been ritually murdered by Jews in 1144, and whose story informed "Lost Hearts". The following year MRJ attended a meeting in Trinity at which Benson offered his thoughts on Emanuel Swedenborg, the Christian mystic whose writings underlie Joseph Sheridan Le Fanu's classic tale of diabolical persecution, "Green Tea" (1869) and his novel *Uncle Silas* (1864)—works that MRJ is known to have revered. The two men also shared an interest in the Elizabethan philosopher and occultist John Dee.

But Benson's fascination with alternative spiritual traditions and the paranormal was practical as well as historical. As an undergraduate he experimented with hypnotism, spiritualism, and crystal gazing; and Bosanquet recalled a not altogether successful investigation into telepathy: "So far as I can remember, half a dozen of us in one room were told to focus our thoughts on the weather-cock on the University church, and after a time the medium in the next room, was aware of a cow [sic] perched on a steeple."

Having changed from Classics to Theology, Benson left Cambridge in 1893 with a third class degree and a half-hearted ambition to take holy orders. He was ordained deacon in the Church of England the following year by his father, who was then Archbishop of Canterbury; but his spiritual restlessness persisted and in 1903, to the consternation of family and friends, he was received into the Roman Catholic Church.

It was in Rome the following year, when he was training for the priesthood, that Benson began writing the stories that were collected in 1907 as *A Mirror of Shalott*—from which "Father Bianchi's Tale", printed here, comes. Set in the fictional Canadian Church of San Filippo in Rome, the book presents a circle of storytelling priests of various nationalities who, over a number of evenings, tell each other true tales from their ministries, tales of "a spiritual world . . . crammed full of energy and movement and affairs".

With its lively characters, speeches, and discussions, the impression is of a kind of popish Chit-Chat Club. Indeed it's possible that faint echoes of the Cambridge institution can be detected in the book. "Father Maddox's Tale" begins with the taking of snuff; and the narrator of "Mr. Bosanquet's Tale" surely borrows his name from Benson's friend and fellow member.

Benson was still working on *A Mirror of Shalott* when he moved back to Cambridge in 1906. Most of the tales first appeared in Catholic periodicals, and at least one of them was first composed to be read aloud. "I have written a ghost-story for . . . Christmas . . . that makes my hair stand up," Benson told a friend. "I hardly dared to go to sleep last night at all. Booh! It is an account of an exorcism." This was "Father Meuron's Tale", in which a young missionary's scepticism about the reality of demonic possession is tested by his experience on a Caribbean island.

Shane Leslie, who would himself convert to Roman Catholicism under Benson's influence, attested to his power as a storyteller, and recalled him "sitting in the firelight of my room at King's, unravelling a weird story about demoniacal substitution, his eyeballs staring into the flame, and his nervous fingers twitching to baptise the next undergraduate he could thrill or mystify into the fold of Rome". Elsewhere Leslie notes that in his ghostly fireside performances Benson's "only rival was the Provost of King's, whose *Ghost Stories of an Antiquary* was being read to nervous listeners at the time".

In "Some Remarks on Ghost Stories" (*The Bookman*, 1929) MRJ himself dismissed *A Mirror of Shalott* as "too ecclesiastical", which seems on the face of it to be a strange criticism from a storyteller whose own works make such regular and effective use of church buildings, officials, and services. What he surely meant was that there was too obvious a religious message behind Benson's tales, too heady a theological tone. And it can't be denied; *A Mirror of Shalott* sets out frankly to look at how far "supernatural" occurrences can be taken as corroborative of Christian belief. As one of the priestly narrators says, "My religion teaches me that there is a spiritual world of indefinite size, and that things not only may, but must, go on there which have nothing particular to do with me." The collected tales tell of a number of intrusions of this spiritual realm into the material world.

Father Bianchi provides the voice of scepticism within the priestly circle, but his tale (the implications of which he passionately denies) suggests an interesting—and enlightened—attitude to ancient paganism on Benson's part; positing the idea that the popular Roman deity Mithras was not simply a demonic rival to Christianity, an evil aberration, but the pathetic embodiment of an incomplete truth—"one of those shadows of reality . . . of which pagan religions are so full". In this, "Father Bianchi's Tale" offers a contrast to MRJ's "Lost Hearts" (1893) where it's implied that Mithraism plays a part in Mr. Abney's murderous pagan belief system.

"Too ecclesiastical": it was an obvious criticism of Benson's fiction, but he didn't care. Just as his brother Arthur, and Herbert Tatham, wrote supernatural tales for the moral edification of their Eton pupils, so Benson's—arguably more imaginative and gripping—stories are intended to instruct as well as entertain. And entertain they do, much of the time.

For all their sincere religiosity, at their best R. H. Benson's ghost stories also impart the same thrill of uncertainty that he himself used to feel as a child, when confronted with a darkened room:

> " 'What,' he was asked, 'do you expect to happen to you?'
> 'To fall,' he replied between a stammer and shudder,
> 'Over a mangled corpse, squish! Into a pool of blood!' "

# Father Bianchi's Tale

### R. H. Benson

Father Bianchi, as the days went on, seemed a little less dogmatic on the theory that miracles (except, of course, those of the saints) did not happen. He was warned by Monsignor Maxwell that his turn was approaching to contribute a story, and suddenly at supper announced that he would prefer to get it over at once that evening.

"But I have nothing to tell," he cried, expostulating with hands and shoulders, "nothing to tell but the nonsense of an old peasant woman."

When we had taken our places upstairs, and the Italian had again apologised and remonstrated with raised eyebrows, he began at last, and I noticed that he spoke with a seriousness that I should not have expected.

"When I was first a priest," he said, "I was in the south of Italy, and said my first mass in a church in the hills. The village was called Arripezza."

"Is that true?" said Monsignor suddenly, smiling.

The Italian grinned brilliantly. "Well, no," he said, "but it is near enough, and I swear to you that the rest is true. It was a village in the hills, ten miles from Naples. They have many strange beliefs there; it is like Father Brent's Cornwall. All along the coast, as you know, they set lights in the windows on one night of the year, because they relate that our Lady once came walking on the water with her divine Child, and found none to give her shelter. Well, this village that we will call Arripezza was not on the coast. It was inland, but it had its own superstitions to compensate it—superstitions cursed by the Church.

"I knew little of all this when I went there. I had been in the seminary until then. The *parrocho* was an old man, but old! He could say mass sometimes on Sundays and feasts, but that was all, and I went to help him. There were many at my first mass as the custom is, and they all came up to kiss my hands when it was done.

"When I came back from the sacristy again there was an old woman waiting for me, who told me that her name was Giovannina. I had seen her before as she kissed my hands. She was as old as the *parrocho* himself I cannot tell how old—yellow and wrinkled as a monkey.

"She put five *loie* into my hands.

" 'Five masses, Father,' she said, 'for a soul in purgatory.'

" 'And the name?'

" 'That does not matter,' she said. 'And will you say them, my Father, at the altar of S. Espedito?'

"I took the money and went off, and as I went down the church, I saw her looking after me, as if she wished to speak, but she made no sign, and I went home; and I had a dozen other masses to say, some for my friends, and a couple that the *parrocho* gave me, and those, therefore, I began to say first. When I had said the fifth of the twelve, Giovannina waited for me again at the door of the sacristy. I could see that she was troubled.

" 'Have you not said them, my Father?' she asked. 'He is here still.'

"I did not notice what she said, except the question, and I said no; I had had others to say first. She blinked at me with her old eyes a moment, and I was going on, but she stopped me again.

" 'Ah! Say them at once, my Father,' she said; 'he is waiting.'

"Then I remembered what she had said before and I was angry.

" 'Waiting!' I said; 'and so are thousands of poor souls.'

" 'Ah, but he is so patient,' she said; 'he has waited so long.'

"I said something sharp, I forget what, but the *parrocho* had told me not to hang about and talk nonsense to women, and I was going on, but she took me by the arm.

" 'Have you not seen him too, my Father?' she said.

"I looked at her, thinking she was mad, but she held me by the arm and blinked up at me, and seemed in her senses. I told her to tell me what she meant, but she would not.

"At last I promised to say the masses at once. The next morning I began the masses, and said four of them, and at each the old woman was there close to me, for I said them at the altar of S. Espedito that was in the nave, as she had asked me, and I had a great devotion to him as well, and she was always at her chair just outside the altar-rails. I scarcely saw her, of course, for I was a young priest and had been taught not to lift my eyes when I turned round, but on the fourth day I looked at her at the *Orate fratres* and she was staring not at me or the altar, but at the corner on the left. I looked there when I turned, but there was nothing but the glass case with the silver hearts in it to S. Espedito.

"That was on a Friday, and in the evening I went to the church again to hear confessions, and when I was done, the old woman was there again.

" 'They are nearly done, my Father?' she said, 'and you will finish them to-morrow?'

"I told her Yes; but she made me promise that whatever happened I would do so. Then she went on, 'Then I will tell you, my Father, what I would not before. I do not know the man's name, but I see him each day during mass at that altar. He is in the corner. I have seen him there ever since the church was built.'

"Well, I knew she was mad then, but I was curious about it, and asked her to describe him to me; and she did so. I expected a man in a sheet or in flames or something of the kind, but it was not so. She described to me a man in a dress she did not know—a tunic to the knees, bareheaded, with a short sword in his hand. Well, then I saw what she meant, she was thinking of S. Espedito himself. He was a Roman soldier, you remember, gentlemen?

" 'And a cuirass?' I said. 'A steel breastplate and helmet?'

"Then she surprised me.

" 'Why, no, Father; he has nothing on his head or breast, and there is a bull beside him.'

"Well, gentlemen, I was taken aback by that. I did not know what to say."

Monsignor leant swiftly forward.

"Mithras," he said abruptly.

The Italian smiled.

"Monsignor knows everything," he said.

Then I broke in, because I was more interested than I knew.

"Tell me, Monsignor, what was Mithras?"

The priest explained shortly. It was an Eastern worship, extraordinarily pure, introduced into Italy a little after the beginning of the Christian era. Mithras was a god, filling a position not unlike that of the Second Person of the Blessed Trinity. He offered a perpetual sacrifice, and through that sacrifice souls were enabled to rise from earthly things to heavenly, if they relied upon it and accompanied that faith by works of discipline and prayer.

"I beg your pardon, Father Bianchi," he ended.

The Italian smiled again.

"Yes, Monsignor," he said, "I know that now, but I did not know it for many years afterwards, and I know something else now that I did not know then. Well, to return. I told my old woman that she was dreaming, that it could not be so, that there was no room for a bull in the corner, that it was a picture of S. Espedito that she was thinking of.

" 'And why did you not get the masses said before?' I asked.

"She smiled rather slyly at me then.

" 'I did get five said once before,' she said, 'in Naples, but they did him no good. And when once again I told the *parrocho* here, he told me to be off; he would not say them.'

"And she had waited for a young priest, it seemed, and had determined not to tell him the story till the masses were said, and had saved up her money meanwhile.

"Well, I went home, and got to talking with the old priest, and led him on, so that he thought that he had introduced the subject, and presently he told me that when the foundation of the church had been laid forty years before, they had found an old cave in the hill, with heathen things in it. He knew no more than that about it, but he told me to fetch a bit of pottery from a cupboard, and showed it me, and there was just the tail of a bull upon it, and an eagle."

Monsignor leaned forward again.

"Just so," he said, "and the bull was lying down?"

The Italian nodded, and was silent.

We all looked at him. It seemed a tame ending, I thought. Then Father Brent put our thoughts into words.

"That is not all?" he said.

Father Bianchi looked at him sharply, and at all of us, but said nothing.

"Ah! that is not all," said the other again persistently.

"Bah!" cried the Italian suddenly. "It was not all, if you will have it so. But the rest is madness, as mad as Giovannina herself. What I saw, I saw because she made me expect it. It was nothing but the shadow, or the light in the glass case."

A perceptible thrill ran through us all. The abrupt change from contempt to seriousness was very startling.

"Tell us, Father," said the English priest; "we shall think no worse of you for it. If it was only the shadow, what harm is there in telling it?"

"Indeed you must finish," went on Monsignor; "it is in the contract."

The Italian looked round again, frowned, smiled and laughed uneasily.

"I have told it to no one till to-day," he said, "but you shall hear it. But it was only the shadow—you understand that?"

A chorus, obviously insincere, broke out from the room.

"It was only the shadow, Padre Bianchi."

Again the priest laughed shortly; then the smile faded, and he went on.

"I went down early the next morning, before dawn, and I made my meditation before the Blessed Sacrament; but I could not help looking across once or twice at the corner by S. Espedito's altar; it was too dark to see anything clearly; but I could make out the silver hearts in the glass case. When I had finished, Giovannina came in.

"I could not help stopping by her chair as I went to rest.

" 'Is there anything there?' I asked.

"She shook her head at me.

" 'He is never there till mass begins,' she said.

"The sacristy door that opens out of doors was set wide as I came past it in my vestments; and the dawn was coming up across the hills, all purple."

Monsignor murmured something, and the priest stopped.

"I beg your pardon," said Monsignor; "but that was the time the sacrifice of Mithras was offered."

"When I came out into the church," went on the priest, "it was all gray in the light of the dawn, but the chapels were still dark. I went up the steps, not daring to look in the corner, and set the vessels down. As I was spreading the corporal the server came up and lighted the candles. And still I dared not look. I turned by the right and came down, and stood waiting till he knelt beside me.

"Then I found I could not begin. I knew what folly it was, but I was terribly frightened. I heard the server whisper, *In nomine Patris . . .*

"Then I shut my eyes tight, and began.

"Well, by the time I had finished the preparation, I felt certain that something was watching me from the corner. I told myself, as I tell myself now," snapped the Italian fiercely—"I told myself it was but what the woman had told me. And then at last I opened my eyes to go up the steps, but I kept them down, and only saw the dark corner out of the side of my eyes.

"Then I kissed the altar and began.

"Well, it was not until the Epistle that I understood that I should have to face the corner at the reading of the Gospel; but by then I do not think I could have faced it directly, even if I had wished.

"So when I was saying the *Munda cor* in the centre, I thought of a plan, and as I went to read the Gospel I put my left hand over my eyes, as if I were in pain, and read the Gospel like that. And so all through the mass I went on; I always dropped my eyes when I had to turn that way at all, and I finished everything and gave the blessing.

"As I gave it, I looked at the old woman, and she was kneeling there, staring across at the corner; so I knew that she was still dreaming she saw something.

"Then I went to read the last Gospel."

The priest was plainly speaking with great difficulty; he passed his hands over his lips once or twice. We were all quiet.

"Well, gentlemen, courage came to me then; and as I signed the altar I looked straight into the corner."

He stopped again, and began resolutely once more; but his voice rang with hysteria.

"Well, gentlemen, you understand that my head was full of it now, and that the corner was dark, and that the shadows were very odd."

"Yes, yes, Padre Bianchi," said Monsignor easily, "and what did the shadows look like?"

The Italian gripped the arms of the chair, and screamed his answer.

"I will not tell you, I will not tell you. It was but the shadow. My God, why have I told you the tale at all?"

# J. K. Stephen
## *(1859-1892)*

*"[Stephen] was extremely good-natured . . . extraordinarily and perennially amusing, and he had the most copious and prodigious flow of elaborate bad language that ever issued from human lips."*

– A. C. Benson, *The Leaves of the Tree* (1911)

T he qualities that A. C. Benson appreciated in his old school friend, James Kenneth "Jem" Stephen seem to have lasted the latter's whole, tragically truncated life. When Stephen died—aged thirty-two, from self-starvation, in a lunatic asylum—the warmest of tributes were paid by those who'd known and loved him, as an Eton schoolboy, a Cambridge undergraduate, a journalist, a wit, and a poet. Looking today at his modest literary legacy—two volumes of light verse and a handful of magazine articles—it's not easy to account for the adulation that he attracted in his lifetime. It was perhaps in his vocal and physical presence that his attested genius shone forth. Certainly, he was the central figure of many friendships in Cambridge in the late nineteenth century.

Stephen was a welcome guest at the Chit-Chat though he was never formally a member. His older brothers, Harry and Herbert, both joined however, and Stephen was still a schoolboy when he attended a meeting on 21 April 1877, to hear Herbert talk on "The Probability of War Becoming Extinct". In November the following year, recently arrived at King's to read History, he was invited to another meeting, in the rooms of M. R. James's older brother Sydney. The host's talk on "The Defects of University Society" might not have been the most stimulating, and around the same time, Stephen joined the Apostles, the senior, reputedly more intellectual society, which met at the same time on Saturday evenings.

In March 1891 Stephen made an indirect contribution to a Chit-Chat meeting when his poem "Organgrinder" was recited by Arthur Bather, while MRJ, E. F. Benson, and Robert Carr Bosanquet each read out verse compositions of their own. All these men were also members of the Twice a Fortnight club, the Chit-Chat's more informal off-shoot, which Stephen had founded as an undergraduate in the late 1870s. He can be seen at the centre of the 1891 photo of the group, pipe clenched between his teeth, his hair in charismatic disarray.

Stephen was also a popular guest at the house parties that Felix Cobbold, the bursar of King's, held each New Year in Felixstowe, the model for Burnstow in MRJ's "Oh, Whistle, and I'll Come to You, My Lad" (1904). And it was while staying at Cobbold's palatial seaside villa, The Lodge, in 1886, that he suffered an accident which changed—and almost certainly cut short—his life. Accounts differ about exactly what happened. Arthur Benson has it that he injured his head while examining a pumping-mill. Within the Stephen family it was said that he was struck by a projection from a passing train. There are suggestions that the horse he was riding was frightened by a whistle, or a gust of wind blowing a leaf, and bucked its rider to the ground. But while the details are unclear, it's certain that on 29 December 1886, Stephen suffered a blow to the head and was never the same again. "He began to form sanguine and unbalanced plans," recalled Benson in *The Leaves of the Tree*, "to be extravagant in money matters, and to display emotional tendencies of a rather vehement type."

Part of this erratic behaviour was the establishment of *The Reflector*, a weekly magazine devoted to political comment, literary criticism, poetry, and fiction. Stephen was himself publisher, editor, and distributor of *The Reflector*, as well as its chief contributor—although Cambridge friends did their bit, among them Chit-Chat members, like F. W. Maitland, the donor of the club's snuff box, who wrote a long editorial on local government for the 5 February 1888 issue; and Francis Holland, who composed "Handless and Harmless" (29 January 1888), a macabre poem based on "the Greek superstition that it was possible to lay the ghost of a murdered man by cutting off his hands and binding them under his arms". (It's not as good as it sounds . . . )

MRJ contributed a "Letter from Cyprus", where he was at that time involved in an archaeological dig. Published on 14 April 1888, this jokey, deliberately non-scholarly missive, begins "Mr. Reflector, I conceive that it is not altogether with you as with me. Unless indeed you are sitting upon a towel, yourself lightly attired in flannels, under the shade of the eastern wall of the Temple of Venus at Paphos, and that I am sorry to notice is not the case . . . " Later the same year MRJ gave a paper to the Chit-Chat on Cyprus, perhaps covering the same ground.

"Man Stories", printed here, appeared in the fourth issue of *The Reflector*, on 22 January 1888. There was no name attached, but in his bound volume of the magazine's run, now in Cambridge University Library, Harry Stephen confidently attributed it to his younger brother, whose many contributions he marked "J." The beautifully timed first paragraph perhaps gives us an idea of what the author was like at the height of his conversational powers. It suggests, too, how

widespread supernatural chit-chat was in educated society at
the time. With its post-prandial debate about "the existence of
men", it brings to mind the opening of "Oh Whistle, and I'll
Come to You, My Lad". And the sceptical credo of Mr. Smith
could have been spoken by a phantasmal Professor Parkins:

> "There are plenty of things I can't understand . . . and
> plenty of things I can't see. I am not going to go believing
> in men merely for the purpose of increasing the aggregate
> of the incomprehensible to respectable dimensions."

The central joke is successfully sustained throughout: a ghost
bemoans the "grossly spiritualistic age" in which he lives; a
ghostess declares that after hearing a man story "she would not
dare go in to a lighted room by herself" (*mutatis mutandis* the
same response that the Cambridge Lecturer on Morphology
has to the terrifying drawing in "The Scrap-book of Canon
Alberic"). But the object of the satire is specific, for the ghostly
Somical Society parodies the earnestly open-minded Society
for Psychical Research (SPR), which had been set up six years
earlier "with the purpose of investigating mesmeric, psychical,
and 'spiritualist' phenomena in a purely scientific spirit".

Two years before "Man Stories" appeared, the SPR had
published *Phantasms of the Living* (1886) by Edmund
Gurney, Frederic W. H. Myers, and Frank Podmore. Many
of the 701 witness statements collected in this lengthy
investigation into telepathy, describe apparitions of physi-
cally-distant friends and loved ones at the moment of death.
And the criticism of veridical man stories that is voiced by the
crotchety old ghost at the end of Stephen's sketch, could fairly
be applied to the typical entry in this exhaustive compilation:

> "It is not harrowing, or dramatic, or bloodcurdling. You
> don't try to amuse or interest me; you try to convince

me. You overload your wretched tale with uninteresting details of what Brown said, and what Robinson said, and what Jones said, all to show that it is true. What does it matter whether it is true or not? The point is whether it is amusing . . . "

—at which I imagine MRJ, beneath the walls of the temple in Paphos, chuckling to himself and nodding in agreement.

After seventeen issues, Stephen ran out of money and *The Reflector* folded, to his intense disappointment. In 1890 he returned to Cambridge and for a while his friends and family sensed an improvement in his mood and behaviour. He published two volumes of poetry: *Lapsus Calami* and *Musa, quo tendis.* And he was a guest at the Chit-Chat again; his last recorded attendance was on 9 May 1891, when he heard a paper by Charles Trevelyan on "The Coming Russian Revolution".

Six months later, however, he suffered what A. C. Benson described as "an acute attack of brain disturbance", and on 24 November his landlady found him standing at the window of his lodgings in the centre of Cambridge, naked, screaming, and throwing his belongings onto the street below. He was convinced that a warrant was out for his arrest. His brothers arrived from London, calmed him and accompanied him to a psychiatric hospital in Northampton, where he was admitted suffering from "extreme depression". He died on 3 February 1892, from "mania, refusal of food, and exhaustion".

# Man Stories

## J. K. Stephen

The guests were sitting round the table, and the meal was drawing to a close. A pleasant darkness pervaded the room, and the good fare set before the members of the party had helped to produce those weird and grisly sensations which are necessary to a state of perfect contentment. A clammy coldness filled the air; the plates and the glasses seemed to be misty shadows of themselves; the tones of the party sounded vague and distant to each other. So much of their faces as could be seen shone pallid and green under the flickering rays of intermittent light; in fact, no single condition was wanting to make everybody perfectly comfortable, and thoroughly disposed to enjoy the good things set before him. There had, however, occurred one of those pauses which are incidental to the best regulated conversations; and it was in the midst of an otherwise unbroken silence that the daughter of the house was addressed by her neighbour in these words: "Do you believe in men?"

Now, it was not the first time by very many that this question had been addressed to the daughter of the house. Like the rest of the party she was a ghost, and ghosts are very much given to speculating about the existence and the nature of men. The commonplace mind of an average ghost rejects the existence of men as the fanciful creation of feeble minds. But there are many ghosts who have a vague, uncertain belief in men, holding at the least that their non-existence is not yet known; and there are some who believe persistently and firmly, and can give reasons for the faith that is in them. The topic of men, in truth, possesses a fascination alike for those ghosts who must talk about something for the sake of not being silent, and for those to whom it furnishes an opportunity of forcing an elaborate theory down the throats of their hearers, insomuch that it has come to pass that many ghosts who are fitted for the higher kinds of conversational exercise, and who are not believers in any theory of things subternatural, look upon the subject as nothing less than a bore. In any case the present question was one which the fair young ghostess who was addressed had already answered on many occasions, and she was at no loss for a reply.

"Well," she said, "I don't exactly believe in men, but after all, you know, Mr. Smith, I think there must be something in it. There are so many stories, especially about the man of a ghost appearing to a friend when the ghost is just dying. They cannot all have been made up. Besides, I think it is only natural that there should be something in the world besides what we can see or understand, don't you, Mr. Smith?"

"There are plenty of things I can't understand," said Mr. Smith, "and plenty of things I can't see. I am not going to go believing in men merely for the purpose of increasing the aggregate of the incomprehensible to respectable dimensions."

Mr. Smith was aware that his presence at this and other dinner-parties was due to his being generally considered as a "clever young ghost", and it was his habit to use rather long words in order to keep up his reputation. The ghostess at his side was not, however, very susceptible to this kind of brilliancy, and she continued to talk in a placid and equable way, keeping on the respectable border-land between faith and scepticism, and showing a complete mastery of all the ordinary gossip about men. She also drew from time to time on a decent repertoire of commonplace man stories. She was interrupted by her neighbour, a bald and middle aged ghost, with a very acrimonious manner, who made the following remark with an air of preternatural sagacity: "There are very pretty stories, no doubt, and I have not a word to say against them; but perhaps you will kindly answer me two simple questions. Did you ever see a man? and do you know anyone who ever did see a man?"

The old gentle-ghost asked these questions with such a crushing air of a brilliant cross-examining counsel, that an ignorant observer might have supposed that nobody had ever thought of that particular way of criticising a man-story before. As it happens, however, these questions are asked as a matter of course whenever the conversation takes a manly turn, and the daughter of the house had been expecting to hear them for some time. She complacently replied that she herself had never seen a man, and had not the least desire ever to see one. She further admitted that she had never met with any one who had positively seen a man, but that she knew several ghosts and ghostesses who had seen and talked with people who had seen men. At this the old Q.C.—for such was his rank—gave a triumphant chuckle.

"Just so," he said; "you say that you have seen some one who says he has seen some one who says that he has seen a man. We are always expected to believe these astonishing tales on evidence which would not suffice to convict a ghost of stealing a pocket handkerchief."

This retort was exactly what the daughter of the house had expected. She considered that the topic of men had now served its turn, and began to consider whether she should introduce politics or cricket as the next topic. Unable to solve this question, she decided to wait for one of her neighbours to start the ball of conversation afresh.

But at this point the subject of men was taken up again by a ghost sitting on the opposite side of the table, and he began to speak in such an authoritative voice and manner that the whole party became attentive to his words, and the various conversational groups of two and three were merged into a circle unanimously bent upon the discussion of a single topic. And, to tell the truth, those who were present were right in giving a more than common attention to a somewhat commonplace subject, for the ghost who now entered the arena was no less a person than one of the Vice-Presidents of the Somical Society. The Somical Society is sometimes miscalled the Somatological, though in fact it devotes its attention to somics, a far more abstruse and refined science than the old-fashioned department of ghostly knowledge known as somatology. The Vice-President addressed himself to the Q.C., who was directly opposite him. "I think," said he, "you are unnecessarily strict in refusing to accept any story which is not told to you at first or second hand. Suppose a perfectly credible person tells you a story, on the authority of another person, also known to you to be perfectly credible; why should you utterly disbelieve it on the score of remoteness? You have not got the best evidence, it is true. You have not got such evidence as would rightly be required by a judge or jury. You have not got such evidence as would be furnished if there were a tribunal to be convinced, nor such as could be obtained by a person who was anxious thoroughly to sift the case and to examine all the persons alleged to be concerned. But you have got pretty good evidence, and such as would serve to bring practical if not literal conviction to your mind, were it not for the vulgar prejudice which denies the existence of men. Assume that men do exist, but that their appearances are not exceedingly numerous. What would happen? Well, you would hear a good deal about men and their appearances. But only one ghost in a thousand would ever see a man, and only one in a hundred would ever know any one who had ever seen one. Now, there is no particular connection between you and men, and you are not on the look-out for men or men-seers. Therefore in all probability what would happen is this: you would never see a man, and never see anyone who had seen a man; but you would hear plenty of stories about men, on good authority, at third or fourth hand. Now this is exactly what does happen. In other words, your experience is, to put it at the lowest, perfectly compatible with the theory that the beings vulgarly called men really exist and appear."

The sceptic made a rather scornful answer to this argument, but the Vice-President of the Somical Society proceeded with unruffled imperturbability to remark that he for his part had made it his business to inquire particularly into the existence of men, and to examine at first hand every alleged appearance of men of which he heard. In consequence he had seen and corresponded with nearly five thousand persons who asserted that they had actually seen, felt, heard, or in some cases smelt, either men or some species of human manifestation. He had not himself seen a man; it was a great disappointment to him not to have been among the ghosts so specially favoured. But he heard, at first hand, more man stories than he could count. He declined to tell any man stories to the present company. He considered that the amusing or harrowing side of a man story was an incidental and almost a regrettable feature in a piece of scientific evidence. He would gladly submit his evidence to any one who cared to examine it in a scientific spirit; but he did not consider it to be any better fitted for the conversational stock-in-trade of a diner out, than the evidence collected by a geologist or an astronomer.

Upon being pressed by some of those present the Vice-President consented, not, indeed, to tell a man story, but to explain some of the main principles of his theory of men, which he considered to be irrefutably proved by the evidence which could stand any test that lawyers or ghosts of science could apply. In fact, it was evident that the Vice-President considered himself and his colleagues to possess very remarkable gifts for the testing of evidence. He had disproved, and consigned to the waste-paper basket, almost as many man stories as he had converted into scientific specimens; and he had established a system of small committees of highly trained observers, who were entrusted with the investigation of different kinds of phenomena, and who had discomfited a dozen impostors for every possessor of extraordinary somical qualities, whom they had unearthed and guaranteed as genuine. The Q.C. was particularly sceptical about the inquisitorial capacity of the Vice-President and his colleagues; but when the Vice-President courteously pressed him to accept a place on one of his committees, he excused himself on the ground of more practical and lucrative engagements. The theory which the Vice-President proceeded to develop was somewhat to the following effect:

"We live," said the Vice-President, "in a grossly spiritualistic age. The very existence of matter is openly denied, and ghosts devote themselves to satisfying their petty spiritual needs, and have no care whatever for their higher material interests. And yet every religion that has ever existed asserts and emphasises the existence of matter. Matter is a real and living thing, and until we have ascertained the laws of its being, and come to understand its workings, our minds will be narrow and our knowledge will be incomplete. Is it possible that we can rest content with our present knowledge on the great topic of death? We all understand death in its merely spiritual aspect. The doomed ghost grows fat and ruddy, his eyes brightens, the texture of his body becomes firm and solid, and at last one day the body disappears altogether. We say the ghost is dead. Is it not possible that the material part of him has become too purely material to be perceived by our senses? Meanwhile the spirit only is left. We bury that, and we know that and we know that dissolution and corruption must ensue. But religion teaches us that the body does not cease to exist, and it is the function of the Somical Society to find out what are the actual relations between that body freed from its spiritual bondage and the survivors whom it leaves behind. The evidence we have collected, and the scientific laws we have been able to ascertain about the dealings of unspirited bodies with our own, help us to realise the true nature of matter." The Vice-President continued at some length to summarise the kinds of evidence which he possessed, and to indicate the laws which he had discovered. He concluded his remarks with a passage of some eloquence. "In short," he exclaimed, "there is a whole world about us of beings not unlike ourselves, but purely material, and therefore not perceptible to our spiritual senses. The bodies of those whom we have known, of those whom we have loved, inhabit the world. They may be thronging, for aught I know, in this very room. Some of us, when our material part is more active than usual, perceive for a moment what we call the men, but what are really the liberated bodies of our dead or dying friends. As time goes on we may all become more sensitive to such manifestations. Meanwhile, every fresh link in the chain of evidence is a step towards the discovery of a new and immeasurably valuable science. The sphere of ghostly knowledge is growing day by day. Its growth is largely due to the work of the Somical Society. The head office of that society is at 101, Skeleton Street; membership is open to all, and the annual subscription is only three and four-pence."

When the Vice-President had finished his eloquent monologue there was silence for a little while, and then a bashful stockbroker, encouraged by what had been urged in support of his favourite belief to brave the sceptical eyes of the Q.C., boldly uttered the electric words, "I once saw a man." A ripple of excitement and anticipation ran round the room. Here was something better than the logic and the eloquence of a professor of somics. A little city ghost in a new dress coat and carefully tied white tie, who had actually seen a man with his own watery and protruding eye! Every one listened attentively. It must be owned, however, that the story of the stockbroker was more distinguished by its length and by the extraordinary complications which it comprised than by any very great aptitude to astonish, amuse, or horrify the listeners. Everything just failed to fit into everything else; all the coincidences just did not come off; countless opportunities for the wonderful and the alarming had been, as it were, deliberately missed. The things which the man had said just failed to illustrate the old family legend. The object which it put into someone's hand was there all right the next morning, only it had no possible significance or importance. No secrets were revealed, no difficulties removed, no prospects opened up. When at last the end of the story was reached, everybody was left just where he was at the beginning. Still there was a real genuine man in the story, and that was something. It was also a consolation to reflect that the stupidity of the story was evidence of its truth. Nobody could have been at the pains to invent such a hopelessly dull, ill-managed, and obscure piece of work. A ghost who was not scrupulously truthful could not have resisted the opportunity of touching it up in the telling. The Vice-President made a few notes in a little book which he always carried with him, and determined to cross-examine the stockbroker in the drawing room.

The ice being once broken, man stories began to be told in great numbers in every part of the room. One ghost was well acquainted with a major-general who at the age of four had distinctly seen the woman of his great-grandmother making a gesture which the old lady was herself making upon her death-bed, many thousands of miles away, at that very moment, allowance made for the difference of clocks. Old-fashioned stories of cheerful sounds, ruddy glows, bright and glowing faces, and substantial forms, heard, felt or seen as the clock struck twelve at mid-day were told with great effect. A few young ghostesses got nervous, and longed for the clanking chains and lurid glare of their own sitting-rooms. One of them declared that she would not dare go in to a light room by herself or sit up at day for weeks to come. But these old-fashioned stories were not so numerous as the statistics of simultaneous appearances, the stories explicable by the doctrine of telepathy, and the mysterious occurrences which had happened under the most commonplace circumstances. The Vice-President was getting near the end of his note-book, and foresaw weeks of testing and sifting. At last an old gentle-ghost, who had slept through the Vice-President's remarks, and sat perfectly silent during the storm of anecdotes, arose and spoke as follows:

"I am sorry to leave this hospitable board abruptly, but I cannot and will not sit here any longer to listen to the dullest and most irritating form of conversational mania yet discovered. Time was when a man story was a man story, and one or two of them, told under suitable circumstances, were perhaps worth listening to. But nowadays the thing has come to be a nuisance. You don't understand that it is possible to have too much of a good thing, and, I may add, impossible to have too little of a bad thing. And a modern man story is a bad thing. It is not harrowing, or dramatic, or bloodcurdling. You don't try to amuse or interest me; you try to convince me. You overload your wretched tale with uninteresting details of what Brown said, and what Robinson said, and what Jones said, all to show that it is true. What does it matter whether it is true or not? The point is whether it is amusing. You cut down the emotional part to the smallest possible limits, and tell it in the most business-like and prosaic way. As for believing in men, I do not believe or disbelieve in particular stories. But I disbelieve in any theory, by whatever evidence it may be supported, which conflicts with my cardinal and essential beliefs about the conditions of ordinary life. And without being a pure spiritualist, or a disbeliever in the subternatural, I do firmly believe this fact: that a ghost once dead is dead for good, and will trouble his friends and family no more. And so, ladies and gentlemen, good day." And with these words he called for his hat and coat and left the room.

# A. C. Benson
## *(1862-1925)*

*"I did derive immense intellectual stimulus from my Cambridge life . . . for I belonged to a little society that met weekly, and read papers on literary and ethical subjects, prolonging a serious, if fitful, discussion late into the night."*

– *The House of Quiet* (1904)

Though it doesn't name it, this passage from Arthur Christopher Benson's autobiographical novel *The House of Quiet*, first published anonymously in 1904, must allude to the Chit-Chat. Benson had joined the Club in November 1881, almost as soon as he arrived in Cambridge from Eton, and he was a regular attendee and speaker throughout his undergraduate career, sharing his thoughts on a number of subjects: "Coleridge" (1882); "Rossetti" (1882); "Buddhism" (twice—1883 and 1884); "The relation of the artistic & moral instincts" (1883); and "Lord Herbert of Cherbury" (1884), a seventeenth century soldier, philosopher, and poet.

Benson's description in *The House of Quiet* and the subjects of his papers suggest an earnestness that was perhaps less dominant in the Chit-Chat by the time his younger brother, E. F. Benson, became a member seven years later. Indeed the younger Benson's characterisation of another undergraduate group, the Apostles, as a "mystical and elevated society who . . . were supposed in their lighter moments to chat about Determinism" (*As We Were*, 1930), could have been applied to the Chit-Chat that his brother had joined in 1881, when we indeed find records of papers with titles like "Pain", "Free Will", and, yes, "The Standpoint of Determinism".

But as well as intellectual stimulation, the club perhaps also offered Benson distraction and respite, because his membership coincided with the first of several crippling bouts of depression that were to blight his life. His voluminous diary—over four million words of it—is surprisingly laconic about his undergraduate years, but it does record what he clearly considered to be the essentials: "In 1881 I went up to King's—my first great misfortune in 1882—I have often thought I was nearly out of my mind—& have certainly never quite recovered it—idleness & moody religion followed."

The exact nature of this "great misfortune" remains unclear. In *The House of Quiet* the trauma experienced by Benson's fictional counterpart as an undergraduate is spiritual, triggered by a Revivalist meeting in Cambridge, an event that turns him "in an instant from a careless boy into a troubled man". The narrator describes how the words of the preacher "burnt into my soul . . . [and] fell on me like the stabs of a knife", and yet "pierced as I was to the heart by contrition and anguish, I knew that this was not for me . . . I went out into the night like one dizzied with a sudden blow". A by-product of this spiritual agony is an impulse on the narrator's part "to find in the great redeemers of mankind, in Buddha, Socrates, Mahomet, Confucius, Shakespeare, the secret of self conquest, of reconciliation", which might account for Benson's apparent fixation with Buddhism in his Chit-Chat talks.

An earlier autobiographical novel, *The Memoirs of Arthur Hamilton* (1886), however, suggests that the crisis was emotional rather than spiritual, and arose from "a moral wound" inflicted by a former schoolmate whose behaviour had "disappointed" the protagonist. "We were great friends once," the offender is quoted as saying, "but he cuts me now; he had to give me up, you see, because he didn't approve of me. Justice, mercy, and truth, and all the rest of it". Interestingly, in a tribute written after Benson's death, M. R. James recommended this novel to "anyone who wants a key to [Benson's] 'outlook' at this time" (*Arthur Christopher Benson: As Seen by Some Friends,* 1925).

It's all deliberately, frustratingly vague; but whatever the precise background to Benson's anguish, it's clear that in November 1882, exactly a year after joining the Chit-Chat, he experienced a psychological shock that cast a dark shadow over his undergraduate life. In 1885, not long after leaving Cambridge, he noted in his diary that "for more than two years, I have not had one happy day".

It's been suggested that an agnostic tendency at the Chit-Chat might have exacerbated Benson's crisis, and it's notable that during the years of his membership the club produced many more lawyers, for instance, than clergymen. But the foundations for a serious depression were likely laid long before Benson came up to Cambridge. His family background ensured that he would have felt more acutely than most young men of his day the pain of religious doubt. A few weeks after the onset of his 1882 crisis, his father, Edward Benson, having held a succession of important positions in the Church of England, was appointed Archbishop of Canterbury. This energetic, irascible man—himself prone to debilitating bouts of melancholy—bore an intense, suffocating love for his children. "[He] exercised a powerful effect [on us]," Benson recalled in the biography of his father that he published in 1899, "but our feeling was almost as much awe as love; he did not always clearly remember the rules he had laid down, so that there was an element of uncertainty about his justice. He never punished us, but his displeasure was frightful to bear."

Benson's relationship with his father was complicated further in 1878, when his intellectually gifted and pious older brother Martin died suddenly, aged seventeen, from suspected meningitis. Arthur was now the eldest son and he bore the weight of his grief-stricken father's expectations. He did not feel equal to them, and after graduating from Cambridge, and reading "enough Theology to very nearly wreck my religion", rather than joining the Church, he returned to Eton to teach Classics, full of self-doubt and literary ambition.

He wasn't a happy schoolmaster, though he was popular with pupils, like Maurice Baring and Robert Carr Bosanquet whose literary pursuits Benson encouraged. A Sunday evening ritual of reading specially composed supernatural tales to the boys in his house was remembered with fondness after his death: "There was considerable competition for the sofa and armchairs," wrote E. H. Ryle. "Those who failed to obtain a seat of any kind sprawled upon the floor. Exactly at the appointed moment 'my Tutor' would emerge from his little privy writing-room . . . He would turn up the light in a green-shaded reading-lamp on a table, bury himself in his great, deep leathern armchair, frown prodigiously at his hands clasped before his face and, from out of the deathly stillness, inquire, 'Where had we got to . . . ?' "

The stories read at these gatherings were collected in *The Hill of Trouble and Other Stories* in 1903 and *The Isles of Sunset* in 1904. They have what Benson described as "a semi-medieval atmosphere", and were written with a frank moral purpose: "to show life as a pilgrimage to a far-off but glorious goal, with seductive by-paths turning off the narrow way, and evil shapes, both terrifying and alluring, which loitered in shady corners, or even sometimes straddled horribly across the very road". A contemporary reviewer described them, not unfairly, as "painfully kind". But not all of Benson's supernatural fiction was aimed at the young.

At Christmas 1903, he was one of a party of bachelors who gathered in King's College to enjoy the hospitality of MRJ. Henry Luxmoore, another Eton master, was there too, and a letter that he wrote on Christmas Eve that year reveals a remarkable programme of entertainment: "A ghost story of diabolical eeriness is written and read most evenings. Dr. James led off with 'No. 13' & 'Fur flebis'. Arthur Benson followed with 'The House at Trehele' [sic] which lasted two nights.

Benson's contribution to the eerie festivities that year was published posthumously in 1926 under the title "Basil Netherby", one of several unpublished ghost stories found among his papers, of which only two were preserved—"The Uttermost Farthing" was the other.

The author's tendency to use his own life as a source for his fiction is evident in "Basil Netherby", which is set in a part of Cornwall that Benson knew well. The names Treheale and St. Sibby are inventions, but Grampound, where the narrator alights his train, is only a few miles from Lis Escop, the much-loved house that the Benson family occupied while Edward Benson was Bishop of Truro. It's described in detail in E. F. Benson's nostalgic ghost story "Pirates" (1928).

The narrator of "Basil Netherby", Leonard Ward, is weary, professionally unfulfilled and prone to moody reflections, much like Benson himself in the early 1900s. And the author's own thoughts, you sense, must lie behind Netherby's observation about the life of the teacher: "A pretty poor business, isn't it? . . . I would rather pick oakum myself. Here I live in a fine house, for next to nothing, and write, write, write—there's a life for a man."

There's something of Benson, too, in the melancholy housekeeper Mrs. Hall, dominated as she is by the deceased master of the house who, it his is strongly hinted, is also her father. Indeed, the painted portrait of the wilful, energetic Heale that makes such an impression on Ward, could be that of Archbishop Benson himself: "It showed a face of great power, a big forehead, clear-cut features, and a determined chin, with extraordinarily bright large eyes; evidently the portrait of a man of great physical and mental force, who would do whatever he took in hand with all his might."

Theologically, Heale and Archbishop Benson could not be further apart, but both exercise power over their respective houses from beyond the grave, and both excite in their surviving offspring ambiguous feelings of fear and loyalty. The Archbishop died of heart failure in 1896 and, for several years after, his eldest son was occupied in compiling a vast two-volume biography—a task that Benson felt as both a burden and a privilege. This was published in 1899, and by 1903, when he wrote "Basil Netherby", there had been a marked change in Benson's life. A few weeks before the Christmas holiday at King's, he'd hosted a farewell dinner to mark his leaving Eton after eighteen years. He'd given up picking intellectual oakum and was preparing to embark upon a full-time life of letters. In doing so, did he feel that he had liberated himself finally from the shadow of his father? Had he, like Mrs. Hall at the end of the story, somehow "prevailed"?

Heale's death-resisting personality is one of the most impressive aspects of "Basil Netherby". He is not—like Mr. Abney or Karswell—simply a fallen scholar, an irredeemable black magician. There's a depth of character, a hinterland of suffering, that MRJ's necromancers lack—although the temptation to compare him to a particular Jamesian villain is irresistible, given the strong echo of "Count Magnus" (1904) that resounds when Horton is shown Heale's desecrated tomb in the local church: " 'I daresay he sleeps sound enough in spite of it all.' [Netherby] stamped his foot on the pavement as he did so, which returned a hollow sound. 'Are you inside?' said Basil, laughingly; 'perhaps not at home?' "

There are, arguably, too many elements to "Basil Netherby", too many plums in the pudding: the cursed music, the Jekyll and Hyde personality of Netherby, Heale's Faustian pact, the "being" in the passageway, the view "behind the veil". And as Luxmoore's observation that the author spent two nights telling it suggests, it does go on for a long time. It risks outstaying its welcome. Benson lacks MRJ's pace and economy of expression—not to mention his comic timing.

But perhaps it's too easy to dismiss A. C. Benson as a verbose miserabilist. Let's leave the last word to a man who, by the time of Benson's death in 1925, had known him longer than anyone else alive. In *As Seen by Some Friends*, MRJ writes:

"I have an uneasy feeling that future generations, who derive their ideas of Arthur Benson from . . . [his] books . . . may conceive of him as a pale and ghost-like figure, bowed with *Weltschmerz*, and seldom speaking but in a level musical tone. That would be a great pity. Nobody enjoyed the pleasant things in life more than he: nobody laughed more, or more infectiously, when he was in the mood: nobody had a greater zest or gust (as Dr. Johnson might say) for simple jokes . . . When you read the delicate introspective books, you have to reckon also with the fact that the writer of them was a person capable of boisterous mirth and amused by jokes of a simplicity as elemental as the butter slide at the pantomime."

# Basil Netherby

## A. C. Benson

It was five o'clock in the afternoon of an October day that Basil Netherby's letter arrived. I remember that my little clock had just given its warning click, when the footsteps came to my door; and just as the clock began to strike, came a hesitating knock. I called out, "Come in," and after some fumbling with the handle there stepped into the room I think the shyest clergyman I have ever seen. He shook hands like an automaton, looking over his left shoulder; he would not sit down, and yet looked about the room, as he stood, as if wondering why the ordinary civility of a chair was not offered him; he spoke in a husky voice, out of which he endeavoured at intervals to cast some viscous obstruction by loud hawkings; and when, after one of these interludes, he caught my eye, he went a sudden pink in the face.

However, the letter got handed to me; and I gradually learnt from my visitor's incoherent talk that it was from my friend Basil Netherby; and that he was well, remarkably well, quite a different man from what he had been when he came to Treheale; that he himself (Vyvyan was his name) was curate of St. Sibby. Treheale was the name of the house where Mr. Netherby lived. The letter had been most important, he thought, for Mr. Netherby had asked him as he was going up to town to convey the letter himself and to deliver it without fail into Mr. Ward's own hands. He could not, however, account (here he turned away from me, and hummed, and beat his fingers on the table) for the extraordinary condition in which he was compelled to hand it to me, as it had never, so far as he knew, left his own pocket; and presently with a gasp Mr. Vyvyan was gone, refusing all proffers of entertainment, and falling briskly down—to judge from the sounds which came to me—outside my door.

I, Leonard Ward, was then living in rooms in a little street out of Holborn—a poor place enough. I was organist of St. Bartholomew's, Holborn; and I was trying to do what is described as getting up a connection in the teaching line. But it was slow work, and I must confess that my prospects did not appear to me very cheerful. However, I taught one of the Vicar's little daughters, and a whole family, the children of a rich tradesman in a neighbouring street, the piano and singing, so that I contrived to struggle on.

Basil Netherby had been with me at the College of Music. His line was composing. He was a pleasant, retiring fellow, voluble enough and even rhetorical in *tête-à-tête* talk with an intimate; but dumb in company, with an odd streak of something—genius or eccentricity—about him which made him different from other men. We had drifted into an intimacy, and had indeed lodged together for some months. Netherby used to show me his works—mostly short studies—and though I used to think that they always rather oddly broke down in unexpected places, yet there was always an air of aiming high about them, an attempt to realise the ideal.

He left the College before I did, saying that he had learnt all he could learn and that now he must go quietly into the country somewhere and work all alone—he should do no good otherwise. I heard from him fitfully. He was in Wales, in Devonshire, in Cornwall; and then some three months before the day on which I got the letter, the correspondence had ceased altogether; I did not know his address, and was always expecting to hear from him.

I took up the letter from the place where Mr. Vyvyan had laid it down; it was a bulky envelope; and it was certainly true that, as Mr. Vyvyan had said, the packet was in an extraordinary condition. One of the corners was torn off, with a ragged edge that looked like the nibbling of mice, and there were disagreeable stains both on the front and the back, so that I should have inferred that Mr. Vyvyan's pocket had been filled with raspberries—the theory, though improbable, did not appear impossible. But what surprised me most was that near each of the corners in front a rough cross of ink was drawn, and one at the back of the flap.

I had little doubt, however, that Mr. Vyvyan had, in a nervous and absent mood, harried the poor letter into the condition in which I saw it, and that he had been unable to bring himself to confess to the maltreatment.

I tore the letter open—there fell out several pages of MS. music, and a letter in which Basil, dating from Treheale, and writing in a bold firm hand—bolder and firmer, I thought, than of old—said that he had been making a good deal of progress and working very hard (which must account for his silence), and he ventured to enclose some of his last work which he hoped I would like, but he wanted a candid opinion. He added that he had got quarters at a delightful farmhouse, not far from Grampound. That was all.

Stay! That was not all. The letter finished on the third side; but, as I closed it, I saw written on the fourth page, very small, in a weak loose hand, and as if scribbled in a ferocious haste, as a man might write (so it came oddly into my head) who was escaped for a moment from the vigilance of a careful gaoler, a single sentence. "Vyvyan will take this; and for God's sake, dear Leonard, if you would help a friend who is on the edge (I dare not say of what), come to me tomorrow, UNINVITED.

You will think this very strange, but do not mind that—only come—unannounced, do you see . . . "

The line broke off in an unintelligible flourish. Then on each corner of the last page had been scrawled a cross, with the same ugly and slovenly haste as the crosses on the envelope.

My first thought was that Basil was mad; my next thought that he had drifted into some awkward situation, fallen under some unfortunate influence—was perhaps being black-mailed—and I knew his sensitive character well enough to feel sure that whatever the trouble was it would be exaggerated ten times over by his lively and apprehensive mind. Slowly a situation shaped itself. Basil was a man, as I knew, of an extraordinary austere standard of morals, singularly guileless, and innocent of worldly matters.

Someone, I augured, some unscrupulous woman, had, in the remote spot where he was living, taken a guileful fancy to my poor friend, and had doubtless, after veiled overtures, resolved on a bolder policy and was playing on his sensitive and timid nature by some threat of nameless disclosures, some vile and harrowing innuendo.

I read the letter again—and still more clear did it seem to me that he was in some strange durance, and suffering under abominable fears. I rose from my chair and went to find a time-table, that I might see when I could get to Grampound, when again a shuffling footstep drew to my door, an uncertain hand knocked at the panel, and Mr. Vyvyan again entered the room. This time his confusion was even greater, if that were possible, than it had previously been. He had forgotten to give me a further message; and he thereupon gave me a filthy scrap of paper, nibbled and stained like the envelope, apologised with unnecessary vehemence, uttered a strangled cough and stumbled from the room.

It was difficult enough to decipher the paper, but I saw that a musical phrase had been written on it; and then in a moment I saw that it was a phrase from an old, extravagant work of Basil's own, a Credo which we had often discussed together, the grim and fantastic accompaniment of the sentence "He descended into hell."

This came to me as a message of even greater urgency, and I hesitated no longer. I sat down to write a note to the father of my family of pupils, in which I said that important business called me away for two or three days. I looked out a train, and found that by catching the ten o'clock limited mail I could be at Grampound by six in the morning. I ordered a hasty dinner and I packed a few things into a bag, with an oppressive sense of haste. But, as generally happens on such occasions, I found that I had still two or three hours in hand; so I took up Netherby's music and read it through carefully.

Certainly he had improved wonderfully in handling; but what music it was! It was like nothing of which I had ever even dreamed. There was a wild, intemperate voluptuousness about it, a kind of evil relish of beauty which gave me a painful thrill. To make sure that I was not mistaken, owing to the nervous tension which the strange event had produced in me, I put the things in my pocket and went out to the house of a friend, Dr. Grierson, an accomplished and critical musician who lived not far away.

I found the great man at home smoking leisurely. He had a bird-like demeanour, like an ancient stork, as he sat blinking through spectacles astride of a long pointed nose. He had a slight acquaintance with Netherby, and when I mentioned that I had received some new music from him, which I wished to submit to him, he showed obvious interest. "A promising fellow," he said, "only of course too transcendental." He took the music in his hand; he settled his spectacles and read. Presently he looked up; and I saw in the kind of shamefaced glance with which he regarded me that he had found something of the same incomprehensible sensuality which had so oddly affected myself in the music. "Come, come," he said rather severely, "this is very strange stuff—this won't do at all, you know. We must just hear this!" He rose and went to his piano; and peering into the music, he played the pieces deliberately and critically.

Heard upon the piano, the accent of subtle evil that ran through the music became even more obvious. I seemed to struggle between two feelings—an over-powering admiration, and a sense of shame at my own capacity for admiring it. But the great man was still more moved. He broke off in the middle of a bar and tossed the music to me.

"This is filthy stuff," he said. "I should say to you—burn it. It is clever, of course—hideously, devilishly clever. Look at the progression—F sharp against F natural, you observe" (and he added some technical details with which I need not trouble my readers).

He went on: "But the man has no business to think of such things. I don't like it. Tell him from me that it won't do. There must be some reticence in art, you know—and there is none here. Tell Netherby that he is on the wrong tack altogether. Good heavens," he added, "how could the man write it? He used to be a decent sort of fellow."

It may seem extravagant to write thus of music, but I can only say that it affected me as nothing I had ever heard before. I put it away and we tried to talk of other things; but we could not get the stuff out of our heads. Presently I rose to go, and the Doctor reiterated his warnings still more emphatically. "The man is a criminal in art," he said, "and there must be an end once and for all of this: tell him it's abominable!"

I went back; caught my train; and was whirled sleepless and excited to the West. Towards morning I fell into a troubled sleep, in which I saw in tangled dreams the figure of a man running restlessly among stony hills. Over and over again the dream came to me; and it was with a grateful heart, though very weary, that I saw a pale light of dawn in the east, and the dark trees and copses along the line becoming more and more defined, by swift gradations, in the chilly autumn air.

It was very still and peaceful when we drew up at Grampound station. I enquired my way to Treheale; and I was told it was three or four miles away. The porter looked rather enquiringly at me; there was no chance of obtaining a vehicle, so I resolved to walk, hoping that I should be freshened by the morning air.

Presently a lane struck off from the main road, which led up a wooded valley, with a swift stream rushing along; in one or two places the chimney of a deserted mine with desolate rubbish-heaps stood beside the road. At one place a square church-tower, with pinnacles, looked solemnly over the wood. The road rose gradually. At last I came to a little hamlet, perched high up on the side of the valley. The scene was incomparably beautiful; the leaves were yellowing fast, and I could see a succession of wooded ridges, with a long line of moorland closing the view.

The little place was just waking into quiet activity. I found a bustling man taking down shutters from a general shop which was also the post-office, and enquired where Mr. Netherby lived. The man told me that he was in lodgings at Treheale—"the big house itself, where Farmer Hall lives now; if you go straight along the road," he added, "you will pass the lodge, and Treheale lies up in the wood."

I was by this time very tired—it was now nearly seven—but I took up my bag again and walked along a road passing between high hedges. Presently the wood closed in again, and I saw a small plastered lodge with a thatched roof standing on the left among some firs. The gate stood wide open, and the road which led into the wood was grass-grown, though with deep ruts, along which heavy laden carts seemed to have passed recently.

The lodge seemed deserted, and I accordingly struck off into the wood. Presently the undergrowth grew thicker, and huge sprawling laurels rose in all directions. Then the track took a sudden turn; and I saw straight in front of me the front of a large Georgian house of brown stone, with a gravel sweep up to the door, but all overgrown with grass.

I confess that the house displeased me strangely. It was substantial, homely, and large; but the wood came up close to it on all sides, and it seemed to stare at me with its shuttered windows with a look of dumb resentment, like a great creature at bay.

I walked on, and saw that the smoke went up from a chimney to the left. The house, as I came closer, presented a front with a stone portico, crowned with a pediment. To left and right were two wings which were built out in advance from the main part of the house, throwing the door back into the shadow.

I pulled a large handle which hung beside the door, and a dismal bell rang somewhere in the house—rang on and on as if unable to cease; then footsteps came along the floor within, and the door was slowly and reluctantly unbarred.

There stood before me a little pale woman with a timid, downcast air. "Does Mr. Netherby live here?" I said.

"Yes; he lodges here, sir."

"Can I see him?" I said.

"Well, sir, he is not up yet. Does he expect you?"

"Well, not exactly," I said, faltering; "but he will know my name—and I have come a long way to see him."

The woman raised her eyes and looked at me, and I was aware, by some swift intuition, that I was in the presence of a distressed spirit, labouring under some melancholy prepossession.

"Will you be here long?" she asked suddenly.

"No," I said; "but I shall have to stay the night, I think. I travelled all last night, and I am very tired; in fact I shall ask to sit down and wait till I can see Mr. Netherby."

She seemed to consider a moment, and then led me into the house. We entered a fine hall, with stone flags and pillars on each side. There hung, so far as I could see in the half-light, grim and faded portraits on the walls, and there were some indistinct pieces of furniture, like couched beasts, in the corners. We went through a door and down a passage and turned into a large rather bare room, which showed, however, some signs of human habitation. There was a table laid for a meal.

An old piano stood in a corner, and there were a few books lying about; on the walls hung large pictures in tarnished frames. I put down my bag, and sat down by the fire in an old armchair, and almost instantly fell into a drowse. I have an indistinct idea of the woman returning to ask if I would like some breakfast, or wait for Mr. Netherby. I said hastily that I would wait, being in the oppressed condition of drowsiness when one's only idea is to get a respite from the presence of any person, and fell again into a heavy sleep.

I woke suddenly with a start, conscious of a movement in the room. Basil Netherby was standing close beside me, with his back to the fire, looking down at me with a look which I can only say seemed to me to betoken a deep annoyance of spirit. But seeing me awake, there came on to his face a smile of a reluctant and diplomatic kind. I started to my feet, giddy and bewildered, and shook hands.

"My word," he said, "you sleep sound, Ward. So you've found me out? Well, I'm very glad to see you; but what made you think of coming? and why didn't you let me know? I would have sent something to meet you."

I was a good deal nettled at this ungenial address, after the trouble to which I had put myself. I said, "Well, really, Basil, I think that is rather strong. Mr. Vyvyan called on me yesterday with a letter from you, and some music; and of course I came away at once."

115

"Of course," he said, looking on the ground—and then added rather hastily, "Now, how did the stuff strike you? I have improved, I think. And it is really very good of you to come off at once to criticise the music—very good of you," he said with some emphasis; "and, man, you look wretchedly tired—let us have breakfast."

I was just about to remonstrate, and to speak about the postscript, when he looked at me suddenly with so peculiar and disagreeable a glance that the words literally stuck in my throat. I thought to myself that perhaps the subject was too painful to enter upon at once, and that he probably wished to tell me at his own time what was in the background.

We breakfasted; and now that I had leisure to look at Basil, I was surprised beyond measure at the change in him. I had seen him last a pale, rather haggard youth, loose-limbed and untidy. I saw before me a strongly-built and firmly-knit man, with a ruddy colour and bronzed cheek. He looked the embodiment of health and well-being. His talk, too, after the first impression of surprise wore off, was extraordinarily cheerful and amusing. Again and again he broke out into loud laughter—not the laughter of an excited or hectic person, but the firm, brisk laugh of a man full to the brim of good spirits and health.

He talked of his work, of the country-people that surrounded him, whose peculiarities he seemed to have observed with much relish; he asked me, but without any appearance of interest, what I thought about his work. I tried to tell him what Dr. Grierson had said and what I had felt; but I was conscious of being at a strange disadvantage before this genial personality. He laughed loudly at our criticisms. "Old Grierson," he said, "why, he is no better than a clergyman's widow: he would stop his ears if you read Shakespeare to him. My dear man, I have travelled a long way since I saw you last; I have found my tongue—and what is more, I can say what I mean, and as I mean it. Grierson indeed! I can see him looking shocked, like a pelican with a stomach-ache."

This was a felicitous though not a courteous description of our friend, but I could find no words to combat it; indeed, Basil's talk and whole bearing seemed to carry me away like a swift stream and in my wearied condition I found that I could not stand up to this radiant personality.

After breakfast he advised me to have a good sleep and he took me, with some show of solicitude, to a little bedroom which had been got ready for me. He unpacked my things and told me to undress and go to bed, that he had some work to do that he was anxious to finish, and that after luncheon we would have a stroll together.

I was too tired to resist, and fell at once into a deep sleep. I rose a new man; and finding no one in Basil's room, I strolled out for a moment on to the drive, and presently saw the odd and timid figure of Mrs. Hall coming along, in a big white flapping sort of sun-bonnet, with a basket in her hand. She came straight up to me in a curious, resolute sort of way, and it came into my mind that she had come out for the very purpose of meeting me.

I praised the beauty of the place, and said that I supposed she knew it well. "Yes," she said; adding that she was born in the village and her mother had been as a girl a servant at Treheale. But she went on to tell me that she and her husband had lived till recently at a farm down in the valley, and had only been a year or so in the house itself. Old Mr. Heale, the last owner, had died three or four years before, and it had proved impossible to let the house. It seemed that when the trustees gave up all idea of being able to get a tenant, they had offered it to the Halls at a nominal rent, to act as caretakers. She spoke in a cheerless way, with her eyes cast down and with the same strained look as of one carrying a heavy burden. "You will have heard of Mr. Heale, perhaps?" she said with a sudden look at me.

"The old Squire, sir," she said; "but I think people here are unfair to him. He lived a wild life enough, but he was a kind gentleman in his way—and I have often thought it was not his fault altogether. He married soon after he came into the estate—a Miss Tregaskis from down to St. Erne—and they were very happy for a little; but she died after they had been married a couple of years, and they had no child; and then I think Mr. Heale went nearly mad—nothing went right after that. Mr. Heale shut himself up a good deal among his books—he was a very clever gentleman—and then he got into bad ways; but it was the sorrow in his heart that made him bad—and we must not blame people too much, must we?" She looked at me with rather a pitiful look.

"You mean," I said, "that he tried to forget his grief, and did not choose the best way to do it."

"Yes, sir," said Mrs. Hall simply. "I think he blamed God for taking away what he loved, instead of trusting Him; and no good comes of that. The people here got to hate him—he used to spoil the young people, sir—you know what I mean—and they were afraid of seeing him about their houses. I remember, sir, as if it were yesterday, seeing him in the lane to St. Sibby. He was marching along, very upright, with his white hair—it went white early—and he passed old Mr. Miles, the church-warden, who had been a wild young man too, but he found religion with the Wesleyans, and after that was very hard on everyone.

"It was the first time they had met since Mr. Miles had become serious; and Mr. Heale stopped in his pleasant way, and held out his hand to Mr. Miles; who put his hands behind him and said something—I was close to them—which I could not quite catch, but it was about fellowship with the works of darkness; and then Mr. Miles turned and went on his way; and Mr. Heale stood looking after him with a curious smile on his face—and I have pitied him ever since. Then he turned and saw me; he always took notice of me—I was a girl then; and he said to me,

" 'There, Mary, you see that. I am not good enough, it seems, for Mr. Miles. Well, I don't blame him; but remember, child, that the religion which makes a man turn his back on an old friend is not a good religion'; but I could see he was distressed, though he spoke quietly—and as I went on he gave a sigh which somehow stays in my mind. Perhaps, sir, you would like to look at his picture; he was painted at the same time as Mrs. Heale in the first year of their marriage."

I said I should like to see it, and we turned to the house. She led me to a little room that seemed like a study. There was a big bookcase full of books, mostly of a scientific kind; and there was a large kneehole table much dotted with inkspots. "It was here," she said, "he used to work, hour after hour." On the wall hung a pair of pictures—one, that of a young woman, hardly more than a girl, with a delightful expression, both beautiful and good. She was dressed in some white material, and there was a glimpse of sunlit fields beyond.

Then I turned to the portrait of Mr. Heale. It represented a young man in a claret-coloured coat, very slim and upright. It showed a face of great power, a big forehead, clear-cut features, and a determined chin, with extraordinarily bright large eyes; evidently the portrait of a man of great physical and mental force, who would do whatever he took in hand with all his might. It was very finely painted, with a dark background of woods against a stormy sky.

I was immensely struck by the picture; and not less by the fact that there was an extraordinary though indefinable likeness to Mrs. Hall herself. I felt somehow that she perceived that I had noticed this, for she made as though to leave the room. I could not help the inference that I was compelled to draw. I lingered for a moment looking at the portrait, which was so lifelike as to give an almost painful sense of the presence of a third person in the room. But Mrs. Hall went out, and I understood that I was meant to follow her.

She led the way into their own sitting-room, and then with some agitation she turned to me. "I understand that you are an old friend of Mr. Netherby's, sir," she said.

"Yes," I said; "he is my greatest friend."

"Could you persuade him, sir, to leave this place?" she went on. "You will think it a strange thing to say—and I am glad enough to have a lodger, and I like Mr. Netherby—but do you think it is a good thing for a young gentleman to live so much alone?"

I saw that nothing was to be gained by reticence, so I said, "Now, Mrs. Hall, I think we had better speak plainly. I am, I confess, anxious about Mr. Netherby. I don't mean that he is not well, for I have never seen him look better; but I think that there is something going on which I don't wholly understand."

She looked at me suddenly with a quick look, and then, as if deciding that I was to be trusted, she said in a low voice, "Yes, sir, that is it; this house is not like other houses. Mr. Heale—how shall I say it?—was a very determined gentleman, and he used to say that he never would leave the house—and—you will think it very strange that I should speak thus to a stranger—I don't think he has left it."

We stood for a moment silent, and I knew that she had spoken the truth. While we thus stood, I can only say what I felt—I became aware that we were not alone; the sun was bright on the woods outside, the clock ticked peacefully in a corner, but there was something unseen all about us which lay very heavily on my mind. Mrs. Hall put out her hands in a deprecating way, and then said in a low and hurried voice, "He would do no harm to me, sir—we are too near for that"—she looked up at me, and I nodded; "but I can't help it, can I, if he is different with other people? Now, Mr.

Hall is not like that, sir—he is a plain good man, and would think what I am saying no better than madness; but as sure as there is a God in Heaven, Mr. Heale is here—and though he is too fine a gentleman to take advantage of my talk, yet he liked to command other people, and went his own way too much."

While she spoke, the sense of oppression which I had felt a moment before drew off all of a sudden; and it seemed again as though we were alone.

"Mrs. Hall," I said, "you are a good woman; these things are very dark to me, and though I have heard of such things in stories, I never expected to meet them in the world. But I will try what I can do to get my friend away, though he is a wilful fellow, and I think he will go his own way too." While I spoke I heard Basil's voice outside calling me, and I took Mrs. Hall's hand in my own. She pressed it, and gave me a very kind, sad look. And so I went out.

We lunched together, Basil and I, off simple fare; he pointed with an air of satisfaction to a score which he had brought into the room, written out with wonderful precision. "Just finished," he said, "and you shall hear it later on; but now we will go and look round the place. Was there ever such luck as to get a harbourage like this? I have been here two months and feel like staying for ever. The place is in Chancery. Old Heale of Treheale, the last of his stock—a rare old blackguard—died here. They tried to let the house, and failed, and put Farmer Hall in at last. The whole place belongs to a girl ten years old. It is a fine house—we will look at that tomorrow; but today we will walk round outside. By the way, how long can you stay?"

"I must get back on Friday at latest," I said. "I have a choir practice and a lesson on Saturday."

Basil looked at me with a good-natured smile. "A pretty poor business, isn't it?" he said. "I would rather pick oakum myself. Here I live in a fine house, for next to nothing, and write, write, write—there's a life for a man."

"Don't you find it lonely?" said I.

"Lonely?" said Basil, laughing loud. "Not a bit of it. What do I want with a pack of twaddlers all about me? I tread a path among the stars—and I have the best of company, too." He stopped and broke off suddenly.

"I shouldn't have thought Mrs. Hall very enlivening company," I said. "By the way, what an odd-looking woman! She seems as if she were frightened."

At that innocent remark Basil looked at me suddenly with the same expression of indefinable anger that I had seen in his face at our first meeting; but he said nothing for a moment. Then he resumed: "No, I want no company but myself and my thoughts. I tell you, Ward, if you had done as I have done, opened a door into the very treasure-house of music, and had only just to step in and carry away as much as one can manage at a time, you wouldn't want company."

I could make no reply to this strange talk; and he presently took me out. I was astonished at the beauty of the place. The ground fell sharply at the back, and there was a terrace with a view over a little valley, with pasture-fields at the bottom, crowned with low woods—beyond, a wide prospect over uplands, which lost themselves in the haze. The day was still and clear; and we could hear the running of the stream below, the cooing of doves and the tinkling of a sheepbell. To the left of the house lay large stables and barns, which were in the possession of the farmer.

We wandered up and down by paths and lanes, sometimes through the yellowing woods, sometimes on open ground, the most perfect views bursting upon us on every side, everything lying in a rich still peace, which came upon my tired and bewildered mind like soft music.

In the course of our walk we suddenly came upon a churchyard surrounded by a low wall; at the farther end, beyond the graves, stood a small church consisting of two aisles, with a high perpendicular tower. "St. Sibby," said Basil, "whether he or she I know not, but no doubt a very estimable person. You would like to look at this? The church is generally open."

We went up a gravel path and entered the porch; the door was open, and there was an odd, close smell in the building. It was a very plain place, with the remains of a rood-loft, and some ancient woodwork; but the walls were mildewed and green and the place looked neglected.

"Vyvyan is a good fellow," said Basil, looking round, "but he is single-handed here; the Rector is an invalid and lives at Penzance, and Vyvyan has a wretched stipend. Look here, Leonard; here is the old Heale vault." He led me into a little chapel near the tower, which opened on to the church by a single arch. The place was very dark; but I could see a monument or two of an ancient type and some brasses. There were a couple of helmets on iron supports and the remains of a mouldering banner. But just opposite to us was a tall modern marble monument on the wall. "That is old Heale's monument," said Basil, "with a long, pious inscription by the old rector. Just look at it—did you ever see such vandalism?"

I drew near—then I saw that the monument had been defaced in a hideous and horrible way. There were deep dints in the marble, like the marks of a hammer; and there were red stains over the inscription, which reminded me in a dreadful way of the stains on the letter given me by Vyvyan.

"Good Heavens!" I said, "what inconceivable brutality! Who on earth did this?"

"That's just what no one can find out," said Basil, smiling. "But the inscription was rather too much, I confess—look at this: 'who discharged in an exemplary way the duties of a landowner and a Christian.' Old Heale's idea of the duties of a landowner was to screw as much as he could out of his farmers—and he had, moreover, some old ideas, which we may call feudal, about his relations with the more attractive of his tenants: he was a cheerful old boy—and as to the Christian part of it, well, he had about as much of that, I gather, as you take up on a two-pronged fork. Still, they might have left the old man alone. I daresay he sleeps sound enough in spite of it all." He stamped his foot on the pavement as he did so, which returned a hollow sound. "Are you inside?" said Basil, laughingly; "perhaps not at home?"

"Don't talk like that," I said to Basil, whose levity seemed to me disgusting.

"Certainly not, my boy," he said, "if you don't like it. I daresay the old man can look after himself." And so we left the church.

We returned home about four o'clock. Basil left me on the terrace and went into the house to interview Mrs. Hall on the subject of dinner. I hung for a time over the balustrade, but, getting chilly and still not feeling inclined to go in; I strolled to the farther end of the terrace, which ran up to the wood. On reaching the end, I found a stone seat; and behind it, between two yews, a little dark sinister path led into the copse.

I do not know exactly what feeling it was which drew me to enter upon the exploration of the place; the path was slippery and overgrown with moss, and the air of the shrubbery into which it led was close and moist, full of the breath of rotting leaves. The path ran with snakelike windings, so that at no point was it possible to see more than a few feet ahead. Above, the close boughs held hands as if to screen the path from the light. Then the path suddenly took a turn to the left and went straight to the house.

Two yews flanked the way and a small flight of granite steps, slimy and mildewed, led up to a little door in the corner of the house—a door which had been painted brown, like the colour of the stone, and which was let into its frame so as to be flush with the wall. The upper part of it was pierced with a couple of apertures like eyes filled with glass to give light to the passage within. The steps had evidently not been trodden for many months, even years; but upon the door, near the keyhole, were odd marks looking as if scratched by the hoofs of some beast—a goat, I thought—as if the door had been impatiently struck by something awaiting entrance there.

I do not know what was the obsession which fell on me at the sight of this place. A cold dismay seemed to spring from the dark and clutch me; there are places which seem so soaked, as it were, in malign memories that they give out a kind of spiritual aroma of evil. I have seen in my life things which might naturally seem to produce in the mind associations of terror and gloom. I have seen men die; I have seen a man writhe in pain on the ground from a mortal injury; but I never experienced anything like the thrill of horror which passed through my shuddering mind at the sight of the little door with its dark eye-holes.

I went in chilly haste down the path and came out upon the terrace, looking out over the peaceful woods. The sun was now setting in the west among cloud-fiords and bays of rosy light. But the thought of the dark path lying like a snake among the thickets dwelt in my mind and poisoned all my senses.

Presently I heard the voice of Basil call me cheerfully from the corner of the house. We went in. A simple meal was spread for us, half tea, half dinner, to which we did full justice. But afterwards, though Basil was fuller than ever, so it seemed to me, of talk and laughter, I was seized with so extreme a fatigue that I drowsed off several times in the course of our talk, till at last he laughingly ordered me to bed.

I slept profoundly. When I awoke, it was bright day. My curtains had been drawn, and the materials for my toilette arranged while I still slept. I dressed hastily and hurried down, to find Basil awaiting me.

That morning we gave up to exploring the house. It was a fine old place, full from end to end of the evidences of long and ancestral habitation. The place was full of portraits. There was a great old dining-room—Basil had had the whole house unshuttered for my inspection—a couple of large drawing-rooms, long passages, bedrooms, all full of ancient furniture and pictures, as if the family life had been suddenly suspended. I noticed that he did not take me to the study, but led me upstairs.

"This is my room," said Basil suddenly; and we turned into a big room in the left-hand corner of the garden-front. There was a big four-post bed here, a large table in the window, a sofa, and some fine chairs. But what at once attracted my observation was a low door in the corner of the room, half hidden by a screen. It seemed to me, as if by a sudden gleam of perception, that this door must communicate with the door I had seen below; and presently, while I stood looking out of the great window upon the valley, I said to Basil, "And that door in the corner—does that communicate with the little door in the wood?"

When I said this, Basil was standing by the table, bending over some MSS. He suddenly turned to me and gave me a very long, penetrating look; and then, as if suddenly recollecting himself, said, "My dear Ward, you are a very observant fellow—yes, there is a little staircase there that goes down into the shrubbery and leads to the terrace. You remember that old Mr. Heale of whom I told you—well, he had this room, and he had visitors at times whom I daresay it was not convenient to admit to the house; they came and went this way; and he too, no doubt, used the stairs to leave the house and return unseen."

"How curious!" I said. "I confess I should not care to have this room—I did not like the look of the shrubbery door."

"Well," said Basil, "I do not feel with you; to me it is rather agreeable to have the association of the room. He was a loose old fish, no doubt, but he lived his life, and I expect enjoyed it, and that is more than most of us can claim."

As he said the words he crossed the room, and opening the little door, he said, "Come and look down—it is a simple place enough."

I went across the room, and looking in, saw a small flight of stairs going down into the dark; at the end of which the two square panes of the little shrubbery door were outlined in the shadow.

I cannot account for what happened next; there was a sound in the passage, and something seemed to rush up the stairs and past me; a strange, dull smell came from the passage; I know that there fell on me a sort of giddiness and horror, and I went back into the room with hands outstretched, like Elymas the sorcerer, seeking someone to guide me. Looking up, I saw Basil regarding me with a baleful look and a strange smile on his face.

"What was that?" I said. "Surely something came up there . . . I don't know what it was."

There was a silence; then, "My dear Ward," said Basil, "you are behaving very oddly—one would think you had seen a ghost." He looked at me with a sort of gleeful triumph, like a man showing the advantages of a house or the beauties of a view to an astonished friend. But again I could find no words to express my sense of what I had experienced. Basil went swiftly to the door and shut it, and then said to me with a certain sternness, "Come, we have been here long enough—let us go on. I am afraid I am boring you."

We went downstairs; and the rest of the morning passed, so far as I can remember, in a species of fitful talk. I was endeavouring to recover from the events of the morning; and Basil—well, he seemed to me like a man who was fencing with some difficult question. Though his talk seemed spontaneous, I felt somehow that it was that of a weak antagonist endeavouring to parry the strokes of a persistent assailant.

After luncheon Basil proposed a walk again. We went out on a long ramble, as we had done the previous day; but I remember little of what passed. He directed upon me a stream of indifferent talk, but I laboured, I think, under a heavy depression of spirit, and my conversation was held up merely as it might have been as a shield against the insistent demands of my companion. Anyone who has been through a similar experience in which he wrestles with some tragic fact, and endeavours merely to meet and answer the sprightly suggestions of some cheerful companion, can imagine what I felt. At last the evening began to close in; we retraced our steps: Basil told me that we should dine at an early hour, and I was left alone in my own room.

I became the prey of the most distressing and poignant reflections. What I had experienced convinced me that there was something about the whole place that was uncanny and abnormal. The attitude of my companion, his very geniality, seemed to me to be forced and unnatural; and my only idea was to gain, if I could, some notion of how I should proceed. I felt that questions were useless, and I committed myself to the hands of Providence. I felt that here was a situation that I could not deal with and that I must leave it in stronger hands than my own. This reflection brought me some transitory comfort, and when I heard Basil's voice calling me to dinner, I felt that sooner or later the conflict would have to be fought out, and that I could not myself precipitate matters.

After dinner Basil for the first time showed some signs of fatigue, and after a little conversation he sank back in a chair, lit a cigar, and presently asked me to play something.

I went to the piano, still, I must confess, seeking for some possible opportunity of speech, and let my fingers stray as they moved along the keys. For a time I extemporised and then fell into some familiar music. I do not know whether the instinctive thought of what he had scrawled upon his note to me influenced me but I began to play Mendelssohn's anthem *Hear My Prayer*. While I played the initial phrase, I became aware that some change was making itself felt in my companion; and I had hardly come to the end of the second phrase when a sound from Basil made me turn round.

I do not think that I ever received so painful a shock in my life as that which I experienced at the sight that met my eyes. Basil was still in the chair where he had seated himself, but instead of the robust personality which he had presented to me during our early interviews, I saw in a sudden flash the Basil that I knew, only infinitely more tired and haggard than I had known him in life. He was like a man who had cast aside a mask, and had suddenly appeared in his own part. He sat before me as I had often seen him sit, leaning forward in an intensity of emotion. I stopped suddenly, wheeled round in my chair, and said, "Basil, tell me what has happened."

He looked at me, cast an agitated glance round the room—and then all on a sudden began to speak in a voice that was familiar to me of old.

What he said is hardly for me to recount. But he led me step by step through a story so dark in horrors that I can hardly bring myself to reproduce it here. Imagine an untainted spirit, entering cheerfully upon some simple entourage, finding himself little by little within the net of some overpowering influence of evil.

He told me that he had settled at Treheale in his normal frame of mind. That he had intended to tell me of his whereabouts, but that there had gradually stolen into his mind a sort of unholy influence. "At first," he said, "I resisted it," but it was accompanied by so extraordinary an access of mental power and vigour that he had accepted the conditions under which he found himself. I had better perhaps try to recount his own experience.

He had come to Grampound in the course of his wanderings and had enquired about lodgings. He had been referred to the farmer at Treheale. He had settled himself there, only congratulating himself upon the mixture of quiet and dignity which surrounded him. He had arranged his life for tranquil study, had chosen his rooms, and had made the best disposition he could of his affairs.

"The second night," he said, "that I was here, I had gone to bed thinking of nothing but my music. I had extinguished my light and was lying quietly in bed watching the expiring glimmer of the embers on my hearth. I was wondering, as one does, weaving all kinds of fancies about the house and the room in which I found myself, lying with my head on my hand, when I saw, to my intense astonishment, the little door in the corner of the bedroom half open and close again.

"I thought to myself that it was probably Mrs. Hall coming to see whether I was comfortable, and I thereupon said, 'Who is there?' There was no sound in answer, but presently, a moment or two after, there followed a disagreeable laughter, I thought from the lower regions of the house in the direction of the corner. 'Come in, whoever you are,' I said; and in a moment the door opened and closed, and I became aware that there was someone in the room.

"Further than that," said Basil to me in that dreadful hour, "it is impossible to go. I can only say that I became aware in a moment of the existence of a world outside of and intertwined with our own; a world of far stronger influences and powers—how far-reaching I know not—but I know this, that all the mortal difficulties and dilemmas that I had hitherto been obliged to meet melted away in the face of a force to which I had hitherto been a stranger."

The dreadful recital ended about midnight; and the strange part was to me that our positions seemed in some fearful manner to have been now reversed. Basil was now the shrinking, timorous creature, who only could implore me not to leave him. It was in such a mood as this that he had written the letter. I asked him what there was to fear. "Everything," he said with a shocking look. He would not go to bed; he would not allow me to leave the room.

Step by step I unravelled the story, which his incoherent statement had only hinted at. His first emotion had been that of intense fright; but he became aware almost at once that the spirit who thus so unmistakably came to him was not inimical to him; the very features of the being—if such a word can be used about so shadowy a thing—appeared to wear a smile. Little by little the presence of the visitant had become habitual to Basil: there was a certain pride in his own fearlessness, which helped him.

Then there was intense and eager curiosity; "and then, too," said the unhappy man, "the influence began to affect me in other ways. I will not tell you how, but the very necessaries of life were provided for me in a manner which I should formerly have condemned with the utmost scorn, but which now I was given confidence to disregard. The dejection, the languorous reflections which used to hang about me, gradually drew off and left me cheerful, vigorous, and, I must say it, delighting in evil imaginations; but so subtle was the evil influence, that it was not into any gross corruption or flagrant deeds that I flung myself; it was into my music that the poison flowed.

"I do not, of course, mean that evil then appeared to me, as I can humbly say it does now, as evil, but rather as a vision of perfect beauty, glorifying every natural function and every corporeal desire. The springs of music rose clear and strong within me and with the fountain I mingled from my own stores the subtle venom of the corrupted mind. How glorious,

I thought, to sway as with a magic wand the souls of men; to interpret for each all the eager and leaping desires which maybe he had dully and dutifully controlled. To make all things fair—for so potent were the whispers of the spirit that talked at my ear that I believed in my heart that all that was natural in man was also permissible and even beautiful, and that it was nothing but a fantastic asceticism that forbids it; though now I see, as I saw before, that the evil that thwarts mankind is but the slime of the pit out of which he is but gradually extricating himself."

"But what is the thing," I said, "of which you speak? Is it a spirit of evil, or a human spirit, or what?"

"Good God!" he said, "how can I tell?" and then with lifted hand he sang in a strange voice a bar or two from *Stanford's Revenge.*

"Was he devil or man? He was devil for aught they knew."

This dreadful interlude, the very flippancy of it, that might have moved my laughter at any other time, had upon me an indescribably sickening effect. I stared at Basil. He relapsed into a moody silence with clasped hands and knotted brow. To draw him away from the nether darkness of his thoughts, I asked him how and in what shape the spirit had made itself plain to him.

"Oh, no shape at all," said he; "he is there, that is enough. I seem sometimes to see a face, to catch the glance of an eye, to see a hand raised to warn or to encourage; but it is all impossibly remote; I could never explain to you how I see him."

"Do you see him now?" I asked.

"Yes," said Basil, "a long way off—and he is running swiftly to me, but he has far to go yet. He is angry; he threatens me; he beats the air with his hands."

"But where is this?" I asked, for Basil's eyes were upon the ground.

"Oh, for God's sake, man, be silent," said Basil. "It is in the region of which you and others know little; but it has been revealed to me. It lies all about us—it has its capes and shadowy peaks, and a leaden sea, full of sound; it is there that I ramble with him."

There fell a silence between us. Then I said, "But, dear Basil, I must ask you this—how was it that you wrote as you did to me?"

"Oh! he made me write," he said, "and I think he over-reached himself—or my angel, that beholds the Father's face, smote him down. I was myself again on a sudden, the miserable and abject wretch whom you see before you, and knowing that I had been as a man in a dream. Then I wrote the despairing words, and guarded the letter so that he could not come near me; and then Mr. Vyvyan's visit to me—that was not by chance. I gave him the letter and he promised to bear it faithfully—and what attempts were made to tear it from him I do not know; but that my adversary tried his best I do not doubt. But Vyvyan is a good man and could not be harmed.

"And then I fell back into the old spell; and worked still more abundantly and diligently and produced this—this accursed thing which shall not live to scatter evil abroad." As he said these words he rose, and tore the score that lay on the table into shreds and crammed the pieces in the fire. As he thrust the last pieces down, the poker he was holding fell from his hands.

I saw him white as a sheet, and trembling. "What is the matter?" I said.

He turned a terrible look on me, and said, "He is here—he has arrived."

Then all at once I was aware that there was a sort of darkness in the room; and then with a growing horror I gradually perceived that in and through the room there ran a thing like the front of a precipice, with some dark strand at its foot on which beat a surge of phantom waves. The two scenes struggled together. At one time I could plainly see the cliff-front, close beside me—and then the lamp and the fire-lit room was all dimmed even to vanishing; and then suddenly the room would come back and the cliff die into a steep shadow.

But in either of the scenes Basil and I were there—he standing irresolute and despairing, glancing from side to side like a hare when the hounds close in. And once he said—this was when the cliff loomed up suddenly—"There are others with him." Then in a moment it seemed as if the room in which we sat died away altogether and I was in that other place; there was a faint light as from under a stormy sky; and a little farther up the strand there stood a group of dark figures, which seemed to consult together.

All at once the group broke and came suddenly towards us. I do not know what to call them; they were human in a sense—that is, they walked upright and had heads and hands. But the faces were all blurred and fretted, like half-rotted skulls—but there was no sense of comparison in me. I only knew that I had seen ugliness and corruption at the very source, and looked into the darkness of the pit itself.

The forms eluded me and rushed upon Basil, who made a motion as though to seize hold of me, and then turned and fled, his arms outstretched, glancing behind him as he ran—and in a moment he was lost to view, though I could see along the shore of that formless sea something like a pursuit.

I do not know what happened after that. I think I tried to pray; but I presently became aware that I was myself menaced by danger. It seemed—but I speak in parables—as though one had separated himself from the rest and had returned to seek me. But all was over, I knew; and the figure indeed carried something which he swung and shook in his hand, which I thought was a token to be shown to me. And then I found my voice and cried out with all my strength to God to save me; and in a moment there was the fire-lit room again, and the lamp—the most peaceful-looking room in England.

But Basil had left me; the door was wide open; and in a moment the farmer and his wife came hurrying along with blanched faces to ask who it was that had cried out, and what had happened.

I made some pitiful excuse that I had dozed in my chair and had awoke crying out some unintelligible words. For in the quest I was about to engage in I did not wish that any mortal should be with me.

They left me, asking for Mr. Netherby and still not satisfied. Indeed, Mrs. Hall looked at me with so penetrating a look that I felt that she understood something of what had happened. And then at once I went up to Basil's room. I do not know where I found the courage to do it; but the courage came.

The room was dark, and a strong wind was blowing through it from the little door. I stepped across the room, feeling my way; went down the stairs, and finding the door open at the bottom, I went out into the snake-like path.

I went some yards along it; the moon had risen now. There came a sudden gap in the trees to the left, through which I could see the pale fields and the corner of the wood casting its black shadow on the ground.

The shrubs were torn, broken, and trampled, as though some heavy thing had crashed through. I made my way cautiously down, endowed with a more than human strength—it was a steep bank covered with trees—and then in a moment I saw Basil.

He lay some distance out in the field on his face. I knew at a glance that all was over; and when I lifted him I became aware that he was in some way strangely mangled, and indeed it was found afterwards that though the skin of his body was hardly contused, yet that almost every bone of the body was broken in fragments.

I managed to carry him to the house. I closed the doors of the staircase; and then I managed to tell Farmer Hall that Basil had had, I thought, a fall and was dead. And then my own strength failed me, and for three days and nights I lay in a kind of stupor.

When I recovered my consciousness, I found myself in bed in my own room. Mrs. Hall nursed me with a motherly care and tenderness which moved me very greatly; but I could not speak of the matter to her, until, just before my departure, she came in, as she did twenty times a day, to see if I wanted anything. I made a great effort and said, "Mrs. Hall, I am very sorry for you. This has been a terrible business, and I am afraid you won't easily forget it. You ought to leave the house, I think."

Mrs. Hall turned her frozen gaze upon me, and said, "Yes, sir, indeed, I can't speak about it or think of it. I feel as if I might have prevented it; and yet I have been over and over it in my mind and I can't see where I was wrong. But my duty is to the house now, and I shall never leave it; but I will ask you, sir, to try and find a thought of pity in your heart for him"—I knew she did not mean Basil—"I don't think he clearly knows what he has done; he must have his will, as he always did. He stopped at nothing if it was for his pleasure; and he did not know what harm he did. But he is in God's hands; and though I cannot understand why, yet there are things in this life which He allows to be; and we must not try to be judges—we must try to be merciful. But I have not done what I could have done; and if God gives me strength, there shall be an end of this."

A few hours later Mr. Vyvyan called to see me; he was a very different person to the Vyvyan that had showed himself to me in Holborn.

I could not talk much with him but I could see that he had some understanding of the case. He asked me no questions, but he told me a few details. He said that they had decided at the inquest that he had fallen from the terrace. But the doctor, who was attending me, seems to have said to Mr. Vyvyan that a fall it must have been, but a fall of an almost inconceivable character. "And what is more," the old doctor had added, "the man was neither in pain nor agitation of mind when he died." The face was absolutely peaceful and tranquil; and the doctor's theory was that he had died from some sudden seizure before the fall.

And so I held my tongue. One thing I did: it was to have a little slab put over the body of my friend—a simple slab with name and date—and I ventured to add one line, because I have no doubt in my own mind that Basil was suddenly delivered, though not from death. He had, I supposed, gone too far upon the dark path, and he could not, I think, have freed himself from the spell; and so the cord was loosed, but loosed in mercy—and so I made them add the words:

"And in their hands they shall bear thee up."

I must add one further word. About a year after the events above recorded I received a letter from Mr. Vyvyan, which I give without further comment.

"St. Sibby, Dec., 18, 189—.

"Dear Mr. Ward,

"I wish to tell you that our friend Mrs. Hall died a few days ago. She was a very good woman, one of the few that are chosen. I was much with her in her last days, and she told me a strange thing, which I cannot bring myself to repeat to you. But she sent you a message which she repeated several times, which she said you would understand. It is simply this: 'Tell Mr. Ward I have prevailed.' I may add that I have no doubt of the truth of her words, and you will know to what I am alluding.

"The day after she died there was a fire at Treheale: Mr. Hall was absolutely distracted with grief at the loss of his wife, and I do not know quite what happened. But it was impossible to save the house; all that is left of it is a mass of charred ruins, with a few walls standing up. Nothing was saved, not even a picture. There is a wholly inadequate insurance, and I believe it is not intended to rebuild the house.

"I hope you will bear us in mind; though I know you so little, I shall always feel that we have a common experience which will hold us together. You will try and visit us some day when the memory of what took place is less painful to you. The grass is now green on your poor friend's grave; and I will only add that you will have a warm welcome here. I am just moving into the Rectory, as my old Rector died a fortnight ago, and I have accepted the living. God bless you, dear Mr. Ward.

"Yours very sincerely,
"JAMES VYVYAN."

# H. W. Tatham
## (1861-1909)

*"A man of impassive countenance and acute sense of humour, [Tatham] was a dreadful neighbour when anything mirth-provoking happened in school or church . . . There would be a sharp nudge from his elbow in your ribs, and the bench would tremble under his massive form . . . Rather brutal I thought him when I first came across him, but he developed into the champion of all suffering things. 'I like toads,' he said, 'they're dry and weak.' He was very sympathetic, too, with cats."*

– M. R. James, *Eton and King's* (1926)

M. R. James enjoyed Herbert Tatham's quiet irreverence and good humour when they were schoolboys, and it's easy to see why they remained friends at Cambridge and beyond. A year older than MRJ, Tatham went to read Classics at Trinity College in October 1881, and joined the Chit-Chat a year later. He was responsible for some of the more engaging-sounding papers in his day. For while Arthur Benson challenged his listeners with "The relation of the artistic & moral instincts", and Charles Waldstein pondered "The Aesthetic aspects of Ethics", Tatham got straight to the point with "Dreams", "War", "Wit and Humour", "Novels", and, one night in 1884, "Ghosts".

MRJ was there to hear "Ghosts", and it would be interesting to know more about the paper's content and tone, as well as the discussion that followed—the minute book gives us nothing more than the title. It might have been a reflection on the foundation two years earlier of the Society for Psychical Research, whose first president, Henry Sidgwick, was a prominent senior member of Trinity.

Tatham succeeded Arthur Benson as secretary of the Chit-Chat in November 1884, but less than a year later, a line in the minute book, in MRJ's hand, sounds an uncharacteristically rueful note: "The society expressed its regret and disappointment at the conduct of Mr. Tatham."

It's not possible to gauge the tone in which this brief minute is to be read, but secretary Tatham had earned his friends' censure—serious or otherwise—by forsaking his post and defecting to the Apostles. This rival undergraduate society met, like the Chit-Chat, on Saturday nights, to snack on anchovy toast and debate philosophical questions, and it too drew its membership largely from Trinity and King's. It was the elder of the two clubs, and its purposes were thought to be the more elevated. MRJ records in *Eton and King's* (1926) that in his day the Chit-Chat was seen as a nursery for Apostles, a representative of whom "would invite you to take a walk with him one afternoon, and would then probe your capacity for philosophic speculation". MRJ never got the summons himself, but during the co-existence of the two clubs, at least twenty-four Chit-Chat members did shift their loyalties.

Tatham sounds like an unlikely candidate for this band of high-flying *penseurs*. He was, as MRJ recalled, "incurably unambitious", and after taking a first in Classics, in 1886 he returned to Eton where he remained, teaching Latin and Greek, for the rest of his life. A. C. Benson had made the same move the year before, and it was as young housemasters at the school that the two men established a close bond. "The boy who in his Sunday questions illustrated the friendship of David and Jonathan by that of Mr. Tatham and Mr. Benson was right," recalled a contemporary, and Benson described Tatham as his "best and dearest friend". In 1892 they co-wrote a book—*Men of Might: Studies of Great Characters*—a collection of inspiriting biographical lectures on the likes of "Socrates the Athenian", "Mahomet", and "George Washington". They also collaborated, more informally, on supernatural fiction.

In Spring 1902, on a hiking tour of Wales, A. C. Benson recorded in his diary that "we talk out plots as we walk and Tatham is very inventive". The product of this holiday was a story, "The Hill of Trouble", which was published in 1903, the title work in a collection of moralising supernatural tales that Benson had originally composed to read aloud to his pupils on Sunday evenings. Tatham is said to have provided his friend with the idea for one of these, "The Grey Cat". But he was, at the same time, composing his own stories, intended, like Benson's, to be read aloud for the edification of the schoolboys in his charge, and in 1910 these were published.

The stories collected in *The Footprints in the Snow* are not all supernatural, though many deal with divine justice and hint at the miraculous. Several have the flavour of fairy tales or parables, and all have a simple, clear Christian moral; they extol the virtues of patience, modesty, generosity, and forgiveness. They're gentle, good-hearted homilies, aimed at listeners who, like the author in his own schooldays, sometimes found it difficult to concentrate in chapel.

But if Tatham's collection lacks the thrills and tension that mark out MRJ's best work, his stories do have something of the same dry wit; and the "impassive countenance and sense of humour" that MRJ cherished in his friend are evident in the tale reprinted here.

"The Phonograph Bewitched" stands out in Tatham's small oeuvre for having a contemporary setting. It is supernatural, though perhaps better classed as science fiction than ghost story. With its self-deprecating portrayal of a vain Classics master, and its quiet, compassionate denunciation of bullying, it's amusing and ultimately poignant rather than chilling. But the mystical ending, the careful pacing, the control of tone and the deft manipulation of emotion, hint at what the author might have achieved had he flexed his imagination—and ambition—more.

Tatham did not live to see his stories published, however. On 4 August 1909, while on a mountaineering holiday in the Alps, he slipped and fell from a path near the Montanvert Hotel in Chamonix. He struck his head on a rock and never regained consciousness.

# The Phonograph Bewitched

## H. F. W. Tatham

A few years ago, there lived in a back street of an old country town in the West of England an old man. He was a strange, bent, wrinkled creature, who looked, when he came out-of-doors, like an owl in the daylight, and was the object of ridicule to most of the boys of his quarter of the town. But by dint of hard work, added to a good natural capacity, he had attained great skill as a mechanician. Indeed, he made his living almost entirely by odd jobs of mending machines and other articles, often succeeding in cases where famous and experienced workmen had declared repair to be impossible.

During the best years of his life he had been greatly attracted by the inventions of Edison, more especially by the phonograph and similar contrivances. The uncanny reproduction of the human voice appealed to his imagination as much as the skilful workmanship to his intellect, and it was supposed in the town that he was devising some new form of the machine, from which great results were expected, though some threw doubt upon the report. However, it was true enough, and on the night of the first of November 189— the machine was nearing completion. The old man sat in the back room of his house, and was lovingly putting the finishing touches to his work. It was quite different from the ordinary kind of phonograph, though it is needless to say in what the difference lay. But somehow the old man was not satisfied. "I wish—I wish—" he said to himself; and just then something tapped at the window. Rising up, he went to it and looked out. But he could see nothing; the moonlight lay in white strips on the yard behind; and there was really nothing there. But there had certainly been a tapping, and there was no branch or anything hanging loose that could have caused it. It must have been fancy; so at least he told himself, as he went back to the table and his work, and presently he fell to wishing again. And again something tapped at the window, so loudly and unmistakeably that he could not believe his eyes when he saw again that the yard was empty. But empty it was, and there was no use in staring out into it. So once again to work; and this time he put the last finishing touches to the machine. Then he sat for a while and stared at it; and then, again, "I wish—I wish—" he said; and with that there came such a loud tapping that the window shook and rattled, and the old man ran to it and flung it wide.

Was it fancy, or did something brush past him into the room? He never knew, I think; certainly he never told anyone; for the next morning he was found sitting in the chair by the table quite dead, with such an odd smile on his face; and the finished phonograph stood beside him.

The old man did not leave much money, and his stock of instruments, materials, machines, etc. was quickly sold up and the proceeds divided among his heirs, who were in no way inclined to continue the business. The phonograph passed into the hands of a schoolmaster. This schoolmaster thought it would be a very interesting thing if he took the phonograph into the room where he held his class, so that an impression of the sounds might be taken and then reproduced afterwards for the amusement of himself and his friends. But there was a peculiarity about the phonograph on which he did not reckon.

The schoolmaster was a man who prided himself on the manner in which he enlivened, for instance, a long and dull construing-lesson with remarks on some topic more or less closely—sometimes very remotely—connected with the subject in hand. So much was he addicted to this that sometimes, led away by his own fluency and the plentiful supply of general knowledge he possessed, he found the hour had almost slipped away before he was aware of it, and some of the regular lesson had to be omitted or hastily construed by himself—not altogether to the sorrow of the boys in the class.

On this occasion he took in the phonograph, and placed it in a position favourable for recording the sounds uttered in the room. He laid himself out to be more than usually interesting—indeed, his description of the various kinds of torpedoes in use in modern navies, which arose out of the account of the ramming of a ship in the battle of Salamis, was wonderful, he thought, in its clearness and grasp of facts. It was not till just before the end of school that he noticed that the ten hardest lines of the lesson remained unconstrued, and hastily (but, as he thought, remarkably clearly and idiomatically) translated them to the division himself.

He stayed behind after dismissing the boys and turned on the phonograph to reproduce the lesson. Of course he expected to hear the lesson reproduced—the slow and stammering construing of the boys—his own ironical comments—the fluent English that he substituted for their bad renderings—finally his eloquent and scientific discourse on the use of the torpedo in modern warfare. But what he really heard was quite different.

All that he had thought the important part was reproduced in a low and hurried voice, through which, now and again, broke loud remarks either quite disconnected with the lesson—referring, in fact, to engagements and appointments of an athletic or social nature—or connected with it in a way that was singularly painful to the hearer; for instance, questions as to the place, or the correct rendering of words in the part of the lesson yet unconstrued, or suggestions made in a friendly spirit to help out a comrade in a difficulty. One remark in particular cut the hearer to the heart. It was a suggestion made to a boy whose intelligent questions had often gratified him that he should get "old So-and-so to jaw about something" for the rest of school, so as to avoid the construing of the harder part of the lesson. He was grieved to think how well the artifice had succeeded.

In fact, it was only too plain that the phonograph, perhaps owing to its peculiar construction, but more likely through the influence of the thing that had come in through the mechanician's window on that November night, recorded remarks in a most contradictory manner—bringing out in a loud tone those which the speaker meant to be low, and *vice versa*. The mechanism was unusually complicated, and the schoolmaster, examining and poking about the handles and screws that he saw, was surprised on touching one to hear a loud whirring sound that lasted for a few seconds and then ceased. He did not realise he had made a startling change in the machine by this, and, after taking out and obliterating the record of the school just passed, he carried the machine back to his house. On going in, for some reason or other it was necessary for him to enter one of the boys' rooms and speak to the owner, and putting down the phonograph he stayed there for a while, and then, as often happens, when he went out he left it behind him on the table. Moreover, oddly enough, he seemed to forget its existence from that time forward; but it is said that after that day his talk in school was less discursive in character.

The boy in whose room the phonograph was left was the captain of the eleven, and otherwise an important personage. It was not long before he noticed the phonograph, and, being of a mechanical turn, saw how to set it going; and it struck him that it would be amusing to place it so that it would record the conversation of some friends who were shortly coming to see him.

The friends presently arrived, and were very courteous in their conversation, laughing at all the captain's jokes, and otherwise showing a great desire to ingratiate themselves with him. It is true that they were boys who were candidates for the eleven. All the same, flattery is pleasant even when the motive is not altogether unguessable, and the captain was gratified. By and by the friends took their leave, and the captain, when they had gone, turned on the mechanisms to reproduce the conversation. But the words that came out made him sit up very straight and turn very red, and finally kick the phonograph across the room, so that it lay fizzing feebly in a corner and finally became silent.

For this was the kind of remark that clearly came from the machine. "What rot it is to have to sit here and listen to jokes a silly ass like B. chooses to make, and all because he can put me in the eleven or not if he likes!" "Besides, he is really not much good himself." "He is awfully bad", said another voice. "It is a pity he did not leave last half; he's been here much too long, and C. would have made a much better captain." And much more to a like effect.

Now it was plain, though the captain did not know it, that the turning of that handle had made a change in the machine. It now took no notice of spoken remarks, but recorded thoughts only; and these thoughts were often quite at variance with the words which were heard by the ear.

I do not know if the two boys who had just left the room got into the eleven or not; let us hope that the captain went by their merits, and felt no grudge against them for their thoughts. Our business is to follow the adventures of the phonograph.

It was all bent and apparently hopelessly damaged by the kick and the fall into the corner of the room, and the captain was only too anxious to be rid of it. So he was glad enough when his fag took it away. The fag was an odd, awkward boy, very shy and reticent, solitary in his habits, with no gifts for work or play; unpopular, unattractive, sometimes unhappy; even, the other boys said, a little mad. He also had some turn for mechanics, and he poked the phonograph about till it was more or less in working order; but its fall in the corner of the room had had an effect on it, which we shall presently see.

Now the boy in whose possession it was had the habit that many solitary and eccentric people have of talking to himself when alone, apparently in quite long conversations, with pauses for the answers, uttered, not clearly and distinctly, but in a low voice, of which the words could not be distinguished through walls or doors, and accordingly baffled the curiosity of his neighbours. But, when they learnt of the existence of the machine in his room, they thought they now had an opportunity of hearing what the remarks really were; so they watched for their opportunity, and left the machine ready to take the record. Then, after a long enough interval, getting the owner out of the room on some pretext, they carried the phonograph away.

It was some time before the experiment was over. But of the four boys who listened to it only one was then left, and, as he re-joined his comrades who had stolen from the room one by one, he seemed strangely moved. It was not only that instead of the broken mumblings they had expected, the boy's voice had come out clear and true; it was not only that the words he spoke had a beauty all their own and a sense that they could but half appreciate; it was not only that the words somehow or other were not afterwards to be recalled; but that there was another voice that spoke with him. It was a voice that may speak to all, but not to most in words audible to the outward ear, and the words were words such as never man spake, and the sound was as the sound of many waters; Moses on the mount, when the cloud came down in darkness and the voice of the trumpet waxed exceeding loud; Elijah in the wilderness, when after the fire came a still small voice; St. John on the barren isle of Patmos in the Spirit on the Lord's Day—those had heard it; and now it was heard one more, as it talked with the despised boy whom his companions called mad.

As for the phonograph, it would record nothing more after that, and was sold for old metal.

"Useless things, these phonographs," said a customer in a shop where it lay neglected and dirty in a corner; "none of them ever did any good. What use has that thing ever been in the world? None, I would wager a good deal."

But the phonograph knew better.

# Maurice Baring
## (1874-1945)

Maurice Baring never completed his degree, but years later when he looked back on his brief time at Cambridge in his autobiography, *The Puppet Show of Memory* (1922), he was able to summon happy memories:

> "Summer afternoons in King's College gardens, and the light streaming through the gorgeous glass of the west window in King's chapel . . . crowds of youths with well-brushed hair and straw hats telling stories in front of the fireplace . . . the present Provost of Eton [M. R. James] mimicking the dons; and the endless laughter of those who could say: 'We were young, we were merry, we were very, very wise, / And the door stood open to our feast.'"

That final couplet, from "Unwelcome" by Mary Elizabeth Coleridge, could work as a motto for the Chit-Chat Club. Baring, who came from a family of prodigiously wealthy bankers, joined the club on 4 November 1893, the same night as Will Stone, and a week after MRJ's reading of "The Scrap-book of Canon Alberic" and "Lost Hearts".

As an Eton schoolboy Baring had already forged links with several Chit-Chat members, past and future. A. C. Benson had been an inspiring influence as his housemaster; and a few months before going up to Cambridge, he'd stayed at the

Benson family home and read the proofs of E. F.'s debut novel *Dodo*. At school he'd been close to Gerald Warre Cornish, and fellow pupil Desmond MacCarthy was to be a lifelong friend. MRJ, twelve years Baring's senior, was closer to his older brothers: he travelled to Greece with Cecil Baring in the summer of 1885, and in October 1882 he described, in a letter home, a visit to John Baring's rooms in Trinity where . . . . the usual rag supervened and we had great sport altogether." But despite the difference in ages, he and Maurice attended several of the same Chit-Chat meetings—and as the quotation above shows—MRJ's skills as a comedian made a lasting impression on the younger man. Baring himself only ever gave one talk to the club, about the German poet Heinrich Heine, whose work he'd first read when studying in Germany the year before coming up to Cambridge, an experience referenced in his story "The Shadow of a Midnight", printed here.

Like MRJ, Baring had a gift for languages but was hopeless with numbers, and it was this mathematical ineptitude that put a premature end to his university career. In order to take a full degree in the Cambridge of Baring's day, an undergraduate had to pass the "Little-Go", a set of preliminary exams designed to test proficiency in Latin, Greek, Scriptural Knowledge, and Mathematics. At the end of his first year, unable to convince the university authorities that he had grasped even the basics of arithmetic and algebra, Baring was forced to give up his place at Trinity College.

But if he failed academically, his abbreviated time at Cambridge was not wasted. In the summer term of 1894 he edited a magazine, *The Cambridge ABC*, which published Robert Carr Bosanquet's "Red Gold", and which bore an original cover illustration by Aubrey Beardsley.

He was also at Cambridge long enough to develop a distrust of religious scepticism. At Trinity, as he recalled in

*The Puppet Show of Memory*, he skirted the fringes of "a small but highly intellectual world of which the apex was the mysterious Society of the Apostles, who discussed philosophy in secret". A representative of this group one day tried to persuade him that he "ought not to go to chapel as it was setting a bad example". In fact, by the time he'd gone up to Cambridge, Baring had already shed the vague Christian assumptions of his childhood—"as easily as a child loses a first tooth"—and he rarely attended Chapel. But in spite of this, he had little time for atheistic proselytising. "Dogmatic disbelief was to me always an intolerable thing," he later wrote, and something of this impatience finds its way into his story "The Ikon".

The protagonist, Ferrol, is scathingly drawn in the opening paragraphs. A dogmatically disbelieving Cambridge man—a Mathematics graduate—he is, Baring tells us, "the kind of man who had nothing in him you could positively dislike, but to whom you could not talk for five minutes without having a vague sensation of blight". With his misplaced intellectual pride, Ferrol has something of MRJ's Professor Parkins about him, though his scepticism ranges more widely and aggressively—"he had come to the conclusion by the age of twenty-five that all men were stupid, irreclaimably, irredeemably stupid; that everything was wrong; that all literature was really bad, all art much overrated, and all music tedious in the long run."

Ferrol is, it emerges, particularly immune to the power of religious art. He can appreciate rarity, beauty, and antiquity, but just as Anderson in "The Scrap-book of Canon Alberic" wonders at the sacristan's emotionally charged response to a painted altarpiece ("how could a daub of this kind affect anyone so strongly?"), so Ferrol is contemptuous of the idea that his idols and ikons can carry any more than their material value. You sense early on that a catastrophe is looming, but

Baring still succeeds, I think, in providing a shock of pity at the end.

With its apparently spontaneous iconoclasm, and tensions between Christian and pagan art, "The Ikon" shares themes with Vernon Lee's remarkable story "Marsyas in Flanders", in which a mutilated pagan statue causes upheaval in a medieval church. Baring had met Lee in Florence in 1893, not long before going up to Cambridge, and the two writers enjoyed a long friendship. "Marsyas in Flanders" was first published in 1900, nine years before "The Ikon", but Lee later included it in her 1927 collection *For Maurice: Five Unlikely Stories*, which was dedicated to Baring.

Mathematical shortcomings did nothing to hinder Maurice Baring's post-Cambridge career. His linguistic brilliance and impeccable social connections led him first to the diplomatic service. As an attaché at the British Legation in Copenhagen, he befriended Constantine Benckendorff, the Russian Ambassador to Denmark, and this led to a lifelong fascination with the history and literature of Russia. He was a foreign correspondent for the *Morning Post* during the Russo-Japanese War, 1904-1905, and until the outbreak of World War One he lived for much of the time in Moscow. During this period he got to know fellow journalist Hugh Hector Munro, whose sardonic, sometimes supernatural, stories written under the pseudonym "Saki" he greatly admired. Baring wrote extensively about Russian life and both "The Ikon" and "Shadow of a Midnight" owe something to his extensive travels in the country. Both stories were first collected in *Orpheus in Mayfair* in 1909, the same year that Baring was accepted into the Roman Catholic Church: "the only action in my life" he wrote, "which I am quite certain I have never regretted . . . "

# The Shadow of a Midnight

## Maurice Baring

It was nine o'clock in the evening. Sasha, the maid, had brought in the samovar and placed it at the head of the long table. Marie Nikolaevna, our hostess, poured out the tea. Her husband was playing Vindt with his daughter, the doctor, and his son-in-law in another corner of the room. And Jameson, who had just finished his Russian lesson—he was working for the Civil Service examination—was reading the last number of the *Rouskoe Slovo*.

"Have you found anything interesting, Frantz Frantzovitch?" said Marie Nikolaevna to Jameson, as she handed him a glass of tea.

"Yes, I have," answered the Englishman, looking up. His eyes had a clear dreaminess about them, which generally belongs only to fanatics or visionaries, and I had no reason to believe that Jameson, who seemed to be common sense personified, was either one or the other. "At least," he continued, "it interests me. And it's odd—very odd."

"What is it?" asked Marie Nikolaevna.

"Well, to tell you what it is would mean a long story which you wouldn't believe," said Jameson; "only it's odd—very odd."

"Tell us the story," I said.

"As you won't believe a word of it," Jameson repeated, "it's not much use my telling it."

155

We insisted on hearing the story, so Jameson lit a cigarette, and began:—

"Two years ago," he said, "I was at Heidelberg, at the University, and I made friends with a young fellow called Braun. His parents were German, but he had lived five or six years in America, and he was practically an American. I made his acquaintance by chance at a lecture, when I first arrived, and he helped me in a number of ways. He was an energetic and kind-hearted fellow, and we became great friends. He was a student, but he did not belong to any Korps or Bursenschaft, he was working hard then. Afterwards he became an engineer. When the summer semester came to an end, we both stayed on at Heidelberg. One day Braun suggested that we should go for a walking tour and explore the country. I was only too pleased, and we started. It was glorious weather, and we enjoyed ourselves hugely. On the third night after we had started we arrived at a village called Salzheim. It was a picturesque little place, and there was a curious old church in it with some interesting tombs and relics of the Thirty Years War. But the inn where we put up for the night was even more picturesque than the church. It had been a convent for nuns, only the greater part of it had been burnt, and only a quaint gabled house, and a kind of tower covered with ivy, which I suppose had once been the belfry, remained. We had an excellent supper and went to bed early. We had been given two bedrooms, which were airy and clean, and altogether we were satisfied. My bedroom opened into Braun's, which was beyond it, and had no other door of its own. It was a hot night in July, and Braun asked me to leave the door open. I did—we opened both the windows. Braun went to bed and fell asleep almost directly, for very soon I heard his snores.

"I had imagined that I was longing for sleep, but no sooner had I got into bed than all my sleepiness left me.

This was odd, because we had walked a good many miles, and it had been a blazing hot day, and up till then I had slept like a log the moment I got into bed. I lit a candle and began reading a small volume of Heine I carried with me. I heard the clock strike ten, and then eleven, and still I felt that sleep was out of the question. I said to myself: 'I will read till twelve and then I will stop.' My watch was on a chair by my bedside, and when the clock struck eleven I noticed that it was five minutes slow, and set it right. I could see the church tower from my window, and every time the clock struck—and it struck the quarters—the noise boomed through the room.

"When the clock struck a quarter to twelve I yawned for the first time, and I felt thankful that sleep seemed at last to be coming to me. I left off reading, and taking my watch in my hand I waited for midnight to strike. This quarter of an hour seemed an eternity. At last the hands of my watch showed that it was one minute to twelve. I put out my candle and began counting sixty, waiting for the clock to strike. I had counted a hundred and sixty, and still the clock had not struck. I counted up to four hundred; then I thought I must have made a mistake. I lit my candle again, and looked at my watch: it was two minutes past twelve. And still the clock had not struck!

"A curious uncomfortable feeling came over me, and I sat up in bed with my watch in my hand and longed to call Braun, who was peacefully snoring, but I did not like to. I sat like this till a quarter past twelve; the clock struck the quarter as usual. I made up my mind that the clock must have struck twelve, and that I must have slept for a minute—at the same time I knew I had not slept and I put out my candle. I must have fallen asleep almost directly.

"The next thing I remember was waking with a start. It seemed to me that some one had shut the door between my room and Braun's. I felt for the matches. The match-box was empty. Up to that moment—I cannot tell why—something—an unaccountable dread—had prevented me looking at the door. I made an effort and looked. It was shut, and through the cracks and through the keyhole I saw the glimmer of a light. Braun had lit his candle. I called him, not very loudly: there was no answer. I called again more loudly: there was still no answer.

"Then I got out of bed and walked to the door. As I went, it was gently and slightly opened, just enough to show me a thin streak of light. At that moment I felt that some one was looking at me. Then it was instantly shut once more, as softly as it had been opened. There was not a sound to be heard. I walked on tiptoe towards the door, but it seemed to me that I had taken a hundred years to cross the room. And when at last I reached the door I felt I could not open it. I was simply paralysed with fear. And still I saw the glimmer through the key-hole and the cracks.

"Suddenly, as I was standing transfixed with fright in front of the door, I heard sounds coming from Braun's room, a shuffle of footsteps, and voices talking low but distinctly in a language I could not understand. It was not Italian, Spanish, nor French. The voices grew all at once louder; I heard the noise of a struggle and a cry which ended in a stifled groan, very painful and horrible to hear. Then, whether I regained my self-control, or whether it was excess of fright which prompted me, I don't know, but I flew to the door and tried to open it. Some one or something was pressing with all its might against it. Then I screamed at the top of my voice, and as I screamed I heard the cock crow.

"The door gave, and I almost fell into Braun's room. It was quite dark. But Braun was waked by my screams and quietly lit a match. He asked me gently what on earth was the matter. The room was empty and everything was in its place. Outside the first greyness of dawn was in the sky.

"I said I had had a nightmare, and asked him if he had not had one as well; but Braun said he had never slept better in his life.

"The next day we went on with our walking tour, and when we got back to Heidelberg Braun sailed for America. I never saw him again, although we corresponded frequently, and only last week I had a letter from him, dated Nijni Novgorod, saying he would be at Moscow before the end of the month.

"And now I suppose you are all wondering what this can have to do with anything that's in the newspaper. Well, listen," and he read out the following paragraph from the *Rouskoe Slovo*: —

"Samara, II, ix. In the centre of the town, in the Hotel ——, a band of armed swindlers attacked a German engineer named Braun and demanded money. On his refusal one of the robbers stabbed Braun with a knife. The robbers, taking the money which was on him, amounting to five hundred roubles, got away. Braun called for assistance, but died of his wounds in the night. It appears that he had met the swindlers at a restaurant."

"Since I have been in Russia," Jameson added, "I have often thought that I knew what language it was that was talked behind the door that night in the inn at Salzheim, but now I know it was Russian."

# The Ikon

## Maurice Baring

Ferrol was an intellectual, and he prided himself on the fact. At Cambridge he had narrowly missed being a Senior Wrangler, and his principal study there had been Lunar Theory. But when he went down from Cambridge for good, being a man of some means, he travelled. For a year he was an honorary Attaché at one of the big Embassies. He finally settled in London with a vague idea of some day writing a magnum opus about the stupidity of mankind; for he had come to the conclusion by the age of twenty-five that all men were stupid, irreclaimably, irredeemably stupid; that everything was wrong; that all literature was really bad, all art much overrated, and all music tedious in the long run.

The years slipped by and he never began his magnum opus; he joined a literary club instead and discussed the current topic of the day. Sometimes he wrote a short article; never in the daily Press, which he despised, nor in the reviews (for he never wrote anything as long as a magazine article), but in a literary weekly he would express in weary and polished phrases the unemphatic boredom or the mitigated approval with which the works of his fellow-men inspired him. He was the kind of man who had nothing in him you could positively dislike, but to whom you could not talk for five minutes without having a vague sensation of blight. Things seemed to shrivel up in his presence as though they had been touched by an insidious east wind, a subtle frost, a secret chill. He never praised anything, though he sometimes condescended to approve. The faint puffs of blame in which he more generally indulged were never sharp or heavy, but were like the smoke rings of a cigarette which a man indolently smoking blows from time to time up to the ceiling.

He lived in rooms in the Temple. They were comfortably, not luxuriously furnished; a great many French books— French was the only modern language worth reading he used to say—a few modern German etchings, a low Turkish divan, and some Egyptian antiquities, made up the furniture of his two sitting-rooms. Above all things he despised Greek art; it was, he said decadent. The Egyptians and the Germans were, in his opinion, the only people who knew anything about the plastic arts, whereas the only music he could endure was that of the modern French School. Over his chimney-piece there was a large German landscape in oils, called "*Im Walde*"; it represented a wood at twilight in the autumn, and if you looked at it carefully and for a long time you saw that the objects depicted were meant to be trees from which the leaves were falling; but if you looked at the picture carelessly and from a distance, it looked like a man-of-war on a rough sea, for which it was frequently taken, much to Ferrol's annoyance.

One day an artist friend of his presented him with a small Chinese god made of crystal; he put this on his chimney-piece. It was on the evening of the day on which he received this gift that he dined, together with a friend named Sledge who had travelled much in Eastern countries, at his club. After dinner they went to Ferrol's rooms to smoke and to talk. He wanted to show Sledge his antiquities, which consisted of three large Egyptian statuettes, a small green Egyptian god, and the Chinese idol which he had lately been given. Sledge, who was a middle-aged, bearded man, frank and unconventional, examined the antiquities with care, pronounced them to be genuine, and singled out for special praise the crystal god.

"Your things are very good," he said, "very good. But don't you really mind having all these things about you?"

"Why should I mind?" asked Ferrol.

"Well, you have travelled a good deal, haven't you?"

"Yes," said Ferrol, "I have travelled; I have been as far east as Nijni-Novgorod to see the Fair, and as far west as Lisbon."

"I suppose," said Sledge, "you were a long time in Greece and Italy?"

"No," said Ferrol, "I have never been to Greece. Greek art distresses me. All classical art is a mistake and a superstition."

"Talking of superstition," said Sledge, "you have never been to the Far East, have you?"

"No," Ferrol answered, "Egypt is Eastern enough for me, and cannot be bettered."

"Well," said Sledge, "I have been in the Far East. I have lived there many years. I am not a superstitious man; but there is one thing I would not do in any circumstances whatsoever, and that is to keep in my sitting-room the things you have got there."

"But why?" asked Ferrol.

"Well," said Sledge, "nearly all of them have come from the tombs of the dead, and some of them are gods. Such things may have attached to them heaven knows what spooks and spirits."

Ferrol shut his eyes and smiled, a faint, seraphic smile. "My dear boy," he said, "you forget. This is the Twentieth Century."

"And you," answered Sledge, "forget that the things you have here were made before the Twentieth Century. B.C."

"You don't seriously mean," said Ferrol, "that you attach any importance to these—" he hesitated.

"Children's stories?" suggested Sledge.

Ferrol nodded.

"I have lived long enough in the East," said Sledge, "to know that the sooner you learn to believe children's stories the better."

"I am afraid, then," said Ferrol, with civil tolerance, "that our points of view are too different for us to discuss the matter." And they talked of other things until late into the night.

Just as Sledge was leaving Ferrol's rooms and had said "Good-night," he paused by the chimney-piece, and, pointing to the tiny Ikon which was lying on it, asked: "What is that?"

"Oh, that's nothing," said Ferrol, "only a small Ikon I bought for two-pence at the Fair of Nijni-Novgorod."

Sledge said "Good-night" again, but when he was on the stairs he called back: "In any case remember one thing, that East is East and West is West. Don't mix your deities."

Ferrol had not the slightest idea what he was alluding to, nor did he care. He dismissed the matter from his mind.

The next day he spent in the country, returning to London late in the evening. As he entered his rooms the first thing which met his eye was that his great picture, "*Im Walde*", which he considered to be one of the few products of modern art that a man who respected himself could look at without positive pain in the eyes, had fallen from its place over the chimney-piece to the floor in front of the fender, and the glass was shattered into a thousand fragments. He was much vexed. He sought the cause of the accident. The nail was a strong one, and it was still in its place. The picture had been hung by a wire; the wire seemed strong also and was not broken. He concluded that the picture must have been badly balanced and that a sudden shock such as a door banging had thrown it over. He had no servant in his rooms, and when he had gone out that morning he had locked the door, so no one could have entered his rooms during his absence.

Next morning he sent for a framemaker and told him to mend the frame as soon as possible, to make the wire strong, and to see that the picture was firmly fixed on the wall. In two or three days' time the picture returned and was once more hung on the wall over the chimney-piece immediately above the little crystal Chinese god. Ferrol supervised the hanging of the picture in person. He saw that the nail was strong, and firmly fixed in the wall; he took care that the wire left nothing to be desired and was properly attached to the rings of the picture.

The picture was hung early one morning. That day he went to play golf. He returned at five o'clock, and again the first thing which met his eye was the picture. It had again fallen down, and this time it had brought with it in its fall the small Chinese god, which was broken in two. The glass had again been shattered to bits, and the picture itself was somewhat damaged. Everything else on the chimney-piece, that is to say, a few matchboxes and two candle-sticks, had also been thrown to the ground—everything with the exception of the little Ikon he had bought at Nijni-Novgorod, a small object about two inches square on which two Saints were pictured. This still rested in its place against the wall.

Ferrol investigated the disaster. The nail was in its place in the wall; the wire at the back of the picture was not broken or damaged in any way. The accident seemed to him quite inexplicable. He was greatly annoyed. The Chinese god was a valuable thing. He stood in front of the chimney-piece contemplating the damage with a sense of great irritation.

"To think that everything should have been broken except this beastly little Ikon!" he said to himself. "I wonder whether that was what Sledge meant when he said I should not mix my deities."

Next morning he sent again for the framemaker, and abused him roundly. The framemaker said he could not understand how the accident had happened. The nail was an excellent nail, the picture, Mr. Ferrol must admit, had been hung with great care before his very eyes and under his own direct and personal supervision. What more could be done?

"It's something to do with the balance," said Ferrol. "I told you that before. The picture is half spoiled now."

The framemaker said the damage would not show once the glass was repaired, and took the picture away again to mend it. A few days later it was brought back. Two men came to fix it this time; steps were brought and the hanging lasted about twenty minutes. Nails were put under the picture; it was hung by a double wire. All accidents in the future seemed guarded against.

The following morning Ferrol telephoned to Sledge and asked him to dine with him. Sledge was engaged to dine out that evening, but said that he would look in at the Temple late after dinner.

Ferrol dined alone at the Club; he reached his rooms about half-past nine; he made up a blazing fire and drew an armchair near it. He lit a cigarette, made some Turkish coffee, and took down a French novel. Every now and then he looked up at his picture. No damage was visible; it looked, he thought, as well as ever. In the place of the Chinese idol he had put his little green Egyptian god on the chimney-piece. The candlesticks and the Ikon were still in their places.

"After all," thought Ferrol, "I did wrong to have any Chinese art in the place at all. Egyptian things are the only things worth having. It is a lesson to me not to dabble with things out of my period."

After he had read for about a quarter of an hour he fell into a doze.

Sledge arrived at the rooms about half-past ten, and an ugly sight met his eyes. There had been an accident. The picture over the chimney-piece had fallen down right on Ferrol. His face was badly cut. They put Ferrol to bed, and his wounds were seen to and everything that was necessary was done. A nurse was sent for to look after him, and Sledge decided to stay in the house all night. After all the arrangements had been made, the doctor, before he went away, said to Sledge: "He will recover all right, he is not in the slightest danger; but I don't know who is to break the news to him."

"What is that?" asked Sledge.

"He will be quite blind," said the doctor.

Then the doctor went away, and Sledge sat down in front of the fire. The broken glass had been swept up. The picture had been placed on the Oriental divan, and as Sledge looked at the chimney-piece he noticed that the little Ikon was still in its place. Something caught his eye just under the low fender in front of the fireplace. He bent forward and picked up the object.

It was Ferrol's green Egyptian god, which had been broken into two pieces.

# Will Stone
## (1872-1901)

*"You ask about Denmark. It was glorious—M. R. James, storks, cathedrals, old towns, handsome people, lakes (lots), plenty to eat, Danish ballads to read. But of course I did not enjoy it properly: I have only just begun to understand the art of enjoying it at all . . . "*

– Will Stone to his sister Lucy (13 October 1900)

In 1904, three books were published which refer to holidays in Denmark taken by M. R. James and his friends, Will Stone and James MacBryde. The most famous of these is *Ghost Stories of an Antiquary*, which includes "Number 13", MRJ's bewildering tale of a dimension-warping hotel room in Viborg. More obscure, but no less entertaining, is *The Story of a Troll Hunt*, an exuberant fantasy written and illustrated by MacBryde, which narrates the adventures of three Cambridge men as they tour Jutland in search of cryptozoologica for the Fitzwilliam Museum. This was printed privately under MRJ's direction as a tribute to its creator after McBryde's sudden death in June 1904. The third book, *The Letters and Memorials of William Johnson Stone*, is obscurer, and perhaps, sadder still. For it contains the scant literary remains of MRJ's other travelling companion who, a few weeks after writing the letter quoted above—just as his new found enjoyment of life was finally kicking in—died of pneumonia, at the age of twenty-eight.

MRJ was ten years older than Stone, but they were close friends and Stone's death quite knocked him off balance. "It is the first time I have lost a companion of that age and those associations," MRJ confided in a letter to his father, Herbert, "and I do not at all know what to make of it." Henry Luxmoore, who'd tutored both men at Eton, recognised the important role that MRJ had played in Stone's life when he wrote, again to Herbert James: "It is pleasant to think that King's and, as I believe, Monty's friendship, were what gave the boy his 'lift' and enabled him to find himself." And this image of Stone as a young man in need of a "lift", is reinforced by the obituary Luxmoore wrote for the *Eton Chronicle*: "When in 1892 he left [school] . . . he was still a small shy boy, though with a twinkle in the eye and a somewhat ready pen that belied his retiring silence."

It was, I suspect, this latent wit, as well as their shared closeness to Luxmoore, that cemented Stone's friendship with MRJ when he arrived at King's in October 1892. The two men were also distantly related: MRJ's paternal great uncle had married Stone's maternal great aunt, and Stone had a cousin who was, remarkably, also called Montague James who had been at Eton and was known to his intimates as "Monty".

In a letter to his brother Ned, written at the start of his first term, Stone proudly listed the names and credentials of the "eminent persons" he had lunched with since coming up to Cambridge: "A. G. Bather, BA; M. S. Dimsdale, MA . . . M. R. James, MA; and A. A. Tilley, MA." All of these men (and Ned himself) were, or had been, members of the Chit-Chat, and Stone himself was elected on 4 November 1893. A letter to his mother written a year later evokes the light-hearted, gently learned mood of the club in his day: "Last night at the Chit-Chat a very amusing paper on the elephant. Ancient ideas of the elephant were very extraordinary; as, that the tusks were horns, that they lived 400 years, that they understood the Indian language and rarely Greek; one of them even wrote a sentence of Greek . . . " The paper was the work of Robert Carr Bosanquet.

But although he clearly enjoyed the meetings, Stone never read a paper himself. His chief literary interest, which he developed at King's—the use of classical metres in English verse—was intense and obscure enough, one would have thought, to have provided material for at least one Saturday night discussion. But again, the impression is of diffidence and introversion, of a boy who held back from playing a full part in the gaieties of undergraduate life.

There's a strong sense of reticence in "A Fable", the only prose fiction to appear in Stone's memorial volume, which is reprinted here for the first time. We don't know when or why this curious allegorical sketch was written, or whether it was published during the author's lifetime. The vague title sheds little light upon its background or interpretation, and one wonders whether it wasn't attached by the compilers of *Letters and Memorials* after Stone's death. It's not strictly a *fable* in the accepted sense of the word, though it does seem to take a strong, if oblique, moral stance, and to conceal a secondary meaning. One might better borrow the title of a strange tale by Walter de la Mare, published in 1903, with which Stone's piece shares a flavour, and call it "A Riddle".

The troubled, hesitant ten-year-old in the story fits the image of its author as a young man not entirely at ease with himself, but it's not an obviously autobiographical piece. When Stone himself was ten, his father was an Eton Classics master and the family home was nothing like that described in the story. He had no dead brother. Nor do the descriptions of the boy's parents in the story chime with what we know of Stone's own mother and father. The fear, confusion and shame felt by the narrator, however, and the presence of secrets connected with the family home, do seem deeply personal.

One can't help wondering what thoughts and experiences lie behind the vivid symbolism and dream-like imagery: the dark forest; the single window that looks into the locked room which somehow consumes those who dare to enter; the great, light-blocking tree that stains and withers the hands, that draws in its branches "as a snail draws in its head", and that "penetrates" men with its black slime.

I hear echoes of MRJ in "A Fable". Stone had joined the Chit-Chat only a week after "Lost Hearts" first aired, and he'd likely have read his friend's story when it was published in the *Pall Mall Magazine* in 1895. His inquisitive, vulnerable young protagonist brings to mind MRJ's Stephen Elliott; the tree-girt garden and fields "made strange by moonlight" recall the park at Aswarby Hall. And, perhaps most strikingly, the apparition of "the face of his brother that was dead . . . acting as one that strove to speak but could not" recalls the spectre of Giovanni Paoli, silently raising his thin arms into the air with "an appearance . . . of unappeasable hunger and longing".

But of all MRJ's stories, "A Fable" has most in common, perhaps, with MRJ's final piece of supernatural writing, "A Vignette". The styles of the two pieces are markedly different, but they share more than a non-committal title. Both are set largely within the enclosed garden of a family home, and deal with the disturbance of a happy, cloistered childhood by a lonely discovery. The protagonists of both feel a reluctance to talk about their experience, and yet nervously seek to bring things to a crisis, to confront the object of fear. And passages within both have a similar dream-like atmosphere.

Stone had been dead for over thirty-five years when "A Vignette" appeared, posthumously, in *The London Mercury* in December 1936. But if, as seems likely, the piece was inspired by a genuine early experience in the garden of MRJ's childhood home in Great Livermere, Suffolk, then Stone might have heard about it when his friend held a modest

celebration there, that was described in a letter from Stone
to his mother in early August 1896:

> "On Saturday, it being his 34th birthday, Monty took
> me and one other to his home on bicycles. The garden at
> Livermere was too charming. We got there at 2.15, ate
> lunch largely, went into the garden, ate gooseberries and
> played skittles; tea at 4, went to Ampton, pressed to have
> more tea, rode to Bury and took 5.38 to Newmarket
> and rode home . . . "

Did MRJ explain to Stone that summer afternoon that the
charm of his parents' garden had been compromised by an
unsettling childhood vision? Between mouthfuls of gooseber-
ries and rounds of skittles, did he point out the plantation and
its gate, and describe their chilling associations? Did the story
cling to Stone's imagination in the same way that it did to
MRJ's? Did it stir familiar feelings and strange recollections?

This is speculation. There is more substantial evidence
that, in one case at least, it was Stone who influenced MRJ.
S. G. Lubbock, who knew both men well, says that the idea
for "Number 13" was first suggested by Stone. It's plausible;
he and MRJ had visited Viborg together in 1900. And a
letter he wrote from the Grand Hotel in Göteborg in August
that year, has correspondences with the opening of MRJ's
story. It also gives the origin of the unusual name of a minor
character, and illustrates well the kind of ghostly folklore that
both men delighted in:

> "At Viborg is a cathedral but only the crypt is as it
> was: all the rest is a restoration. There is also a Black
> Friars Chapel, every pew decorated with pictures
> representing a literal interpretation of some text: e.g.
> a large hand throwing chaff out of the sky to represent

the ungodly. At Viborg too there are two vast lakes: also at dinner there was Röd Gröd (neither *d* must be pronounced), a national pudding of extraordinary deliciousness. It means 'red porridge' and is made of raspberry juice . . . From Viborg we went to Aalborg, from which we paid a visit to an old country house called Vorgoard, now mostly a ruin, but some of it well kept up. The owner was away. He rejoices in the name Scavenius. We had an introduction from the Danish Ambassador and so were rather disappointed. It is of enormous size and very finely decorated in front. Built by Fru Ingeborg Skael in 1588. This exciting woman after she paid for one wing found the expense too great and so when the ships bringing building materials came, had the cables cut just before the storm: the ships were wrecked and she claimed the cargoes as the lady of the manor. The architect's bill was also too heavy. He was requested to appear with the keys and his bill receipted. She would go through the rooms with him first and threw the heavy leys round his neck. After going the round they stood on the drawbridge. Fru Ingeborg called attention to the view and pushed the poor man into the moat, where the heavy keys dragged him to the bottom. She then called assistance. Naturally she walked after death and had to be exorcised into a neighbouring marsh. Every year she advances one cock's step towards the house; the marks are said to be visible because of course the grass won't grow: when she reaches the house it will fall down."

# A Fable

## Will Stone

In the front the house was like other houses: the sun shone upon it and flowers grew plentifully in the gardens. And the boy lived there careless and happy until he was ten years old, playing in the garden or at the windows that looked out upon the street. For of all the windows in the house one only looked out upon the court-yard behind, nor had he ever seen through it, for the room had been forbidden him from his earliest years.

But when he was ten years old he lost his way once in the woods, and darkness came on, so that when he was free of the trees he wandered aimlessly and crying bitterly through fields made strange to him by the moonlight, and it was thus that he first came upon his home from the back, but he knew it not. It was like a great blank wall with one spot of green light in the midst of it. The front was a low wall with a gate, through which he went. Then he saw that the light came from a window, but faintly because of a great black tree that stood before it. At the first fear overcame him, but soon he was approaching it. There was no door in the wall, and it was a leafless tree, so that the branches seemed rotten, yet when he felt them they were firm but covered with black slime, so that his heart sank at it. Then he turned from that court-yard with a strange loathing and went round to the other side of the house, and it was his home.

For many days he told no one of these things, but the finger with which he had touched the tree became black and the nail wrinkled, so that he kept it in the palm of his hand; and in the evenings he would steal round to the back and look with awe upon the window and the tree, until his whole life became shadowed with the thought of it. Each night he went nearer to the window, becoming powerfully drawn to climb the tree, but when his feet stood in the shadow, the face of his brother that was dead appeared above him in the green light acting as one that strove to speak but could not. Then he fled from the place and pondered in his heart whether he should tell his mother. Now his mother was a comfortable woman, to whom sorrow was a satisfaction and sin a thing to talk of in whispers; and his father was a man who thought little because he was afraid where it might lead him. So the boy went to his old nurse, but with trembling because he feared that these were things that men hid in their hearts. And when he had told her, speaking boldly because her eyes were sightless, she rejoiced and said, "You have done well to speak, for in silence the blackness would grow within you and fill you, and to me, for I am old and wise. Sooner or later, all who are born in the house must find the back of it, and because they know its shamefulness they say nothing. Some see it from afar and feel no wish to go near it. Others go near but are saved at the last. But there are some whose soul becomes blackened by the touch, so that they think of nothing besides. And these will climb the tree and gaze nightly into the room, so that their minds become distorted, making them desire the horrible things that are in it. In the daytime they go about like other folk, but within they are penetrated with the black slime of the tree. And at last they will set foot in the room, and from that hour they are heard of no more. But to you my advice is, go home and from henceforth see only the front side of things, lest the seed of blackness which is in every man become strong within you." So said the old nurse but the boy said nothing, and going home thought upon these things, and everything became grey around him. And at last he spoke to his mother and said, "Why did you never tell me the nature of the tree and of the room that I might fall from the danger?" And his mother said it was not customary for children to be told such things and bade him hold his peace.

So for many years he lived peacefully, but at times his finger pained him and at last he learnt that the boy that was his friend was a climber of the tree. Then anger came upon him and he went every night with an axe and would have cut it down. But as he cut the chips flew and covered him over the face and body, and the tree stood firm. Yet he attained this much, that while he cut at it the tree drew in its upper branches as a snail draws in its head, so they that climbed might not see more than the ceiling of the room and could not set foot in it. So for a year he worked but could do no more than this and his hair grew long and his body bent, and all over he was black with the touch of the tree so that people marked him or ran from him, and his father turned him out of doors. And at last he knew that his labour was vain and it came upon him that, if he entered the room and destroyed the monster within it, men might be saved though his life were the forfeit. So with his axe in his hand he climbed the tree and, when he reached the top, the tree shrank back because, though black without, his soul was pure within. Then he leapt at the window and would have reached it, but his brother thrust him back and he fell to the earth stunned.

When he awoke from his trance the moon shone on the house, the tree had put forth its branches and there was his friend stepping in at the window.

# Desmond MacCarthy
## *(1877-1952)*

*"One cannot accuse [MacCarthy] of not being interesting, & in fact the only fault I have to find with him is that we cannot talk for more than five minutes without his plunging out of his depth & dragging me with him; but he is a really strong swimmer even though the water is very deep . . . "*

– Gerald Warre Cornish
in a letter to his father (1895)

Talking was Desmond MacCarthy's forté. Gerald Warre Cornish made the above observation about his friend and fellow Chit-Chat member when they were undergraduates together at Trinity College in 1895. But throughout his life—from his prep-school days, to his career as a broadcaster in the early years of the BBC—MacCarthy's conversational verve won him a multitude of friends and admirers.

He was elected to the Chit-Chat on 9 March 1895, and remained a member until the club's demise two years later, despite also belonging to the rival club, the Apostles. MacCarthy's membership of the two societies, which both met on Saturday nights, might explain why he only ever gave one paper to the Chit-Chat: "Mary Queen of Scots" in 1896. But, divided as his club loyalties might have been, he was closely associated with several other Chit-Chat members who feature in this book. He had been a favourite pupil at Stone House, the private prep school in Kent run by the father of Will Stone. At Eton he had established a lasting friendship with Maurice Baring, "a deep, formal, fashionable relationship that seemed to go on for ever", according to his protégé Cyril Connolly. And in 1906 he married Gerald Warre Cornish's sister, Mollie.

Although MacCarthy was never as close to M. R. James as contemporaries like Will Stone and James MacBryde, he clearly liked and respected him. He was present at a Chit-Chat meeting on 18 May 1895, to hear MRJ talk about "A Medieval Humourist"—probably Walter Map, the author of *De Nugis Curialium* (*Courtiers' Trifles*), a twelfth-century compendium of anecdotes, jokes, and tall tales, which MRJ translated in 1923. And on 27 February 1938—by which time he was one of England's most respected literary critics—MacCarthy used his column in the *Sunday Times* to praise MRJ's memoir *Eton and King's* (1926): "one of those books," he wrote, "which, at expansive moments, when the pleasure of other persons is particularly vivid to us, we thrust into the hands of departing friends: they seldom come back".

As well as bemoaning the fact that *Eton and King's* was remaindered, MacCarthy's article gives a brief but useful analysis of MRJ's supernatural tales: "They follow two sound principles necessary to telling an entertaining ghost story: the supernatural element must represent the powers of darkness (a good ghost is insipid), and the victim of the awful experience should be a thoroughly humdrum, unadventurous person . . . success depends on mixing precise detail with vague suggestions in the right proportions." These were principles that MacCarthy himself observed to good effect in the story reprinted in this volume.

A tale of guilt and supernatural retribution, "Pargiton and Harby" belongs to a tradition that MRJ himself enjoyed and contributed to. MacCarthy was not at Cambridge when MRJ talked to the Chit-Chat about Joseph Sheridan Le Fanu in 1893, but one can sense that he was familiar with the Irish writer's work. The increasingly frantic paranoia of Pargiton, his night terrors, and the final, almost calm acceptance of his fate, recall the experiences of Captain Barton in Le Fanu's "The Familiar" (1872). There are parallels, too, with MRJ's "The Stalls of Barchester Cathedral" (1910) and "A Warning to the Curious" (1925). MacCarthy's story was published only a year after "A Warning to the Curious", and its most striking passage—in which an impossible shadow spooks Harby during a nocturnal walk—brings to mind the "more than a shadow", and the shade-stalked night sortie, in MRJ's tale.

Like MRJ, MacCarthy uses Latin to brilliantly creepy effect in the story. An innocuous enough phrase in its original context, "*nunquam minus solus, quam cum solus*" ("never less alone than when alone") here conjures the same dread and menace as MRJ's Latin tags in "Oh, Whistle, and I'll Come to You, My Lad" (1904) and "A School Story" (1906). And the fact that the words are scrawled in red ink by an unknown hand recalls the latter tale even more strongly. In the 4 January 1912 edition of *The Eye-Witness*, MacCarthy had written an admiring review of MRJ's *More Ghost Stories of an Antiquary* (1911) which includes "A School Story"; and in 1967 the tale would appear alongside "Pargiton and Harby" in Robert Aickman's *Fourth Fontana Book of Great Ghost Stories*.

MacCarthy's story was first published, along with works by Algernon Blackwood, Arthur Machen, and Oliver Onions, in *The Ghost Book* (1926), edited by Lady Cynthia Asquith—another great conversationalist, with whom MacCarthy enjoyed a close friendship. This story appears to be his only foray into supernatural literature—although, intriguingly, on Christmas Eve 1929, 7-7.45 P.M., the BBC broadcast *The Haunted Hour*, listed in the *Radio Times* as "Ghost Stories by Mr. E. F. Benson, Mr. W. W. Jacobs, and Mr. Desmond MacCarthy." No titles are given, but "Pargiton and Harby" is surely too long for the time-slot if it was to be divided equally between the three writers.

MacCarthy was a prolific journalist and an admired literary critic, he operated on the fringes of the Bloomsbury Group, and spoke throughout his life of composing a great literary work; but by the time he died in 1952 (not quite the last Chit-Chat member to pass away, but almost), he had produced little original fiction of any length. His wit and imagination were never in doubt, but his reputation was as a talker rather than as a doer; and as his friend Virginia Woolf noted in her diary: "I can see myself going through his desk one of these days, shaking out unfinished pages from between sheets of blotting paper . . . & making up a small book of table talk, which shall appear as a proof to the younger generation that Desmond was the most gifted of all of us. But why did he never do anything? they will ask."

For an idea of how MacCarthy might have fitted in at the Chit-Chat, we should perhaps picture him in the light of the following observation by Cyril Connolly:

"His voice . . . was both manly and seductive and contained the essence of his charm; warm, friendly, independent and judicious, full of subtleties; the tenor of humanism. It spoke to everyone as if they were all his life-long fellow-guests at some delicious dinner party and seemed to introduce himself to them by a touch of modest urbanity, as if to say, 'I do believe we are going to enjoy ourselves.' "

# Pargiton and Harby

## Desmond MacCarthy

Robert Harby and Thomas Pargiton had known each
other well in youth; indeed, they had once been
devoted to each other; then, for more than twenty
years, their friendship had lapsed. On going down from
Cambridge together they had shared lodgings in London.
Both had had to make their way in the world, but while
Harby dreaded the prospect and would have preferred a
safe civil service or academic career, Pargiton had looked
forward avidly to competitive adventure. At Cambridge
Harby had envied his friend his ambitious temperament,
but he soon began to deplore it. The tough-mindeness he
used to admire at the university showed up in London as
unscrupulousness; and some of the transactions in the city
in which Pargiton had become involved struck Harby as
certainly mean if not positively illegal. He had not been
sorry when, one morning, Pargiton abruptly informed him
that he could no longer afford to live at such "a bad address",
and moved to an ostentatious flat in a fashionable part of
London. After that Harby had seen less and less of Pargiton.
At last he only heard of him now and then; once he saw his
name in the papers in connection with a commercial case
which hinted at blackmail.

Meanwhile, Robert Harby had gone quickly along the path
which opportunity had first opened to him. He had been

employed by a firm of map-publishers which, thanks to the demand for new maps after the war, had prospered, and in course of time he had been taken into partnership. The firm had recently been putting on the market a series of guide books, and this enterprise, which had proved lucrative, was in his particular charge, it necessitated frequent journeys abroad, and it was on one of these expeditions, which combined business and pleasure in proportions agreeable to his temperament, that, after twenty years, he had met Pargiton again.

Harby had just arrived at Dieppe one wet February afternoon, when, looking out of his bedroom window, which faced the cobbled market-place, he noticed a tall man in a brown coat buying sweets at one of the stalls below. His figure struck him as familiar, but when the man moved away to distribute what he had just bought among a group of children, Harby thought he must have been mistaken. The man in the brown coat walked with a heavy limp. He appeared to be making for Harby's hotel. It was—no, was it?—Pargiton! The largess of sweets Harby had just witnessed was not at all like Pargiton, nor was it like him to be staying at a commercial hotel rather than at one of the glittering palaces on the sea-front, and Pargiton was not lame. Still, in spite of that, in spite, too, of that painful hitching gait, Harby felt sure that this was none other than his old friend; but it was curiosity rather than eagerness which the next moment made him descend the corkscrew stairs to meet him. Although he could not see the face of the man who had just entered, for the hall of the hotel was a mere passage and only lit by the open door, he went straight up to him and addressed him by name. It was Pargiton; and Pargiton was glad to see him—pathetically glad, so Harby reflected late that night while he undressed.

After meeting they had repaired at once to one of the cafés under the arches which face Dieppe harbour. There they sat and talked over apéritifs, dinner, and cognacs, watching, through the plate glass, craft of all sorts gently rocking on the dark water, and now and then a train draw up, jangling and panting, on the quay. Harby was starting early next morning for Caen; meanwhile, for the sake of his company, Pargiton contentedly allowed the Newhaven boat to depart without him into the night.

Reviewing their conversation in the train the next day, Harby was surprised to discover how little, after all, Pargiton had told him about the last twenty years. By tacit consent they had gone back to their pre-London memories, and Pargiton had touched him a little by saying, "I have always associated you with my better self," adding, "Now I have found you again, I don't mean to let you go." His career had apparently been chequered, till he had inherited, about two years ago, his elder brother's fortune and tea-broking business. Harby had also gathered that Pargiton's brother had been engaged to a widow at the time of his death, and that the widow's son was now being educated at Oxford at Pargiton's expense, and that it was his intention soon to hand over the business to him.

He had not spoken of his brother directly, but Harby gathered that it was not compulsion, but loyalty, which was actuating him in these matters. This rather astonished Harby, for it came back to him that the brothers had been very indifferent in old days; "My ass of a brother", was a phrase which he remembered had often been on Pargiton's lips. Harby would have supposed that he was probably in love with the widow, had not a question elicited the fact that he had never seen her. As for his lameness (one leg was decidedly shorter than the other), about that, too, Pargiton had been decidedly laconic; he had suffered incessant and awful pain for nine months; now his leg only troubled him sometimes. He was living in a little house at Greenwich to save money, as he would soon have to give up the business to the boy.

Harby must come and see him often, very often. He was lonely and hated new friends, but old friends were different. It was at this point in their talk that Pargiton had touched him by saying, with an almost frightened earnestness, "I have always associated you with my better self." He was certainly changed, very much changed.

Harby's tour in France had lasted some months, during which he had several letters from Pargiton. Near the end of the time a telegram announced that Pargiton would join him at once, but it was followed next day by another, "All well. No need to bother you now. Look forward to your return." Harby had no idea that Pargiton had ever had any "need" of him. Perhaps he had missed a letter while on the move? Two days later he received one which, though it mystified him still more, at least cleared up that point:

Dear Robert,

I am afraid you must have thought from my last letter (so there had been another letter) either that I was making an absurd fuss about nothing or that I was going off my head. I wrote in great agitation. The fact is, I have experienced symptoms of the same kind before, but never as late in the year. January is my bad month, and I thought it was well over, when I suddenly discovered that someone had been marking my books, an annoyance which preceded last time that feeling of never being alone which I told you in my last letter I dreaded. I happened to take down Newman's *Apologia*. (He has changed! thought Harby.) You remember, perhaps, the passage in which he tells how on one of his solitary walks the Provost of Oriel quoted as he bowed and passed, "*Nunquam minus solus, quam cum solus.*" Well, *in my copy these words were underlined in a brownish, deep-red ink.* You will say I must have done this myself and forgotten. But I never mark books, and I have never had red ink in the house. "Never less alone than when alone!" You can imagine how these words alarmed me. I hurriedly pulled out another book. (I must tell you that on occasions I believe my hand is strangely guided.) There was nothing marked in it. I turned over every page. In the third and fourth I examined I also found nothing, but in my Wordsworth, opposite the line, "That inward eye which is the bliss of solitude," was written—in my own hand—the word, "Bliss!" with an ironical exclamation mark after it. You will say that the fact that the writing was exactly like my own proves that I must have done it myself—perhaps in my sleep or in some strange state of unconsciousness. Of course I gave that explanation full weight, but listen. It was Saturday afternoon; I felt that I could not stay in the house. I wired to my chief clerk, who is a good fellow, saying that I was unwell and asking him to come down to Westgate with me for two nights. While we were there, I was burgled. The loss was trifling, a suit-case, a suit of clothes, a shirt or two, sponge, pyjamas, in fact—except—that I had taken my brushes with me—the things one usually packs for a week-end. But that's not all. I must tell you first that I purposely tested my condition while at Westgate. I took a longish walk by myself and I felt all right. The sea-air did me good. I had intended to keep the door between Sparling's room and mine open at night but it was not necessary. I felt perfectly secure, and slept well. The next day I sent my second wire to you. I returned to London on Monday with Sparling, but I begged him to come back to Greenwich with me for the night, as I was not yet absolutely certain that I should be easy in my own home. The maids met us with the story of the senseless theft. They had found the drawers in my bedroom pulled out on Sunday morning, and they had reported the matter to the police. The policeman on duty that night was a new man on the beat; he said he had seen a man come out of the house with a suitcase about 10 p.m., but had thought nothing of it. Now comes the extraordinary and disconcerting thing. The same constable came to see me to ask the necessary questions, and the moment he entered the room I saw him give a start of surprise. He recovered himself quickly and grinned in a rather insolent way. When I asked him point-blank what he meant by his behaviour, he put on a knowing air and said, "I expect *you* can clear this little matter up. It doesn't seem a case for the police." I again asked him to explain himself, and went to the sideboard to mix him a whisky-and-soda. It had the usual propitiatory effect, for he then said, rather apologetically, "Well, sir, the person I see coming out of that front door Saturday night was a gentleman as didn't walk quite easily." At this, my glass shook in my hand so that I had to put it down. I managed, however, to assert pretty emphatically that I was at Westgate with a friend that night. He noticed my agitation, and smiling with a cocksure benevolence terrible to me, he replied, "Gentlemen does sometimes find it handy to be in two places at once. Good evening, sir." I know I dropped into a chair like one stunned. How long I sat there I don't know. I cannot tell you now all the thoughts which rose in my mind in connection with what had happened. Had I better stay where I was, or fly? You will see from the address at the top of the letter that I decided to return to Westgate. I have not been followed. The bad moments I endure are those when I first come into the hotel from a walk. Among the luggage of new arrivals I am always terrified of seeing my lost suitcase. But I am afraid of becoming afraid again.

Robert after our long estrangement, I cannot ask you to leave your work and join me, but if old days still mean anything to you, as, thank God, they seemed to when we met, do not desert me. It is not in the name of affection I ask you to hasten your return and come to me—I have no right to anyone's affection, let alone yours—but take pity on me, help me. Come. Wire that you will come. With you I am my better self, my *old* self; I feel it. Then I am safe.

I must tell you that I took a Shakespeare to Westgate. This morning I picked it up, thinking it might distract my mind. On the page I opened I found these lines marked:

"It will be short: the interim is mine;
And a man's life is no more than to say, One."

I have not dared to look at any more.

Below the signature of the letter was scrawled this:

P.S.: "I have not told you all."

On first reading this letter, Harby concluded that Pargiton was going off his head, but on second thoughts he was inclined to suspend judgment. He would, in any case, be returning shortly to England, so he decided to wire that he would join him at Westgate. He left for England the next day.

On the journey his thoughts were naturally much concerned with Pargiton, and he re-read his letter several times in the train. It was clear that he imagined himself to be the victim of some kind of supernatural persecution. Of course, the most plausible explanation of the facts was that he was suffering from incipient persecution mania, which had been intensified by the odd coincidence of his house having been broken into by a man who was as lame as himself. The marking of the books was certainly an odd feature of the case, but it was probably self-justificatory evidence forged by the unhappy man himself to account for terrors peculiar to his state of mind.

When Harby stepped off the steamer at Dover, almost the first person he noticed in the crowd was Pargiton, who raised his hand in a kind of solemn, Roman gesture of greeting. He wanted to return straight to London.

All attempts on the journey to talk of things in general broke down, and the presence of other people in the carriage prevented confidences. They dined in London, and Pargiton's spirits seemed slightly to revive, but he was not communicative. They drooped again on reaching Greenwich.

His house was, as he had said, a small one; a semi-detached villa standing back from a road shaded by tall old trees.

A short paved path led from the little gate to its pillared but modest portico. Pargiton's sitting room on the ground floor struck Harby as a delightful room. It was lined with books, and a large square mirror over the mantelpiece reflected prettily the green trees outside. Pargiton threw himself into a chair with something like a sigh of relief.

"You're thinking I ought to be happy here. Well, I am—as long as you are with me. I wish, old fellow, we could live together as we used to in old days. Anyhow," he added, "don't leave me yet awhile."

"About your letter," Harby began . . . but Pargiton seemed reluctant to discuss that and proposed a game of chess. "Just like old times," he said, setting the men; "it is the best dope in the world," and for half an hour he appeared to find it so.

Then he suddenly jumped up before the game was finished and said he must have a breath of fresh air before going to bed.

As soon as the small iron wicket had clamped behind them, and they found themselves in the road, Pargiton, taking his friend's arm, said, "You noticed my postscript? I think now I can tell you everything. I have what I want—now, yet it has come to me in a way which has robbed me of all power to enjoy it. You remember I was very set on getting on? I was reckless, unscrupulous; I was also a failure. Do you remember my brother? No, of course you don't, but you must remember my talking about him. It was his death that saved me. I never cared about him, but I wish he hadn't died." He stopped speaking, and for some time they walked on in silence up the road towards the open heights of Blackheath. "My trouble—my trouble, which I wrote to you about it, I'm certain . . . and yet I am not . . . My brother was drowned. Did you see anything about it in the papers?—skating on the lake at his place in the country. I was with him at the time. It was terrible."

They had now emerged from the avenue into the open moonlight and the road lay white before them. Harby's eyes had been for some time fixed on the ground, for he had been filled with that uneasy feeling which possesses us when a companion is endeavouring to speak openly and yet is obviously unable to do so. He couldn't meet Pargiton's eye, who was continually turning his head towards him, as though he hoped to see that he was conveying more than he had actually succeeded in saying. "It was terrible," he began again. "The ice broke whenever he tried to hoist himself on to it." But Harby, though he heard the words, hardly took in their meaning; his eyes were fixed on what was in front of him. He stopped in amazement: their united shadows had unmistakeably three heads. "It was my fault, too," Pargiton went on, still trying to read his face, "I challenged him to a race. If I had not fallen myself and broken my thigh, I should have been done for, too." Part of the composite shadow slowly elongated itself, and a pair of shoulders appeared beneath the extra head. Harby felt a grip on his arm; Pargiton had jerked him round. "Don't you understand?" he said, in a voice of extraordinary tension; "it was partly my fault, *my fault*. My, God, man, what's the matter with you? Listen, you must listen; it seems to me now that it is possible that—I am tortured by the suspicion that I believe I *knew* the ice near the other side of the lake was unsound." Harby again turned his eyes from the agitated man beside him to the road. He was about to point to the shadow, when a cloud covered the moon. Perhaps it had been fancy. Yet, at the back of his mind he still thought he had seen what he had seen. Anyhow, the cat was out of the bag; Pargiton had made his confession, or as complete a one as he could bring himself to make. They presently turned back and descended the avenue together.

It was not abhorrence that Harby felt for his companion; or, if it was, it was so mixed with pity that it amounted only to a neutral feeling of indifference; but the sensation of Pargiton's arm in his had become unpleasant, and he could hardly listen to what he was saying: Pargiton was talking volubly about his past life. He did not mention his brother again, but he began to pour out an account of all he had done and regretted in the past. The past was the past—that was the refrain. A man could make a fresh start, couldn't he? He, Pargiton, was certainly now a different man. Hadn't Harby himself noticed that? A man might be too hard on himself, mightn't he? Might fancy he had been baser than he had been, especially if there really was a lot of good in him? By the time they reached the house, Pargiton had talked himself into a sort of wild gaiety. When they parted on saying good night, he wrung Harby's hand with an earnest squeeze, which made him more anxious than ever to leave the next morning. Pargiton was still standing in the hall. To feel those imploring eyes upon his back as he ascended the stairs was bad enough but to return their gaze was impossible. He passed the landing corner without looking back. How—in what words—should he tell Pargiton in the morning that he could have nothing more to do with him, that he must leave him to his fate? Was it horror at his crime, he asked himself (Harby was quite certain he was guilty), or fear of having to share some horrible experience with him that lay behind his resolve to go? In his mind's eye he saw again that third shadow detach itself from their combined shadows upon the white road. Was it, then, merely fear? In that case, ought he to yield? Did he care for Pargiton? No: that was over long ago. Yet he had undoubtedly begun a kind of friendship with him again—at any rate, he had roused in the wretched man some hope that he would not be in the future left utterly alone. What was the decent thing to do? Of course he could make work an excuse to-morrow, and the easiest way would be to say he must go up to London, then wire that he was detained. But Pargiton would guess; he would insist on coming with him. To be followed by a haunted murderer was unbearable. Yet he could not blame Pargiton for clutching on to him. What *ought* he to do?

He remained awake for hours, so it seemed, his thoughts revolving round and round the same problem, only sometimes interrupting them to strain his ears to catch some tiny noise or other in the dark. Once or twice, when his thoughts were busiest about his own predicament, he had been nearly certain he had heard, not the dreaded creak of Pargiton's footstep on the stairs, but a strange, low, ringing sound, and twice he had switched on the light; but when he concentrated upon listening he could hear absolutely nothing.

At last, without knowing it, he must have fallen asleep. For he found himself standing on the edge of a sheet of black ice. The moon was up, yet daylight had not quite left the sky, and a white mist lay knee-high round the shores of a long lake. Someone was waiting there in a creeping agony of excitement, but Harby could not tell whether it was he himself or another who was experiencing this horrible sense of expectation, for he seemed to be both the man he saw and the disembodied percipient. Again his listening attention caught faint, faint at first, that low, sweet, ringing sound. It was coming nearer now, growing louder, and mingled with it he could distinctly hear the hiss of skates. Presently, he too was moving, travelling with effortless rapidity over a hard slightly yielding surface. He felt the wind of his own speed against his face; he heard the bubbles run chirruping under the sweep of his strokes and tinkle against the frozen edges of the lake; he felt the ice elastic beneath him, and his chest oppressed by a difficulty in breathing which was also somehow indistinguishable from a glow of triumph. Suddenly from the mist in front of him, he heard a crash, a cry. The echo seemed to be still in the room, when with flying heart and shaking hand he touched the switch of his lamp.

His door had been thrown violently open, and in the doorway stood Pargiton.

He was still fully dressed, but Harby only noticed his face. The stricken man stood with his mouth a little open, swaying slightly. Harby went up to him, took him by the hand, led him to the bed, and made him lie down, but neither spoke, till Harby tried to disengage his hand and said, "I'll go and fetch a doctor."

Pargiton, who was lying motionless with open mouth, staring at the ceiling, rocked his head twice upon the pillow, and without moving his lips, breathed out the words: "No use."

"What's your maid's name? I'll call her."

Harby felt the grasp upon his hand tighten: "I mean I'll shout for her," he added, "and tell her to fetch some brandy from downstairs."

"She mustn't go into that room," Pargiton breathed again.

"All right, but what's her name?"

"Bertha."

Without changing position by the bed, Harby began to shout her name. It required considerable effort of courage to raise his voice, but presently two startled women with outdoor coats over their nightgowns appeared. Harby took the situation in hand.

"I want you both to dress at once and go together to the nearest doctor. Your master has been taken ill. And tell him it's a heart case. No; tell him the patient is in bad pain. Tell him anything, to come prepared for anything—restoratives, sedatives. Quick."

A few minutes later the closing of the front door sent a shiver through Pargiton, and the next half-hour was the most painful vigil in Harby's life. For some time the sick man lay still; then he raised the forefinger of his disengaged hand as though he were listening, or bidding his companion listen, while his face became festered with terror. Presently he sat bolt upright, staring into the passage. Harby wrenched away his hand and jumped up to shut the door. As he crossed the room the thought leapt at him that it might not shut—not quite; so vividly had those staring eyes imprinted, even for him, upon the framed oblong of darkness, the sense of something on the threshold. Terrified himself, he flung his shoulder at the door and slammed it with a crash that shook the house. Pargiton sank back in a state of collapse upon the pillow; he seemed to have lost consciousness, and Harby made no attempt to rouse him from that happy state. A little later the sound of the doctor's footsteps on the stairs, however, did so only too effectively; all four of them found themselves engaged in a struggle with a wildly delirious man. At last they succeeded in holding him down while a strong morphia injection brought at last relief. The doctor remained until a trained nurse arrived, and the dusk of early morning had already begun to brighten into day when he left. The same day Pargiton was removed by two trained attendants to a home for mental cases.

It was an inexpressible relief to Harby to find himself again in his own rooms. He went straight to bed, utterly exhausted, and awoke from a short sleep with steadied nerves, though with a strong reluctance either to think over what he had been through or to be alone. He decided to wire to ask an old friend, who was married to a particularly sensible and cheerful wife and surrounded by children of all ages, to receive him for a few days. The suggestion was warmly accepted, and Harby caught a late train. His hosts were puzzled by his looks and the suddenness of his visit, but they were kind enough to ask no questions, and a few days in their company did much to restore his equanimity. The first report he received of Pargiton (he had left directions that he should be kept informed) told him little beyond the fact that the condition of the patient was considered grave; the second, that he had had no more violent attacks, but that his despondent condition required the constant presence of an attendant. His physical state was also alarmingly low. The third report enclosed a letter from Pargiton himself; it ran as follows:

My Dear Harby,

I have enjoyed to-day and yesterday a peace of mind such as I have not experienced for a long time. I know what is the matter with me, and you know, but those who are looking after me do not. I know, too, that my release is near, and I have an inward confidence that it will not come in too cruel a way. I have paid my awful debt—my death is but the small item which still remains due. The worst is over; but I should like at least one other human being to know how bad it has been, and, especially, that you, my old friend, should know what I have had to endure. It may help you to think more mercifully of one whom you have reason to number among the basest of men. Verbally incomplete as my confession was on our walk in Greenwich you grasped the whole truth. I was aware of it, as I watched you go upstairs to bed that night; and when you did not turn to look back at me, I knew that I had lost even the little claim I had upon your sympathy.

I find some difficulty in describing my state of mind at that moment. My confession, shirking, halting—for it concealed from you my certainty of my own guilt— lying as it was, had brought me extraordinary relief, and my courage had been artificially heightened by the whisky I had just drunk. I saw that I was repulsive to you, but depression at that was quickly succeeded by hope. I went into my room and drank another whisky and sat down in that big chair which faces the looking-glass over the fireplace. My thoughts were busy with all I intended to do to atone, with my plans for that boy and his mother—the woman my brother intended to marry—and for you. I have no doubt I was maudlin; but you cannot imagine how sweet it was, even for a while, too feel that I was not a scoundrel. The persecution I have suffered has not come from my poor brother, I am certain. The very nature of it had from the start pointed to a very different origin, even if the revelation I am about to describe had not occurred. Had I been pursued by his revengeful spirit, believe me, I should not have suffered so much, for I am capable of feeling enough genuine remorse to have bowed my head with recognition of its justice. No: my persecutor has been a being so intimately identified with myself that escape from him, or it, has been impossible, and propitiation a contradiction in terms. I have been pursued and tortured by a being who has as good a claim to be myself as the Pargiton you know, but who is now utterly repellent to me, and to whom every attempt on my part to dissociate myself from him—can you imagine the horror of this to one who longs, as I do, to have done with the past?—gives an intensified power of independent action. After every attempt I made to make amends I have felt his power grow stronger. It was not until I first tried to help mother and son that I was conscious of him at all. I think now that it was because in your company I was a better man that he came so close to me after we parted. What followed my confession to you, which was the greatest effort I ever made to reconquer self respect, you shall hear.

How long I had been sitting in my chair planning how I should give up my ill-gotten wealth and lead the life of service, pure devoted service, which seemed miraculously open to me, I do not know. Perhaps I fell asleep; my sleep has been very poor and thin for a long time, hardly filming over a riot of thoughts and consciously created images. My future life was unrolling before me in comforting colours when, suddenly, the series of pictures was shattered by the clash of the iron wicket in the front of the house. I did not start, my new-found happiness was too strong upon me, though the thought occurred to me that the hour was singularly late for anyone—and who could it be?—to come to see me. It was the next sound which set my heart thumping; someone was approaching up the stone path to the porch. Now a lame man learns to know well the rhythm of his own footfalls, especially if he walks alone as often as I do. A heavy step, the click of a stick, a scraping, light step and then a heavy one again—Harby, those approaching steps were my own! I heard the grate of my latch-key in the lock and the heavy breathing of a cripple pausing on the mat. Two lurching steps would bring him, I knew well, within reach of the handle of the study door and from it I could not take my eyes; I tried to cover them, but I could not move my hands. I heard a stumble, a fumble; the brass knob turned and the door began to open slowly—nothing came in!

There are moments of terror so dreadful that nature in man cries out, "This can't be true," and I pray for all men that our death may not be such a moment; but there is, believe me, a terror beyond that, one which carries with it a sensation of absolute certainty against which the brain can raise no protest of frantic disbelief. I spun round in the agony of one who, not finding his assailant in front, looks behind, and I saw a face, an awful face. It was mine. Oh! Sweet relief, I knew in an instant it was my own reflection in the glass; that wild white face was mine, those glaring eyes were mine. I was still alone.

But the profound relief of that moment of recognition did not last. While I was still staring at myself, holding myself at arms' length from the mantelpiece, I thought the lips of my reflection smiled. When I put one hand to my mouth to feel if I too were smiling, the gesture was not repeated by the figure in front of me! The next moment that ultimate terror was on me with the spring of a tiger; though both my hands were clutching the mantelpiece and I could swear to the chill of the stone beneath them, the hands in the mirror were slowly stretching out to reach me. I heard a crash; I must have fallen; I don't remember picking myself up. When consciousness returned I was standing at your bedroom door. You know the rest.

I have only one more thing to tell you. Lying here in this place, where everyone is so kind and no one understands, I have been thinking things out. Those hopes of a new life were all false dreams; I could never live such a life. I see what I must do; I understand now that to go on defying my Past Self, though every act of defiance intensifies his power to destroy me, *is* my proper expiation, and when I think about him in that light I am no longer afraid. What is death without terror? Nothing—an event that isn't part of life. Even my weakling's confession to you almost enabled him to get his hands upon my throat. I have written to my brother's wife—for so I always think of her—telling her how and why the idea entered my head of luring my brother on to ice I had tested and knew did not bear. I have not spared myself. I have of course left everything I possess to her and her boy. My end now is certain. If you care to see me again, come, but don't think I am asking for or depending upon support.

When Harby read this letter he wired to say that he would be with him that afternoon, but a telegram, which crossed with his, informed him that Pargiton had died in his sleep the night before. What had been, Harby wondered, his last dream? In his coffin he looked stern and peaceful, but the faces of the dead tell us nothing.

# Gerald Warre Cornish
## (1875-1916)

Writing after his death, Desmond MacCarthy noted of his brother-in-law Gerald Warre Cornish, that "he wished his stories to be published . . . without any memoir or account of himself". He remains an elusive character, though he came from a well-documented clan.

Cornish was born at Eton where his father was a popular housemaster who later became librarian and Vice-Provost. His mother, Blanche, a cousin of William Thackeray and a novelist herself, was notorious in Eton society for what one admirer called "the pregnant and startling irrelevancies of her conversation". It was said that her "mind moved like a knight in chess, two squares in one direction, and then a turn round the corner", and a compilation of her most treasured sayings, *Cornishiana*, was published in 1935. An example: " 'Tell me,' said Mrs. Cornish to a young lady, 'who would you rather have had for a lover—Shelley, Keats, or Byron?' The young lady being too shy to speak, Mrs. Cornish answered her own question: 'I'd give all three of them for one wild half-hour with Rossetti.' " The Cornishes set up the Eton Shakespeare Society in 1880 of which the seventeen-year-old M. R. James became an early and enthusiastic member.

Gerald's sister Mollie, who married his old prep school friend and fellow Chit-Chat member Desmond MacCarthy in 1906, became a notable figure in the Bloomsbury Group. And his older brother, Hubert, was one of those present to hear MRJ read "Lost Hearts" and "The Scrap-book of Canon Alberic" for the first time. Gerald arrived at King's to read Classics a year later, and joined the Chit-Chat on 13 October 1894—the same meeting at which *The Green Bay Tree* was discussed.

Cornish was the penultimate secretary of the club and a member until it folded, but he only ever read one paper: "Exmoor and Stag Hunting" in 1895. The prosaic title and subject matter are perhaps surprising, when one considers that Cornish wrote the most mind-bending and original story in this book. "Beneath the Surface" is a startlingly original and ambitious piece of mystical fantasy, of which only the ghostliest passage is reprinted here. And it was produced under remarkable circumstances.

In 1899 Cornish had been ordained deacon in the Church of England and went on to hold a succession of ecclesiastical posts. In 1911 he left the church to become a lecturer in Greek and Latin at the University of Manchester, but at the outbreak of World War One he volunteered for Army service and was attached to the 6th Battalion of the Somerset Light Infantry, where he became a Major. According to Desmond McCarthy's introduction to the collection *Beneath the Surface and Other Stories* (1918), the story was "written in spare hours while he was training in this country with his regiment . . . and finished while they were actually serving in France."

The extract printed here occurs just over half-way through the story, as the narrator, Horton, an archaeologist, and his employer, Fin Lund, are sailing down the Euphrates, ostensibly to survey the river for the German government, but in reality for a much stranger purpose.

Lund is an explorer, well-known but derided by the academic establishment for his outlandish theories and speculations. The particular idea under investigation as we join him here, is that the site of the biblical Garden of Eden is to be found in the Valley of the Euphrates. This is risible enough in itself to Horton's scholarly colleagues, but what underlies the expedition, and Lund's life's work, is a grander, madder theory still: that of "universal flow"; the idea, that all observable phenomena—trees, sun, moon, Milky Way, ghosts—"have been left as they are by the movement of a deeper power". On his Euphrates journey Lund is in reality travelling back to "the source of created things—to the point from which creation streams out from the infinite".

This stream lies *beneath the surface* of the visible world, and few are able to perceive, let alone follow it. But, early on in the story, as Horton stares out of his window onto a dreary London street, he has an experience that leaves him in thrall to Lund: "I looked down, and felt more than ever the impression of movement, flowing *from* me now, and onward to a great distance. I felt as if I could see through the public-house below, and catch a glimpse of some great robe of sliding atmosphere beyond it. As I looked, the impression deepened, and . . . I thought it was accompanied by a sound, soft as feathers, but deep like thunder . . . " The fictional worlds of MRJ and E. F. Benson feel very far away.

And so we join Horton and Lund here, as they float along the ancient stream of the Euphrates and the still more ancient, metaphysical current beneath, encountering "many ghosts, as many almost as appeared to Ulysses beside the River Cocytus".

Learned and vividly described, Cornish's account of the ancient site on the river and the phantasms that inhabit it is an antiquarian ghost story of a different kind to that pioneered by MRJ. The past is visibly, thrillingly present, but Cornish's ghosts are not malicious or frightening. Far from being menacing "dim presences", they're as vivid yet insubstantial and incapable of causing physical harm as the images on a strip of film. And they're peripheral to the main narrative—in Lund's words, merely "waste products of creation's energy". Historical silt. Ultimately the ghosts that Horton encounters excite pathos rather than terror, and later on he is weighed down with "the pity, almost the despair, of death and decay . . . "

The journey culminates in an extraordinary, sustained, ecstatic, visionary passage, as Lund reaches the end of his journey. And so forceful and persuasive are some of the descriptions of Horton's spiritual fear and confusion towards the end, that one is tempted to read in them a crisis of faith on the author's part.

But Cornish's religious faith, though doubtless sorely tested in the trenches of France, in the end outlived him. "He was killed," MacCarthy tells us, "on September 16, 1916, the second day of the main advance on the Somme, while leading his company in an attack upon the German trenches in front of the village of Gueudecourt, south of Flers." Among his belongings was found a mud-spattered notebook containing another, more conventional but no less earnest, literary work—a free translation from the Greek of the New Testament Epistles to the Corinthians and Ephesians. This was published in 1937 as *St. Paul from the Trenches*.

AN EXTRACT FROM

# "Beneath the Surface"

### Gerald Warre Cornish

I have now to record certain things which I saw, which will not easily be believed. How far these things were real, I shall not attempt to define. Although I believe myself, and Lund certainly believed, that they were hallucinatory, yet they belonged to a consciousness which was not purely subjective, not simply my own or Lund's. It seemed that this wondrous stream, which lay deeper than the immediate grasp of the senses, as it flowed backward to its source, caused a resuscitation of past experience, in some general nature-consciousness, faintly stirring and bringing up to the surface, like bursting bubbles, age-long buried layers of experience—much as the blood rushing over the brain in a peculiar way is said to release memories and images of the past. So this mighty stream began to stir into existence, and release to the surface once more the sights and sounds of former ages of the river's life.

It was after we had begun to notice some of the many ruins of an almost prehistoric civilisation which are so common in these parts that these phenomena began.

On one or two islands I noticed the remains of ancient brick fortifications, and on obtaining leave from Lund to land, I discovered to my intense interest a few of these clay bricks stamped with cuneiform writing, with which some of our museums are now replete.

What we actually saw, however, presented itself to our minds with such an amazing appearance of reality and of actual life, that these sights bore very little relation to any of the relics of those past civilisations with which we are familiar from our museums.

The first phenomenon of the kind happened as follows.

It was towards evening and there was a breeze blowing sufficient to keep me busy at the steerage oar, and with the manipulation of the sail, at which double duty I had become rather skilful since our boatmen had left us. At the same time, so far as I could spare any of my attention, it was given to the sight of some ruins which we were approaching at a bend in the river. I could see quite plainly the bastions of what I judged must at one time have been a city wall jutting into the river-bed. They rose above the dark bushes that grew in the dry and broken channels, and were plainly visible overtopping them in the level evening light. It appeared to me as if the remains had once been strong squat towers and forts built of brick, past which the river had flowed. As we neared them, and turned the promontory on which they stood, I suddenly gave an exclamation of surprise and pleasure. For I saw not far off in front of it a bridge of boats, of a kind I had never seen before. As we drew nearer, I saw plainly the great barges, looming above the water, amid the evening shadows. I also heard the ripple of the water round them, and the splash and creak of the hawsers as the wind drew the great swinging chain of boats up against the breeze. Then with unexpected rapidity we seemed to be close up to them, and I suddenly hurled all my weight on the steerage oar to put the boat about. As we went about (and in doing so I had to turn most of my attention to the boat), I yet saw quite close above me a man standing on the bridge, in a long straight garment reaching his feet. His mouth was open, as if he was shouting at us, yet I could hear no sound coming from it. When I had got the boat about, and was making up and across the stream with the aid of the breeze, I looked round again at once, and to my astonishment and chagrin saw nothing but certain dark shadows and patches on the water. I had waked it seemed from a foolish day-dream, and I turned the boat down-stream again.

All this time Lund had said nothing, although I called out to him to look at the barges. But he only shook his head and smiled. I looked hastily toward the bank. The ruins were real at any rate. I could still see them sleeping there by the river's edge in the evening light. And then I saw that farther on, beyond these brick ramparts there were several mounds of sand. These mounds of sand are not infrequent, and are caused by deposits of dust blown over what were once towers and streets. I now saw that there were people sitting on these mounds, it was a most curious sight. They seemed to have gathered there to watch it go by. There were four mounds in all rising out of the desert, for at this particular spot the sand of the desert reaches up to the river. What these people were doing there, and why they sat so still, I could not say, but something prompted me this time to sail right on, past them, although I kept my eyes fixed hard on the strange groups seated on the mounds, one man stood on the edge of the river, into the waters of which he was gazing intently. When we had passed out of sight of the place, I went up to Lund, who had continued sketching all the time.

"What were those people?" I asked him.

"Pay no attention to them," he said. He was taking an observation at the moment with one of his instruments, and as he spoke, he continued to work at his plan of the river. "You and I are pursuing a more substantial goal than those dreams. They are nothing," and he applied his eye again to his sextant and compass.

"But they have some significance," I said, "they belong to the phenomena of your theory of travel and movement. They are evoked somehow by the undercurrent. How do you explain them?"

He put down his instruments for a moment and passed his fingers over the paper on which he was sketching.

"This old river," he said, smiling, " 'this ancient river, the River Euphrates', is what you might call a kind of sink into which old disused portions of the world's history have settled down, and come to a dead standstill, much as sand silts up a channel. These past ages of history lie round us now invisible to the eyes, but not less present in reality than the stone and brick buildings which were once the scene of their existence—such as that old place we passed just now," pointing up the river behind us. "Now don't you see," he turned towards me with one hand clasping the gunwale of the boat firmly, "as we pass through these surroundings, always nearing the ultimate source, and ever more closely in touch with the real energy of things, even these ghosts of the past become once more faintly apparent? So vigorous and real is this amazing undercurrent of the world's life, that even the earliest strata of history which have remained buried for ages in this channel must for a time be galvanised into some appearance of life."

"But that life is not real?" I asked.

"No, not even though our sense may sometimes be deluded," he said; "these apparitions only *mimic* life, appear to move for a few brief moments with the life they once had, and possess a kind of quasi-being, but they are in reality dead—mere husks and shells. They do not properly belong to my theory of travel. They are only waste products of creation's energy as it renews itself at its own source."

He went back to his map, and I remained leaning on my oar, and pondering on his explanation. I believe that what he said was the correct view. Anyway, whatever the theory, the facts were that during the rest of the journey Lund and I saw many ghosts, as many almost as appeared to Ulysses beside the River Cocytus.

In obedience, however, to his injunction to pay no attention to these appearances, I shall do no more than set down one more such instance.

It happened the evening after passing the ruined city—which I believe to have been the City of Thapsacus—when we were encamped beside an ancient dyke which stood on the banks of the river. These dykes are a feature of this neighbourhood—bulwarks, built of brick, to hold the river in its course. Some of them said to be as old as Semiramis. The whole plain of Mesopotamia abounds with relics of this kind. From our bivouac on a spit of sand by the river's edge we had seen the broken lumps of brickwork emerging from the bushes from some distance along the sweep of the river-bed; and we had followed them up some way. Whilst inspecting them, we came across a kind of causeway or brick platform, which ran up from the river, over the dyke and on to the plain beyond. This broad road or flooring of the river's bed, I took to be the remains of a ford passing over the dyke. The night was warm. I fetched my blankets and lay down to rest at last under this wall of brick. Before closing my eyes I saw the stars shining very large and bright just above the black summit of the wall. When I awoke, the river was red in the early dawn. There had been some wind, and I think it must have been distant dust-clouds which turned the dawn so crimson. The brickwork of the old dyke was on fire. I never saw so blood-red a morning, and the desert too was red. On the horizon these wisps of red dust were creeping murkily across the sky, and standing by the dyke I saw a man. I could see the upper half of his body above the bushes, and his great square black beard, and his belt below it, bound, not round his waist, but round his breasts. He remained motionless, and I began very cautiously to climb the brick dyke behind me, in order that I might see this figure more clearly. When I reached the top, however, I could no longer see the figure amongst the dark bushes, perhaps because it was no longer silhouetted, as I was now above it, and I climbed down again to go in search of him. I pushed my way through the bushes, glancing about me everywhere, making my way towards a bit of higher ground where we had noticed the brick platform or causeway the night before. I scrambled up with as little noise as possible, until I stood on a level with this old road, as it seemed to be, with its broken ruined flooring, out of which grew flowering weeds, and here and there myrtle-bushes with their stiff pointed leaves. And there, standing in the middle of the causeway, I saw the most startling sight that I think I ever beheld. Two horses with plumed heads stood side by side, one a white Arab, the other dark, and behind them was a small light chariot, with solid wooden wheels. Two men stood upright side by side in the car, motionless like the horses. Above their heads two spears pointed upwards to the sky, from which I noticed that the stars had not quite faded, although the eastern horizon was burning like a furnace; for a few moments I watched them. The hair and beard of the man on the side nearest me were plaited, and on his back was a big quiver-box, from which protruded strong red and blue feathered shafts. As I looked, the figures swayed slightly, and I distinctly heard the feathers on the arrows scrape against the man's back. There was something curious about the movement of that chariot. At one moment the picture presented to the eye was the embodiment of strength and power. In the stiff upright forms of the men, and the grip of the horses' hoofs biting the brick-work and the splendid sinews of their out-stretched legs, I saw the balance and power of a grand fighting machine. The wheels of the car revolved, and it passed onward, till I saw it for a moment against the rising sun on the slightly domed summit of the broad dyke. It was magnificent, the appearance of the two warriors in their dark, straight, close-fitting tunics, and the spear-heads flaming above them, and I could see the muscle standing out rigidly across the arm of the driver as he held his horses in a grip of iron—and then, I did not know whether to laugh or cry, for I *knew*—it seemed to be written all over them—that these strange beings were dead and unreal, merely aping and mimicking life with a kind of hope, worse than despair, of inducing me to believe in them. I think perhaps it was the motion of the chariot more than anything which disillusioned me. It was unconvincing. The motion was not perfectly continuous, but it was more like a series of pictures, in reality motionless, but presented rapidly to the eye with a view to producing an appearance of movement and life. I walked boldly up the causeway, my boots ringing cheerfully on the bricks, and, as I expected, I saw nothing of them when I reached the top. Only I saw the river, like a pool of blood, or rather a chain of pools, stretching away league on league into the farthest distance.

I sat down on the top of the dyke. Where was this river leading us? Was it true that under its surface flowed the river that moves with all life, and leads into the everlasting soul of things? Had this restless traveller and world-wanderer really penetrated into it, and was he moving swiftly with it? Was it really true that that stream was so living and real that even the dead shadows of the past stirred into a fictitious life, as we two went by in our boat past the shadowy shores of this outer world?

I looked away to where our boat was beached, and I saw Lund himself seated at his table. Strange—his electric lamp was burning. It shone like a little star even yet, in the shadow of the bank, though the sun was rising. He had been at work all the night, intent on his task of mapping the river's course! Was it a contradiction that one whose heart and mind were settled so deep in the eternal underlying force of Nature, should yet work with such almost infinite patience and pains at the surface details around him, verifying all the observations of previous cartographists, and producing a more truthful and reliable map than any that had hitherto been made? Was this a contradiction, or was it the natural outcome of his greater grasp of reality? As I watched him, his light went out with a wink. I could see his figure in the growing light of day, moving hither and thither about the boat. I scrambled down over the ruins to the water's edge, and found him in the best of spirits, shaking out a clean shirt which he had washed the night before, and anxious to be off as soon as possible.

# The Green Bay Tree

O n 13 October 1894, at the 613th meeting of the Chit-Chat, the minute book records that "Mr. James read extracts from a novel entitled *The Green Bay Tree* in which the proceedings of the Society are slanderously reported."

*The Green Bay Tree: A Tale of To-day* was widely and positively reviewed when it was first published in 1894. The opinion expressed in *The Lady's Pictorial* was typical: "The dovecotes of society and of the political world will be fluttered by the literary bomb which the joint authors have thrown in their midst, and the quidnuncs will be all agog to find the originals of the men and women who figure in *The Green Bay Tree*. This clever novel will attract hundreds by reason of its audacity."

It was a collaboration between two authors, William Wilkins and Herbert Vivian, both of whom had been undergraduates at Cambridge at the same time as M. R. James, and both of whom he is likely to have met. The two were active members of the Cambridge Union Society of which MRJ was librarian in 1885, and he and Vivian had several friends in common.

William Henry Wilkins (1860-1905) attended Clare College from 1884 to 1887, after which he became a political campaigner and writer. In 1892 he published *The Alien Invasion*: not, disappointingly, a pioneering work of science fiction, but a political tract, dedicated to "The Right Honourable the Earl of Dunraven . . . the Leader of the Movement for Protecting our People against the Invasion of the Destitute and Worthless of other Lands." It argued for tighter restrictions on immigration to the United Kingdom, particularly of unskilled Jews from Eastern Europe. Much of Wilkins early career was spent campaigning for this cause; but in 1892 he also started publishing novels, under the pseudonym W. H. de Winton (the aristocratic-sounding Norman flourish was presumably acceptable to admirers of *The Alien Invasion*). He went on to become a respected biographer of minor Royals, and published titles like *The Love of an Uncrowned Queen: Queen Sophie Dorothea Consort of George I* (1900) and *"A Queen of Tears": Caroline Matilda Queen of Denmark and Norway and Princess of Great Britain* (1904).

Wilkins' co-author, Herbert Vivian (1865-1940), was the longer lived, and ultimately more prominent, of the two. It's unclear precisely how their collaboration worked, but it is Vivian's life that provides the model for Walpole Coryton, *The Green Bay Tree*'s main character. Like Coryton he was the son of an MP, and a schoolboy at Harrow—an exact contemporary there of MRJ's close friend, and fellow Chit-Chat and Twice a Fortnight member, Walter Headlam. He went up to Trinity, Cambridge, in 1883, where he pursued an interest in politics and where he knew various Chit-Chat members, with at least one of whom—Ernest Debenham—he was on friendly terms. His memoir, *Myself not Least, being the Personal Reminiscences of "X"* (1925) is helpful in identifying several of the characters who are caricatured in *The Green Bay Tree*.

Vivian shared his co-author's conservative politics and views on immigration control. He was an ardent monarchist and a leading figure in the "Neo-Jacobite" movement, which sought to restore the House of Stuart to the throne of England, Scotland, and Ireland. It was on this platform, in 1891, that he stood unsuccessfully as an MP in Bradford, the sole member of "Individualist Party". *The Green Bay Tree* seems to have been his sole foray into fiction, but he was a prolific travel writer and journalist, with a particular interest in Serbia and Italy. In the 1920s he met Benito Mussolini, for whom he developed an admiration that was expressed in his 1936 book *Fascist Italy*. On balance it is perhaps to the Chit-Chat's credit that neither men were ever members.

The chapter that follows is the one from which MRJ read on the night of 13 October 1894. Its descriptions suggest some first-hand knowledge of the Chit-Chat, and some of the characters described are identifiable with known members. The paper that is delivered at the meeting in the novel, entitled "The Riddle of Life", might have been inspired by "Aims in Life", a real talk delivered to the club by Arthur Llewelyn Davies in 1884. Davies himself must be the model for the novel's Thomas Llewelyn Morgan.

The description of the Apostles as "an inner circle" of the Chit-Chat seems to overstate the relationship between the two clubs—but it adds substance to MRJ's suggestion that the Chit-Chat was a recruiting ground for the older club.

# The Green Bay Tree

## W. H. Wilkins and Herbert Vivian

*"Cherchons donc à voir les choses comme elles sont, et n'ayons pas plus d'esprit que le bon Dieu."*

– Flaubert

The undergraduate with literary aspirations is about as precocious and insufferable a prig as may be found in the whole republic of letters. His ideas are suburban rather than of Grub-street; his idols are under-done poets and incomprehensible essayists; his principles are the give and take of inept admiration; the goal of his ambitions is to take a high degree, go to London, and be elected a member of the Savile Club.

The most pretentious coterie for such young men at Cambridge is a highly exclusive society known as the Chit-Chat. It meets once a week in the rooms of all the members in turn, when the host reads a dogmatic paper on a subject of frivolous solemnity and the other members discuss it. Punch is brewed, dried fruits are consumed, and the club snuff-box is handed round. Every member is bound by honour and tradition to consider all the other members "*frightfully* clever" and to speak to outsiders with bated breath of his membership as the greatest honour which the University had to bestow.

Stay, there is a greater honour yet, but it is too supreme even to be whispered in the ears of the profane. The Chit-Chat has an inner circle, consisting only of the twelve most *frightfully* clever men in the University. They modestly style themselves "The Apostles" and are theoretically only known to each other in that capacity, though they usually take precious good care that the secret shall be only a secret of Polichinelle.

The Chit-Chat and the Apostles have been in existence to minister to the vanity of at least three or four generations of undergraduates, but the sluggish Cam still flows on unfired.

"I want you to reserve me Sunday evening, dear boy," said Coryton to Gaverigan as they walked home together from a card-party at Williams' and Wilmot's rooms.

"By all means. What is it? Poker in your rooms or a prayer-meeting in Victor Sexton's, O thou man of many wiles?"

"No, an infinitely funnier study in human nature than either."

"Human nature! That means vice or something equally humdrum, doesn't it? To my mind 'human nature' is a contradiction in terms. Anything nakedly natural disgusts me. What is there so repulsive as a human being, who seeks to be natural and consequently only succeeds in being foolish?"

"For my part," returned Coryton smiling, "I prefer natural people. One knows just what they will do under given circumstances and one can plan accordingly. But then I am a student of fools, a morologist—to coin a word."

"You are quite right to study fools, if what you labour for is success. For my part I don't believe that anything is worth while. There is no heaven save pleasure, and no hell save satiety."

"But all pleasures are of nature: from women to 'wittles'. Success is my greatest pleasure and that is why I pursue it."

"Philistine! Success is the triumph of art over nature. There is no pleasure in anything where nature has not been completely overshrouded by art. Natural food means bananas or raw potatoes washed down by rainwater, it is to art that we owe our tournedos Rossini and Mouton Rothschild 1874. But you haven't told me what you propose for next Sunday."

"I want you to come to a meeting of the Chit-Chat."

"Why, what on earth is taking you there?"

"I am a member."

Gaverigan looked at Coryton with a curious smile and whistled softly to himself.

"Whew! You are a marvel! Is there a single pie in the whole 'Varsity, where you haven't got your thumb? But why bother your head about such small fry? They can be of little enough use here and none hereafter."

"Everyone has his uses—down to the President of the Catt's debating society. But will you come? They want to elect you a member, but you needn't accept unless you like."

"And I am to come for inspection, as Mauresk did last week. All right, but I won't promise to be on my good behaviour."

"No one would ever expect that of you. Mauresk made a very good story out of his inspection. The show isn't quite so funny as all that. Still it may amuse you, and I know you only live to be amused."

When Sunday came, Gaverigan had forgotten all about the Chit-Chat and was lying comfortably at full length before his fire, enjoying his greatest pleasure of doing absolutely nothing, when Coryton burst in on him like an avalanche.

"You are a nice chap!" he exclaimed. "The Chit-Chat has been waiting for you half an hour—a thing utterly unheard of in its whole history. You are really too provoking."

"My good chap," returned Gaverigan, scarcely turning at his entrance, "I wish you wouldn't burst in like the North wind. You have chilled me to the marrow. I vow I won't stir an inch until you have pledged me in a bumper of this port. It's really not bad—for Cambridge."

"All right, but for Heaven's sake, hurry up!"

217

"Well, where are we to go?" said Gaverigan gloomily, "I sincerely wish I hadn't said I'd come."

"It's in the rooms of a man named MacRonald in the Old Court. He's really rather a clever chap. Older than most undergrads. Came up from Glasgow University or some such place. Wears a truculent yellow moustache. Never came nearer civilisation than Newcastle before his matriculation here and yet has passable manners—outrageously artificial, of course, but then you like artificial things."

"He's '*frightfully* clever', I suppose, like all the rest of them?"

The rooms were very large, like all those in the Old Court at Trinity. Oak panelling gave them a certain air of solid wealth, which was not borne out by the sparse and rather gimcrack furniture, evidently intended for an aspiration after new-fangled art by one who did not quite understand it. A long table in the centre of the room was covered with coffee cups of all sorts and conditions of patterns, which conveyed the impression that "alas, master, they were borrowed".

MacRonald came up smiling, with one hand grasping an end of his Randolphian mustachio. He had cultivated very carefully the appearance of being entirely at his ease on all occasions, and had succeeded in acquiring it to the satisfaction of superficial observers. Coryton used to say that his manners were those of a man who is always in expectation of being kicked downstairs, but then Coryton was a keener observer than most people.

"It is a great pleasure and honour to see you under my poor roof," MacRonald said to Gaverigan, with what he fancied was old-fashioned politeness; "we had half begun to fear we were forgotten."

"Forgotten! 'Twere impossible to forget the high honour of this invitation. I fear me I am not so punctual as is my wont," returned Gaverigan imitating MacRonald. But the humour—as usual—was lost upon the Scotsman.

"I found him sitting over the fire with a bottle of port," put in Coryton brutally.

The procedure at a meeting of the Chit-Chat is to devote the first hour to conversation, or "chit-chatting",—whatever that may be—then to proceed to the election of new members, and to wind up with a paper read by the host.

MacRonald's idea of entertaining had the merit of simplicity. Directly a man came in, he would take him to somebody, introduce them and plant them on a sofa or two chairs close together. Before ten minutes were up, he would pounce upon the man again, whisper in his ear "I want to introduce you to So and So" and carry him off to a *tête-à-tête* with somebody else. There was a game of General Post going on all the time and MacRonald certainly shewed skill in never leaving anybody by himself, or with a man who evidently bored him. At a pinch he would even go further and suggest subjects when the conversation seemed to be flagging.

MacRonald first introduced Gaverigan to an effeminate young man named Freeman. His father was a partner in a well-known firm of wholesale haberdashers, and had thought to turn his son into a gentleman by sending him to a public school and university. The result had been a curious hybrid, in which the shopwalker strain struggled with the veneer of gentility. Freeman had no notion how to talk or where to place his hands and feet, but he had a gushing, almost girlish, disposition, and was liked by people when they got to know him. He was good-looking, almost aristocratic-looking, with a Roman nose and slight, well-curled moustache, and so long as he did not open his mouth, he made an impression on a stranger. He had what members of his father's firm would have called a "good address", which was only rendered tolerable by his intuitive preference for the eloquence of silence. Like so many who have alloyed a pretentious education with middle-class home-life, he had no sense of proportion, mistook for sentiment what was only mawkishness and for philanthropy what was but foolery. He was eaten up with fads, from socialism and esoteric Buddhism to long hair and vegetable foods.

Gaverigan took to him at once. The great quality to him in an acquaintance was that he should be a good audience, and that was Freeman's strong point. Finding that he had a faddist to deal with, Gaverigan poured into his willing ears archaic individualism and epicurean theories, and he was just completing the process of captivating the impressionable youth by avowing a belief in astrology, when MacRonald came up and whispered in his ear that he was anxious to introduce him to Thomas Llewelyn Morgan. This was whispered with some pomposity, as though the proposition were an unusually advantageous one.

"I have known him ever since I was a boy," said Gaverigan, following his host, though he hated Morgan, "his father was up here with mine once upon a time."

Gaverigan at once rose several feet in MacRonald's estimation, for Thomas Llewelyn Morgan was a shining light in this coterie and was even whispered to be of the mysterious inner circle,—the Apostles!

They found him seated on a window-seat, discoursing atheism to a select circle of admirers. "The Bible," he was saying, "is not only a mass of inconsistencies and absurdities, but such hopelessly dull reading, such dismally bad literature."

"There I don't agree with you," said a man named Emery, who was a Positivist by creed and an editor of the *Cambridge Review* by profession, and therefore of course an authority both on religion and literature. "The Bible isn't half a bad book if one can once get rid of his prejudice against it. People who have had it crammed down their throats during childhood can't be expected to approach it impartially. I have had it bound in yellow calf and really, when I come to peruse it like that, I find it far better reading than either the Talmud or Omar Kayam."

"What title did you put on the cover?" asked Morgan contemptuously. "Perhaps if you spelt Bible with a little *b*, it might serve."

"I haven't put a title on yet. I want a good one, if anybody has ideas."

"Of course we all have ideas," said a man called Belgium indignantly, and he scratched a red shock head, without, however, eliciting any.

"*Poems and Fables of the Semites*," suggested Gaverigan in a still, small voice.

A delighted shiver passed through the little audience, and MacRonald rubbed his long bony hands with glee, as he trotted off to arrange further introductions. Morgan looked sulky at being eclipsed on his own territory.

Coryton had been very much bored meanwhile, talking to one of the most precious of the Apostles, a colourless young man named W. P. Jones, known to the intellectual circles of Cambridge as "W. P." and whose "*frightful* cleverness" consisted merely in a knack of passing examinations in Latin and Greek. He had a thin, husky voice, which he used in the most supercilious way, as if it were amazing condescension to consent to speak at all. He was insignificant-looking, with a pug nose and mutton-chop whiskers, but it was the custom of the Chit-Chat to take men at their own valuation, and his was an unusually high one even for these select circles.

Coryton had been flattering him more unblushingly even than his wont, and was beginning to wonder whether there was anything he would not swallow. He had told him with what engrossing interest he had read his article on Pindar in the *Cambridge Review*; he had alluded to him to his face as the cleverest man in the 'Varsity; he had even hinted at unparalleled personal beauty, and suggested the Chit-Chat paying a first-class artist to paint his portrait,—but the man had accepted it all as gospel, without turning a hair.

Coryton was beginning to admit that his powers of blarney must at last have reached their limit, when a welcome relief was afforded by MacRonald taking him away for introduction to Mr. Scott, whom Coryton had heard much about, but somehow had not yet met.

Mr. Scott gave what turned out to be somebody else's lectures in English literature in the hall of Trinity College some half a dozen times a term, to a select audience of Cambridge Apostles and Newnham disciples. The Chit-Chat swore by him, and probably contributed to his vogue. In London, despite persistent logrolling in the *Lickworm Gazette*, he was only known as the writer of washy sonnets of doubtful scansion and as the editor of certain English classics, which required no editing. At Cambridge he was Sir Oracle to a great number of crude young men. He was a podgy little person with glutinous hands, one of which he placed in Coryton's without the least attempt at pressure.

"I am very pleased indeed to make your acquaintance," he said, in an oily voice. "I think I have seen you sometimes at my lectures."

Coryton took the cue and began to express his enjoyment of them, though in reality he had never been there. "I was especially interested in what you said about Milton," he said, "though I confess I do not entirely share your admiration of him."

Mr. Scott's face gathered into a frown. Then he smiled pityingly and said, "Let me hear what you have to say," in the tone of a master asking a lower boy to show cause why he shall not be flogged.

"I take Voltaire's view," said Coryton boldly, for he was getting tired of heaping Pelion on Ossa in flattery of tenth-rate prigs; "he accused Milton of obscurity, unnecessary length, and entire absence of interest, and he pointed out that he was despised by his contemporaries."

Mr. Scott gasped at what seemed to him sheer blasphemy and was about to administer a reproof, when a movement in the room gave warning that the proceedings were going to begin, and everyone settled himself to attention.

"Our first business." said Thomas Llewelyn Morgan, the secretary, with more than the solemnity of a cabinet minister, "is to proceed to the election of new members. I hope it is understood by strangers present," and here he looked biliously at Gaverigan, "that our proceedings are strictly private. If any stranger does not consider himself bound in honour to treat them as such, I have to request that he will withdraw."

He made a long, awkward pause to enable Gaverigan to do so, but as the latter made no move, he proceeded to read out the names of the candidates proposed.

MacRonald took advantage of the pause to whisper in Gaverigan's ear, "That warning is on account of Mauresk. He behaved in a most ungentlemanly way. Came as our guest. Accepted our hospitality. And then went about everywhere, telling the most extravagant tales about what we did."

"Ha! ha! ha! Mauresk is not a respecter of persons," laughed Gaverigan.

"No, but one imagined he was a gentleman," returned the Scotsman severely.

"Mr. Mauresk of King's College," Morgan was reading, "proposed by Mr. W. P. Jones of Trinity College and seconded by Mr. Drake of King's, has been withdrawn."

The announcement was greeted with ironical cheers, in which Gaverigan and Coryton, who knew that Mauresk would never have accepted election at the hands of this society, joined heartily.

"Mr. Bertram Paine of Trinity College is proposed by Mr. MacRonald of Trinity and seconded by Mr. Edward Freeman of the same college," pursued the inexorable Secretary.

There was a pause, while the Chit-Chats pondered among themselves who should cast the first stone.

"Is he *frightfully* clever?" asked a man named Crust presently, sniffing the air.

"I don't think he scintillates particularly," said an over-grown King's man named Drake, his thick lips quivering nervously as he tried to think of a joke and failed.

"He wrote some *frightfully* clever articles in my paper, the *May-Bug*," said MacRonald with some humility, "and really he did coruscate the night he came on approval."

"Heavens!" whispered Gaverigan to Coryton.

"I trust I am not here 'on approval'. Are they all watching to see whether I 'scintillate' or 'coruscate'?"

"No, be quiet. You are watching them to see what funny things they do."

"And he isn't going in for the classical tripos," growled The MacSnorter. "I don't believe anyone can be frightfully clever who doesn't. Paine is a history-man I think.""

"Yes," assented Chortle, "a man whose intellect is nourished on history only is like a boy brought up to eat nothing but bath-buns. Both necessarily lack stamina."

After a long discussion in a similar strain, it was decided to defer the election to next term, and MacRonald proceeded to read his paper. It was not devoid of cleverness, though weighed down by Scottish conceptions of humour. It was entitled "The Riddle of Life" and consisted of emasculated Rabelaisian language, with a few aphorisms modelled on Voltaire peeping out every now and then like truffles in *pâté de foie gras*.

The aphorisms, which were evidently meant to be the strong point of the paper, were of the kind which prompts men to exclaim "How true!" rather than "How strange!"

*"When a woman weeps, she is about to deceive; when she smiles she has betrayed."*

*"Reputations,—like men,—are born of women, and women are not hard to deceive."*

*"When you say 'Good-bye, Colonel' in America, every man within hearing distance takes off his hat; if you exclaimed 'Pretty scamp!' in a London drawing-room, every woman would curtsey."*

*"An amorous man is amorous to his friend's wife."*

*"Love is the distemper of humans."*

*"The man who has a beautiful wife never lacks friends."*

*"A philosopher is one who asks other people questions to the end that he may answer them himself."*

And so on.

Signals for applause were never neglected. "Wonderful!" Drake would gasp to The MacSnorter; "*Frightfully* clever!" Quid, the Johnian history Lecturer, would telegraph with his eyes to Charles of King's; "Ripping!" was the comment of Belgium, who had not yet got into the Chit-Chat jargon.

Coryton's face was that of a sphinx all the time, neither enthusiastic nor bored, but when the essay came to an end in a splutter of scarcely intelligible fireworks, he was the first to rush up and congratulate the author with dulcet emphasis.

A desultory discussion followed, and then the assembly of prigs gradually melted away across the great court in twos and threes, still keeping up their priggish conversation.

As Coryton and Gaverigan walked across the court together, the latter asked, "What are they all going to get out of this, do you suppose?"

"Mutual admiration here," replied the other with a shrug of his shoulders, "and universal contempt hereafter."

"But they are all coming men, aren't they?" said Gaverigan laughing.

"Coming men who never come. Or if they come at all, it will be as third-rate ushers in fourth-rate schools, quill-driving clerks, or literate 'ghosts' for illiterate hacks and quacks, doomed to spend their lives flitting on the top of a 'bus between the suburbs and the British Museum."

The which in point of fact they did.

# Sources

"The Scrap-book of Canon Alberic" was first published in the *National Review* (March 1895); it was collected with the title "Canon Alberic's Scrap-book" in *Ghost Stories of an Antiquary* (London: Edward Arnold, 1904).

"Lost Hearts" was first published in *Pall Mall Magazine* (December 1895); it was collected in *Ghost Stories of an Antiquary* (London: Edward Arnold, 1904).

"The Other Bed" was first published in *The Popular Magazine* (April 1908); it was collected in *The Room in the Tower and Other Stories* (London: Mills & Boon, 1912).

"The Dean's Story" was first published in *The Granta* (April 1891); it was anthologised in *An Anthology of Humorous Verse*, edited by Sir Theodore Andrea Cook (London: H. Virtue & Co. Ltd., 1902).

"Red Gold" was first published in *The Cambridge ABC* (June 1894); it was collected in *Robert Carr Bosanquet: Letters and Light Verse*, edited by Ellen S. Bosanquet (Gloucester: John Bellows, 1938).

"Father Bianchi's Tale" was first published in *The Ecclesiastical Review* , Vol. 35 (1 July 1906); it was collected in *A Mirror of Shalott* (London: Pitman & Sons, 1907).

"Man Stories" was first published in *The Reflector* (22 January 1888).

"Basil Netherby" was first published in *Basil Netherby* (London: Hutchison and Co., 1926).

"The Phonograph Bewitched" was first published in *The Footprints in the Snow* (London: MacMillan & Co., 1910).

"The Ikon" was first published in the *Morning Post* (9 March 1909); it was collected in *Orpheus in Mayfair and Other Stories and Sketches* (London: Mills & Boon, 1909).

"The Shadow of a Midnight" was collected in *Orpheus in Mayfair and Other Stories and Sketches* (London: Mills & Boon, 1909).

"A Fable" was published in *The Letters and Memorials of William Johnson Stone* (Eton College: Privately Printed, 1904).

"Pargiton and Harby" was published in *The Ghost Book: Sixteen New Stories of the Uncanny*, edited by Lady Cynthia Asquith (London: Hutchison & Co., 1926); it was subsequently anthologised in the *Fourth Fontana Book of Great Ghost Stories*, edited by Robert Aickman (London: Collins, 1967).

"Beneath the Surface" was published in *Beneath the Surface and Other Stories* (London: Grant Richards, 1918).

*The Green Bay Tree: A Tale of To-day* by W. H. Wilkins and Herbert Vivian was published by Hutchinson & Co. (London), 1894.

# Acknowledgements

For advice and help while researching and writing the introductory material for this book I'd like to thank Matt Baylis; David Blake; Rob Brown; Jim Bryant; Keith Cavers; Donal Cooper; Katrina Dean at Cambridge University Library; Jonathan Dunlop; Malcolm Gaskell; Taff Gillingham; Nancy Gregory; Timothy J. Jarvis; Peter Johnson of the Society for Psychical Research; Eryl and Nancy Lloyd Parry; Patricia Maguire at King's College, Cambridge; Rosemary Pardoe; Jim Rockhill; Brian J. Showers; Jonathan Smith at Trinity College, Cambridge; and Mark Valentine. Thanks also to John Coulthart for his jacket artwork, Meggan Kehrli for her cover design, Ken Mackenzie for typesetting and Shelagh Bidwell for the editor photograph on the jacket.

Thanks is also due to the Estate of Desmond MacCarthy for permission to reprint "Pargiton and Harby"; to King's College Library, Cambridge, for permission to reproduce the photograph of the Twice a Fortnight club (Keynes Papers RV/1), and the illustration to "Canon Alberic's Scrap-book" by James MacBryde; and to the Syndics of Cambridge University Library for permission to reproduce the invitation to a Chit-Chat Club meeting (Cambridge Papers J 2790).

This book was conceived and begun several months before the Covid-19 pandemic made itself felt, but research was greatly hampered by the closure in March of Cambridge University Library where the minute books of the Chit-Chat Club and many papers related to M. R. James are kept. I must therefore acknowledge a particular debt to Michael Toseland's *Chit Chat Cambridge* (Figaro Publishing, 2014), in particular its appendices, without which much would have gone unnoticed.

## About the Editor

Robert Lloyd Parry is a performance storyteller and writer. In 2005 he began what he now refers to as "The M. R. James Project", with a solo performance of "Canon Alberic's Scrap-book" and "The Mezzotint" in James's old office in the Fitzwilliam Museum, Cambridge. The Project has since encompassed five more one-man theatre shows, several films and audiobooks, two documentaries, a guided walk, and numerous magazine articles.

# SWAN RIVER PRESS

Founded in 2003, Swan River Press is an independent publishing company, based in Dublin, Ireland, dedicated to gothic, supernatural, and fantastic literature. We specialise in limited edition hardbacks, publishing fiction from around the world with an emphasis on Ireland's contributions to the genre.

www.swanriverpress.ie

*"Handsome, beautifully made volumes . . .*
*altogether irresistible."*

– Michael Dirda, *Washington Post*

*"It [is] often down to small, independent, specialist presses*
*to keep the candle of horror fiction flickering . . . "*

– Darryl Jones, *Irish Times*

*"Swan River Press has emerged as one of the most inspiring*
*new presses over the past decade. Not only are the books*
*beautifully presented and professionally produced, but they*
*aspire consistently to high literary quality and originality,*
*ranging from current writers of supernatural/weird fiction*
*to rare or forgotten works by departed authors."*

– Peter Bell, *Ghosts & Scholars*

# GREEN TEA

J. Sheridan Le Fanu

Published alongside "Carmilla" in the landmark collection *In a Glass Darkly* (1872), Le Fanu's "Green Tea" was first serialised in Charles Dickens' magazine *All the Year Round* in 1869. Since its first publication, Le Fanu's tale has lost none of its potency. "Green Tea" tells of the good natured Reverend Jennings, who writes late at night on arcane topics abetted by a steady supply of green tea. Is he insane or have these nocturnal activities opened an "interior sight" that affords a route of entry for an increasingly malignant simian companion? This 150th anniversary edition of "Green Tea", with illustrations by Alisdair Wood and an introduction by Matthew Holness, is the definitive celebration of Le Fanu's masterpiece of psychological terror and despair.

*"Even 150 years after it was published,*
*'Green Tea' has stood firmly against the test of time*
*as a wonderfully eerie and well-crafted ghost story."*

*– Ghosts & Scholars*

*"To paraphrase Little Women, it wouldn't be Christmas*
*without any ghost stories . . . Swan River Press*
*has just issued a beautiful keepsake volume*
*of J. Sheridan Le Fanu's Green Tea."*

– Michael Dirda, *Washington Post*

# CURFEW
### & Other Eerie Tales

Lucy M. Boston

Lucy M. Boston is best remembered today as the Carnegie Medal-winning author of a series of children's novels set in Green Knowe, an ancient, haunted house based on Hemingford Grey Manor near Huntingdon, Cambridge. She began writing these chilling tales when she was already in her sixties, but they were not her first attempts at fiction. A handful of supernatural tales dating from the early 1930s exist among her papers, and these are here published together for the first time, along with her only play, The Horned Man, which has been out of print since 1970. An introduction by Robert Lloyd Parry considers the literary influences on these works and looks at them in the context of Boston's personal life.

*"Boston's tales are written in a solid, classical narrative style,
in the tradition of the great ghost story writers . . .
a charming book unearthing forgotten gems
and apt to delight any ghost story lover."*

– British Fantasy Society

*"Like the Green Knowe . . . these stories appear to have
been written mainly for older children or young adults.
However, Boston makes few concessions to her younger
readers: horror is not avoided, nor altogether survived.
Her writing is straightforward, but not simple or anodyne.
Horrific details are faced unflinchingly . . ."*

– Reggie Oliver, *Wormwood*

# BENDING TO EARTH
*Strange Stories by Irish Women*

edited by Maria Giakaniki
and Brian J. Showers

Irish women have long produced literature of the gothic, uncanny, and supernatural. *Bending to Earth* draws together twelve such tales. While none of the authors herein were considered primarily writers of fantastical fiction during their lifetimes, they each wandered at some point in their careers into more speculative realms—some only briefly, others for lengthier stays.

Names such as Charlotte Riddell and Rosa Mulholland will already be familiar to aficionados of the eerie, while Katharine Tynan and Clotilde Graves are sure to gain new admirers. From a ghost story in the Swiss Alps to a premonition of death in the West of Ireland to strange rites in a South Pacific jungle, *Bending to Earth* showcases a diverse range of imaginative writing which spans the better part of a century.

"Bending to Earth *is full of tales of women walled-up in rooms, of vengeful or unforgetting dead wives, of mistreated lovers, of cruel and murderous husbands.*"

– Darryl Jones, *Irish Times*

"*A surprising, extraordinary anthology featuring twelve uncanny and supernatural stories from the nineteenth century . . . highly recommended, extremely enjoyable.*"

– British Fantasy Society

Lightning Source UK Ltd.
Milton Keynes UK
UKHW010725010822
406672UK00002B/521